BLIND SURRENDER

"I love you, Sarah," Nicholas said, his voice so soft it was as if he stroked her.

"And . . . I love you, too," she whispered, knowing that it was true. She was in love, hopelessly so, and nothing had ever been more certain.

He didn't say anything more, but pulled her into his arms, kissing her fiercely on the lips. It was a hungry kiss, urgent and intense, and she gave herself willingly, her body yielding against him as if she had been fashioned solely for him. Caution flew away on the autumn breeze, and rich desire took its place, arching exquisitely through her and turning her blood to fire as his lips teased and aroused, and she was alive to the hardness of his body against hers.

Sarah was an innocent in a world of lords like Nicholas Stanhope who were used to having what they wanted, and ruthless beauties like Lady Georgette Belvoir who would do anything to have him. All she could trust in was love—and all she could hope was that love would be enou

Cruel
Lord Cranham

by

Sandra Heath

A SIGNET BOOK

SIGNET
Published by the Penguin Group
Penguin Books USA Inc., 375 Hudson Street,
New York, New York 10014, U.S.A.
Penguin Books Ltd, 27 Wrights Lane,
London W8 5TZ, England
Penguin Books Australia Ltd, Ringwood,
Victoria, Australia
Penguin Books Canada Ltd, 10 Alcorn Avenue,
Toronto, Ontario, Canada M4V 3B2
Penguin Books (N.Z.) Ltd, 182–190 Wairau Road,
Auckland 10, New Zealand

Penguin Books Ltd, Registered Offices:
Harmondsworth, Middlesex, England

First published by Signet;
an imprint of Dutton Signet,
a division of Penguin Books USA Inc.

First Printing, October, 1993
10 9 8 7 6 5 4 3 2 1

 REGISTERED TRADEMARK—MARCA REGISTRADA

Printed in the United States of America

For my daughter Sarah

1

IT was snowing outside, and the afternoon light was fading fast as Nicholas Stanhope stood alone in the vast picture gallery at Chalstones, the beautiful Oxfordshire home of the Howard family. The lighted candlestick in his hand cast only a pale, flickering light, and did not keep the gathering shadows at bay.

He was aristocratically handsome, with dark hair and steady gray eyes, and the tanned complexion of a man who liked the open air. His tall, athletic shape was perfect for the day's close-fitting fashions, so that his superbly tailored beige coat, gold brocade waistcoat, and cream cord breeches became him very well indeed, as did the way he wore his coal black hair just a little longer than was strictly the mode. At thirty he was considered to be one of London's most attractive and eligible gentlemen, but no one had as yet led him to the altar. He had considered it, though. Oh, yes, how he had considered it!

His lips twisted with bitterness as he held the candlestick up to examine the portrait he'd discovered of Sarah Howard. She was so lovely, with her long fair curls, pale complexion, and forget-me-not eyes, and nothing could have become her more than the summery sky blue muslin gown she wore. She seemed so sweet, fresh, and innocent, and there was something eminently believable about the candor in her eyes and the openness of her smile. But it was all fairy glamour, for the lady was not at all what she seemed.

A dark pain passed through his eyes, and he turned from the portrait to place the candlestick upon a table, then went to the window to look at the heavily falling snow. It would be dark soon, and to continue his journey in such conditions would be the height of foolishness.

But could he bring himself to stay here? It would be ironic indeed if of all the houses in England, he had to be benighted here at Chalstones. He wished now he had decided against pausing at the one place that meant everything to Sarah Howard and seemed to be filled with her presence.

He gazed down over the white-carpeted park toward the ornamental lake in the tree-filled valley below. Had it really only been October when it had all begun? Had less than two months passed since he had stood like this at the window of his London town house in Duke Street, looking down at St. James's Park as he waited for his cousin Stephen to call?

It had been the height of autumn then, one of the most mellow and clement autumns in living memory, and he had yet to even hear of Miss Sarah Howard. . . .

How peaceful the capital's most beautiful park looked in the sunshine of a late October afternoon. Looking at such a scene, Nicholas found it hard to believe that in this year of 1803 Britain was again at war with France, and that he was soon to set out on a dangerous voyage to take vital documents to the British ambassador in Naples.

His glance moved toward Birdcage Walk, the royal carriageway on the southern boundary of the park. Beyond the drive the elegant seventeenth-century houses of Queen Square caught his eye, and in particular the fine residence of Lady Thurlong, the most formidable Tory hostess in London. She was holding an assembly tonight, and its purpose was twofold. Not only did she wish to drum up support for ex-prime minister Pitt, whom she regarded as the rightful occupant of 10 Downing Street at a time like this, but she also wished to launch her talented nephew upon a political career under Pitt's wing.

Nicholas smiled, and swirled his glass of cognac. Thomas Thurlong was both likable and clever, and blessed with the inborn political brilliance of his influential family. He would probably reach Downing Street himself one day, and make a good fist of it. If he didn't, it wouldn't be for lack of assistance from his aunt, Nicholas thought, given how diligently the Thurlong House servants were hanging countless variegated lanterns in the park.

It was warm in his blue-and-gold drawing room, and Nicholas had taken his coat off and tossed it idly over the back of one of the blue velvet chairs. His frilled shirt was very white, and the silver threads in his embroidered waistcoat shone in the light from the window. The cut of his cream kerseymere breeches was so close and perfect that there wasn't a wrinkle to be seen against his long legs, and his valet had labored for a considerable time to achieve the enviable shine on his top boots.

His expression became pensive, and Lady Thurlong's political ambitions slid from his mind as he thought about the forthcoming journey to Naples. He didn't particularly want to go, for he loathed long voyages, especially hazardous ones at time of war, but it was his duty as a patriotic Englishman. It had its compensations however, for Naples was gratifyingly out of reach of the persistent and increasingly tiresome Lady Georgette Belvoir.

Georgette was regarded as one of the belles of London society, but she was also a determined and unscrupulous creature when it came to getting her own way. She was the youngest of the financially straitened Earl of Hayden's four daughters and the only one still unmarried. Nicholas grimaced for it was his misfortune that her desirous eye had fallen upon him. For several months now she'd pursued him relentlessly, and in that time had stooped to many low stratagems in her attempts to win him. He had managed to elude her without society becoming generally aware of her rather scandalous conduct, but he had long since ceased to have a sense of humor about it, and her father was rumored to be displeased, to say the least. The earl's once capacious purse had suffered considerably of late, after unwise investments and the expensive marrying off of his three other daughters, and his temper was becoming decidedly choleric. In both his and Nicholas's opinion, the sooner a suitable husband was found for her, the better.

A discreet tap came at the door. It was his butler, Blunsden. "Begging your pardon, sir, but Mr. Mannering has called."

"Ah, yes, I'm expecting him. Show him in, if you please." Nicholas straightened and went to pour a second glass of cognac. Stephen Mannering was his maternal cousin, and was about to be asked to handle his affairs during his absence in Naples.

Stephen was admitted. He was a lanky, sandy-haired young man, and as unlike Nicholas as it was possible to be. Dressed in evening attire in readiness for his customary visit to his club in St. James's Street, he rather resembled a redheaded crow, but his smile was ready and likable. The diamond pin in his neckcloth flashed in the firelight as he took a seat and accepted the glass of cognac.

"You wanted to see me, Coz?"

"I have a favor to ask. Some time around the middle of November I have to go to Naples on Whitehall business, and I'd be obliged if you'd take care of matters for me while I'm away, just as you did when I was despatched to Washington and Vienna."

Stephen grinned. "You trust an incorrigible gambler like me with your purse strings? How very rash, to be sure."

Nicholas returned the grin. "You aren't about to be left in control of my purse strings, just my affairs in general. I'm concerned only with the general protection of my finances, problems on my estates, and so on."

"Ah, well, there goes my ignoble hope of being able to fritter away your fortune, but I forgive you. Yes, Coz, of course I shall handle your affairs for you. You may trust me." Stephen's glance went suddenly to the window. "Would you mind raising the sash a little? I know it's damned cold outside, but I cannot abide being entirely closed in."

"Yes, of course." Nicholas went to the nearest window. As he lifted the sash he felt the cool autumn air breathing into the room, but he did not object, for he was accustomed to his cousin's dread of being cooped up in any way. Ever since Stephen had been a child, he had had this fear, and his family all understood.

Stephen smiled again. "Thank you. Now, what was I saying? Oh, yes, it was that you can trust me."

"I know I can." Nicholas took the seat opposite, and then studied him for a moment. "I wish to God you'd give the green baize a miss for once. I take it that you're on your way to your club now?"

"I am, but as it happens my purpose is to watch the play, not to indulge in it."

"Pigs will fly before I believe that."

"It's the truth." Stephen sat forward. "There has been some very deep play of late, very deep indeed, and involving some unlikely people. Your father is there, of course."

Nicholas's smile faded. "I don't wish to talk about my father."

"Yes, but—"

"I'm not interested, except to say that I'm amazed you should think him an unlikely person to be seated at a gaming table. He lives for the turn of a card, and his luck is that of Old Nick himself."

"Actually it wasn't your father's presence that I was referring to as unlikely, but rather that of a certain landowner who usually shuns the tables."

"Can't we leave the subject, Stephen?" Nicholas was estranged from his widowed father, who over a number of years had treated his late mother very shabbily indeed because of a flighty little actress at Drury Lane. The estrangement was complete, although it had not quite come to a matter of disinheritance.

Stephen sighed, and drained his glass. "Have it your own way. Suffice it that I've seldom seen such deep play before."

Nicholas gave a wry smile. "No? How forgetful you have suddenly become. I seem to recall that deep play is your personal forte," he murmured as he rose to pour the other a further measure of the cognac.

Stephen leaned his head back against the chair. "I know I've been somewhat reckless, but my luck has to change soon, damn it."

"The law of averages doesn't always apply, my friend," Nicholas replied, holding out the refilled glass.

"Don't I know it. My promissory notes are to be found in far too many desk drawers, I fear."

"Is anyone pressing for settlement?"

Stephen laughed a little cynically. "They know the lamentable state of my finances, and are prepared to wait because they are aware that next year I'll come into a handsome sum, thanks to my mother's dear departed brother. I am even assured that Geoffrey Belvoir will not dun me until then.''

"Geoffrey Belvoir holds some of the IOU's?"

"Yes, unfortunately. I'm afraid I was a little more rash than usual last month, but at least I have the consolation of knowing that he is fractionally more of a gentleman than his sister is a lady.'' Stephen gave him a sly look. "And how is the delectable Georgette?"

"I neither know nor care. She is enough to drive me insane.''

"Or drive you out of the country. That is the truth of it, eh, Coz? This government business in Naples has come at a fortuitous time, removing you from the lady's desirous reach.''

"I sincerely hope that my absence will cool her ardor, and while I'm waiting to leave, I intend to visit Grandmother in Cheltenham. That's why I've asked you here now. I trust I'm not keeping you from anything important?"

"No, of course not, for the interesting play won't commence until after midnight," Stephen replied with a wry smile.

"I wasn't referring to your damned gambling, but since you mention it again, just have a care, Stephen. You won't inherit until late next year, and in the meantime you could find yourself in debtor's jail. If you fear being enclosed in a room like this, God alone knows how jail would affect you. The Marshalsea isn't renowned for its comfort.''

Stephen shifted uncomfortably, for the thought of jail did indeed frighten him. "I've already told you that everyone is prepared to wait.''

"Do you need any help in the interim?"

"No.''

"Are you sure? I can make a sum over to you, if you wish.''

Stephen shook his head. "There is no need, but thank you all the same.''

"It will be too late once I've left the country," Nicholas warned.

"I've already said that no one is pressing me. I'll manage. Besides, I can't come scuttling to you every time I overindulge. If I did, I'd be on your doorstep every week." Stephen smiled ruefully. "I promise to mend my ways before long."

"See that you do."

Stephen gave him an impish look. "Oh, but I must, Coz, for I wish to be as eligible and pursued as you. I may not have the looks, but I'm much more charming."

"I will gladly surrender Lady Georgette Belvoir to you," Nicholas replied with feeling.

"My dear fellow, fabulously beautiful she may be, but she also terrifies the breeches off me. You may keep her." Stephen drank the second glass of cognac and then rose. "I'll be toddling off, then. If you need me at all, I'm still at the same lodgings in Conduit Street, and while you're away I'll see to it that your business affairs are handled to perfection."

"I'm very grateful, Stephen," Nicholas replied, rising as well.

"Why don't you join me at the club tonight?"

"And risk being beneath the same roof as my father? Thank you, but no."

"I know he's not the world's most pleasant man, but—"

"No, Stephen," Nicholas interrupted quietly.

Stephen shrugged. "As you wish. By the way, when did you say you were leaving for Cheltenham?"

"Within the next few days, I'm not exactly sure when. It will have to be soon if I am to spend any time with Grandmother before sailing."

"Be sure to remember me to her."

"I will."

Stephen smiled. "You may be her favorite grandson, but I'm infinitely more lovable, if she did but know it."

"I'm sure she does know it."

"Good night, Nicholas."

"Good night."

As his cousin left, Nicholas went to close the window, and then resumed his seat by the fire. Stephen might tease him about matters of the heart, but the truth was that in the love stakes he was trailing somewhat miserably behind. Oh, there were ladies in plenty, but no one with whom he could actually fall in love. No doubt there was someone somewhere, although where she was the Lord alone knew. Maybe Dame Fortune would smile upon him in Cheltenham.

2

SEVERAL days later, in the library of Chalstones in the county of Oxfordshire, two young ladies were whiling away the late afternoon in the library. They were close friends, and one of them, Sarah Howard, was the only daughter and heiress of the owner of the estate, Mr. Henry Howard. The other was Julia Thurlong, wife of the same Thomas Thurlong who was in London with his aunt, Lady Thurlong, for the promotion of his new political career. Sarah was reading in a chair by the fireplace, and Julia was supposed to be writing a letter to Thomas, but she was too preoccupied to concentrate.

Her preoccupation concerned Sarah's recent betrothal to Lord Fitzcharles's son and heir, Oliver. The betrothal was formal, but had yet to be announced publicly, and Julia was worried because it was already clear to her that Sarah was making a grave error of judgment. Oliver Fitzcharles was all that was wrong for her. But how could one broach such a delicate subject without causing offense? A blunt statement of fact might result in the severing of a long and close friendship, and yet how else could Sarah be made to face certain unpalatable facts about her betrothed?

Far from being all that was gallant, strong, and dependable, Oliver Fitzcharles was unreliable, weak, and completely under the thumb of his autocratic father. Sarah was happy at the moment and looking forward to the Christmas ball at which the betrothal would be formally announced, but Julia was afraid that the future held a very unpleasant awakening.

Julia wished that Mr. Howard would come home, but Sarah's widowed father was following his custom of spending each autumn in London. He knew little of Lord Fitzcharles and his son, for they had only recently purchased Blackwell Park, an estate adjoining Chalstones, but their wealth and aristocratic breeding, to say nothing of the love which undoubtedly existed between Sarah and Oliver, had been sufficient to convince him that the match was very desirable and advantageous. Julia had been at Chalstones only for a few weeks, having left her home in Cheltenham to spend some time with her friend, prior to joining Thomas in London at Thurlong House, but in that time she had very swiftly recognized Oliver Fitzcharles's failings. If only Sarah could recognize them as well, for behind the dashing manly facade there lurked a mouse.

With a sigh she put her pen down, and sat back in the chair at Mr. Howard's huge writing desk. She was dainty and dark-haired, and wore a crimson dimity gown with a ruff at the throat. Her brown eyes were pensive as she glanced across the library to where Sarah sat by the fire with her book. It seemed to Julia that Oliver's betrothal ring glittered tauntingly in the firelight, almost as if it were defying her to voice her grave doubts about the man who had placed it there.

Sarah read on, blissfully unaware of her friend's quandary. Flame shadows moved over her rose velvet gown as she sat engrossed in a volume of her favorite book, Mr. Richardson's *Clarissa Harlowe*. The same flickering firelight shone in her forget-me-not eyes, and brought out glints of gold in the heavy fair hair piled up in curls on her head. With her slender figure and clear complexion, she was considered very lovely, and since she was also the sole heiress to Chalstones and the Howard family's tolerable fortune, she had not lacked suitors from the moment she'd first come out in society. But it had been upon undeserving Oliver Fitzcharles that her favor had been bestowed.

Julia had been surprised that Lord Fitzcharles had agreed to the match, for he had always made it plain that he wanted a daughter-in-law of noble blood to carry on the line, but before long she realized it was Chalstones that provided the reason.

The estate's eventual acquisition by the Fitzcharles family would mean that when Oliver inherited his father's title, he would be master of a vast portion of the county of Oxfordshire. Without Chalstones, Julia had no doubt

that Sarah Howard would not have been considered at
all, for no matter how much Lord Fitzcharles's son loved
her, or how beautiful she was, her lack of aristocratic
background and her fairly modest financial expectations
would not have suited him. If he did not want Oliver to
marry her, he would not hesitate to forbid the match.
And Oliver would not hesitate to obey.

Julia wished that all these disquieting thoughts hadn't
entered her head, but they had, and now they plagued
her so much she couldn't think of anything else, let alone
write to Thomas.

She pondered Sarah's future father-in-law. There were
few people in society who were not aware of how ruthless
he was, and certainly no one at all in horse-racing circles.
For him the turf was of paramount importance, and the
Fitzcharles colors had to be first past the post no matter
what. He had no scruples or conscience, and certainly
no honor in the accepted sense of the word. His jockeys
were notorious for breaking the rules, and if a horse
caught his eye, Lord Fitzcharles moved heaven and earth
to own it.

From Thomas's letters, Julia knew that at the moment
an elderly gentleman by the name of Sir Gerald Pennyworth was receiving a great deal of unwelcome attention
from Lord Fitzcharles. Sir Gerald owned a blood stallion
named Icarus, which had proved itself in races and as a
sire, and Lord Fitzcharles desperately wished to possess
the animal. For months now he had been pestering Sir
Gerald, whose financial situation was somewhat precari-
ous, but who was proving obstinate in the extreme. It
was being whispered that Sir Gerald's ruin was being
hastened along by Lord Fitzcharles in order to force his
hand, although this was something Sarah had not as yet
been told.

It was a situation of increasing concern to Julia. Oliver
Fitzcharles was incapable of thinking for himself or standing up to his father, but Sarah had been brought up to
show spirit and initiative; it was therefore inevitable that
sooner or later Sarah would fall foul of Lord Fitzcharles,
and when that happened she would expect her husband
to support her. But Oliver would fail her.

Sarah glanced up, at last becoming aware of her friend's

lengthy pensiveness. "Can't you think of anything to write?" she asked.

"Mm? Er, no. The muse isn't with me, I fear."

"Really? That must be the first time ever. You usually manage to write about ten pages."

"I have a great deal on my mind today," Julia answered, getting up from the writing desk and going to one of the tall French windows that faced down over the park toward the tree-edged lake.

The October afternoon was getting very cold now, and the sunset was a blaze of red and gold that was almost matched by the glory of the autumn leaves. A chill mist would soon rise from the lake, and by morning it would lie like a blanket in the valley. This fall had been particularly beautiful, with no gales yet to tear the leaves from the trees, and the English landscape was at its glorious best. The hedgerows were bright with berries, late flowers were still in bloom, and abundant fruit was in the orchards. The war seemed a million miles away from this tranquility.

Sarah misinterpreted her mood. "You're missing Thomas, aren't you? I don't expect you to stay here with me if you'd rather go to London."

"I do miss Thomas, but I'm in no rush to go to London."

Sarah studied her, and then slowly put her book aside. "You're not really thinking about Thomas at the moment, are you?" she said, joining her at the window.

"No."

"Can I help?"

An ironic smile touched Julia's lips. "Sarah, I am the one who wishes to do the helping, and you are the one I wish to help."

Sarah looked curiously at her. "I don't understand."

"We've been friends for a long time now, haven't we? Ever since school in Cheltenham?"

"Miss Worth's Academy for the Daughters of Gentlefolk," Sarah said with a smile. "Yes, we've been friends for a long time."

"Long enough for me to presume upon our acquaintance?

"Presume? Yes, of course. Julia, what is all this about?"

Julia drew a heavy breath, for now that the moment was upon her, she wasn't sure how to commence.

"You're not going to like any of this, Sarah, but I won't be much of a friend unless I say something. It concerns your betrothal to Oliver. In my opinion you're making a terrible mistake." There, it had been said at last.

Sarah stared at her.

Julia went quickly on. "Oliver hasn't any backbone at all when it comes to his father. Have you begun to think what that will mean? Lord Fitzcharles is a tyrant who wants his own way in absolutely everything; indeed he seems more of a despot than Bonaparte himself! And now there is this latest rumor—"

"Rumor?" Sarah was reeling, for Julia's doubts had taken her completely by surprise.

"About Sir Gerald Pennyworth." Julia briefly related what she'd heard. "It may not be true, of course, but the fact that it is believed is surely indicative of Lord Fitzcharles's character. He isn't capable of allowing you and Oliver to live your own lives. Sarah, sooner or later, probably sooner, you are going to cross Lord Fitzcharles, and when that happens you will be on your own. Oliver won't stand up for you. He dances to his father's tune, and always will. You deserve better than that, far better."

Suddenly Sarah felt stung into retaliation. "Are you in any position to point that particular finger? Isn't Thomas in London at this very moment because *he* is dancing to a relative's tune? Hasn't Lady Thurlong dangled her fortune in front of him if he succeeds in political circles?"

Julia colored a little. "It isn't quite the same thing. Thomas *wants* to take up politics, and if it comes to supporting me against his aunt, then I know he will. Sarah, I don't want to quarrel with you over this, nor have I relished upsetting you, but I simply can't stand by any longer. Oliver Fitzcharles is going to make you very unhappy, and I don't want to see that happen. As things are at present, the betrothal isn't public. Please delay any announcement and give yourself time to be absolutely certain."

"But I'm absolutely certain now," Sarah replied a little coolly.

"If your father had been here these past few weeks instead of in London, I'm sure he would have begun to doubt as well; indeed I think he'd be actively considering how best to extricate you from this match. He's brought you up to think for yourself and do what you think is right; that freedom will be denied you time and time again once you're in Fitzcharles's clutches. *Please* think again, I beg of you. It isn't too late to withdraw."

Sarah had no opportunity to say anything more because at that moment there was a timid tap at the library door behind them. She whirled about a little irritably. "Yes? What is it?"

It was her maid, Annie, who'd lingered outside for a moment or so on hearing their slightly raised voices. She was small and dark, with soft brown eyes, and she delivered her message with noticeable reluctance. "Begging your pardon, Miss Sarah, but Mr. Fitzcharles wishes to see you urgently."

Julia turned away in dismay, for Oliver was the last person she wished to see right now.

Sarah collected herself. "Very well, Annie. Show him in."

The maid hesitated. "I can't do that, Miss Sarah."

"Why ever not?"

"Because he's not here, Miss Sarah. He's waiting for you at the grotto by the lake. He sent a man up to the house with the message. It's important that you see him straightaway."

Sarah was astonished. Oliver wished her to go to the grotto? But why, when he was perfectly at liberty to call upon her at the house?

Julia was instinctively uneasy. There was something strange about this.

Annie shuffled a little awkwardly. "It's very urgent, Miss Sarah," she said again.

Sarah nodded. "Very well, I'll go directly. Please bring my cloak."

"Yes, miss." Annie bobbed a curtsy and began to leave, but Julia called after her.

"Bring my cloak as well, if you please."

"Madam." Annie withdrew.

Sarah turned immediately to Julia. "There is no need for you to come," she said, her tone still cool.

"Do you honestly imagine I will let you go alone when it's getting dark? I wouldn't dream of it." Julia gave her a conciliatory smile. "I really don't wish to be at odds with you, you know, and I promise that nothing I've said about Oliver will be repeated elsewhere, not even to Thomas, and least of all to Oliver himself. I've spoken up because I love you, and because I'm so concerned."

After a moment Sarah returned the smile. "I know, but you're wrong about Oliver."

"I hope I am." Julia paused and then took a long breath. "Sarah, why do you think he's asked you to meet him like this? Isn't it rather odd?"

Sarah glanced out the window at the fiery sky. A sense of foreboding had settled over her. Something was wrong—very wrong indeed.

3

IT was colder outside then they'd expected, and they were glad of their fur-lined cloaks as they hurried through the gathering shadows of the park toward the beech wood on the slope above the lake. Their breath was silvery, and the few leaves that had fallen were brushed aside by their hems as they made their way down the barely discernible path.

The western sky was still stained crimson with the sunset, but behind them the darkness of night was approaching. Some local volunteers were drilling on a hillside beyond the park, and the pop-popping of their muskets carried sharply through the evening as Sarah paused for a moment to look back at the house she loved so very much.

Chalstones spread with Palladian symmetry and splendor across the hillside. It was a porticoed mansion, flanked by single-story wings, one containing the library, the other the picture gallery, which now boasted a new portrait of her by Mr. Lawrence. The house was usually very white, but the sunset had blushed it to pink. The pedimented windows glinted in the fading light, as if looking down at her, but it was a friendly gaze. She smiled a little. Nowhere else would ever mean as much to her as Chalstones.

An owl hooted nearby, and the sound wavered through the motionless trees as Julia halted farther along the path. "Come on, it's too cold to linger," she called.

Sarah hurried to her, and together they made their way down to the edge of the lake, where the path became very mossy as it followed the shore toward the outcrop of rocks surrounding the grotto.

The evening calls of water fowl drifted across the mirrored surface of the lake, where the reflection of Sarah's grandfather's Egyptian obelisk shone from its hilltop on the boundary between Chalstones and adjacent Blackwell Park. Visible from every corner of the estate, the obelisk had been brought back from the shores of the Nile at the end of what had been a very lengthy and memorable Grand Tour.

Sarah's apprehension increased with each step now. Oliver wouldn't resort to this behavior unless something were very wrong. There was no need for such subterfuge. They weren't illicit lovers, but had the approval of those who mattered.

She and Julia were close to the grotto now, and the gentle splash of water was audible as the spring trickled over the reclining white marble Venus at the shell-studded entrance. Suddenly a horse whinnied close by, and it was such an abrupt and startling noise that they halted in alarm. The sound had come from some rhododendron bushes on the slope above the grotto, and as they looked they saw Oliver's large black thoroughbred hidden among the shining dark foliage.

There was something very furtive about the animal's concealment, and Sarah glanced unhappily at Julia. "I wish I knew what this is about," she said quietly. "Whatever it is, I've a dreadful feeling that I'm not going to like it."

"I'd be lying if I said I thought everything was all right," Julia replied sympathetically, looking toward the nearby grotto. "I'll wait here, for I'm sure he wishes to speak to you alone."

Sarah walked slowly on, and then down the shallow steps into the dark entrance. There she halted, for everything was silent except for the gurgle of the spring water. "Oliver? Are you here?" The echoes took up her voice, whispering eerily back at her from every side. "Here, here, here . . ."

A shadow moved from the darkness at the rear of the grotto. It was Oliver. He was tall and well made, with wavy brown hair and long-lashed green eyes. His complexion was pale, his mouth full and sensuous, and he was very personable in appearance, but she thought him handsome. He wore a fashionable pine green riding coat and gray corduroy breeches, and a pearl pin in the folds of his starched neckcloth. His hat, gloves, and riding crop lay upon the curving surface of the marble Venus.

He came swiftly to her, taking her in his arms and kissing her so passionately on the lips that he almost bruised her. Then he rested his cheek against her hair. "I love you, my darling, I love you with all my heart," he said softly. The echoes took up his words. "Heart, heart, heart . . ."

Her trepidation increased, and her eyes were large and anxious as she drew back to look up at him. "What is it, Oliver? Why have you asked me to meet you like this?"

Slowly he released her, turning away slightly to run his fingers through his hair. It was a nervous gesture, and one which she knew preceded bad news.

Suddenly he faced her again. "Sarah, no matter what, I want you to know that I will always love you."

A chill finger touched her spine, making her shiver involuntarily. "As I love you, too," she whispered, but then her gaze was drawn to the fourth finger of his left hand. He wasn't wearing the gold ring she'd given him on their betrothal. Slowly her eyes returned to his face. "The betrothal is over, isn't it?" she said quietly. It wasn't a question, more a statement of fact, and the uncanny echoes mocked her. "Over, over, over . . ."

"Sarah, I don't know what this is all about, I know only that my father has written from London to say that I must consider—"

"London? I . . . I thought he was at Blackwell Park with you," she interrupted, a thousand and one emotions spinning wildly through her. She felt numb and unable to take in what he'd said.

He ran his fingers through his hair again. "He, er, went there last week. Something to do with forcing Sir Gerald Pennyworth to part with that damned horse. It seems my father isn't the only one after the nag, for his most bitter foe, Sir Mason Thackeray, is bidding as well."

His words took her back to the library, and Julia's warnings.

Oliver continued. "Anyway, that has nothing to do with this. Suffice it that my father is in London and has written to me from there."

"Saying that the betrothal is over?"

"Yes, and that I am to stay away from you and from Chalstones."

She almost wanted to laugh. There was something ludicrous about the situation. Here they were, meeting secretly at dusk in a grotto to discuss the ending of their betrothal, even though they didn't want it to end and had no idea at all why Lord Fitzcharles had made this seemingly arbitrary decision. She took a long breath to try to steady herself. "Are you certain your father gave no reason?"

"Absolutely certain."

She did laugh then. "This is a jest, isn't it? Tell me April Fool's Day has moved to October, and I will believe you!"

"It isn't a jest, Sarah," he said quietly. "My father's letter was only too clear and concise."

"Did it mention my father?" she asked as a thought suddenly occurred to her.

"Your father? No. Why?"

"Because he is in London as well, and I can only wonder if he and your father have fallen out."

He shook his head. "I don't think it's anything like that."

"Then what *do* you think?" she demanded. Julia's warnings were all around her, and now seemed almost prophetic.

"I don't know what to think; I only know that it would be prudent for the moment if we did as I've been ordered. We can put the betrothal aside temporarily, and—"

"No, Oliver," she interrupted quietly. "I wouldn't believe it today when I was advised that you would never stand up to your father, but now I am forced to admit it is true. You have no idea why he has done this, but you do not question it at all, indeed you rush to comply. The betrothal is over once and for all." She took off her glove and removed the ring from her finger. Her voice was level, but her emotions were in chaos.

He shook his head. "No, Sarah. The betrothal isn't over finally; all I ask is that we—"

"It's over," she said again, and the echoes heard her. "Over, over, over . . ."

"But I love you, Sarah! We love each other!" he pleaded, taking her urgently in his arms again and trying to press his lips over hers.

She pushed him away. In the past his kisses had melted her, but quite suddenly she was seeing him only too clearly. "I wish to end the match, Oliver. Take your ring." She held it out again.

"No!" he cried, anguish bright in his green eyes as he realized she meant what she said. "Please, Sarah! This is only a temporary thing; it will soon be over, and—"

"Defy your father for me," she interrupted levelly. "Tell him to go to perdition and that you will continue with the match whether he likes it or not."

"You know I can't do that."

"Yes, because you are spineless. Good-bye, Oliver." She placed the ring next to his gloves on the marble Venus, and then gathered her skirts to hurry up the few steps toward the path, where Julia was still waiting for her.

He started after her. "Sarah! In God's name, try to understand!"

She turned then, her eyes cold. "I understand only too well, Oliver. I just wish I'd been this wise a little earlier, for then I would never have been gull enough to fall in love with you in the first place." She hurried on, anxious to escape from him.

He halted, unable to believe that this was happening. It hadn't occurred to him that she would react in this way. All his life he had done as his father instructed, and he had expected her to understand and do the same.

There hadn't been a tremor in her voice or any tears in her eyes when she'd faced him, but Sarah was choking back a sob as she reached Julia, who was instantly alarmed. "Sarah? What is it?"

"Please, let's go back to the house."

Julia cast a bitter glance back toward Oliver, and then ushered Sarah away along the path.

Oliver stared after them, and then slowly turned to retrieve his hat and gloves. He looked at the ring as he picked up the riding crop, and for a moment he thought of leaving it there, but then he put it in his pocket and strode from the grotto up to the bushes where he'd hidden his horse. Mounting, he urged it furiously away in the direction of Blackwell Park.

Julia heard the drumming hooves, and made Sarah halt. "Tell me what happened," she said quietly.

"The betrothal is at an end, by order of Lord Fitz-charles," Sarah replied, still striving not to give in to the tears that stung her eyes. She was shaken to the core by

Oliver's conduct. He was everything Julia had said, and she, Sarah Howard, had been to blind and foolish not to see it until now.

Julia was thunderstruck. "But why? What possible reason could there be for—?"

"No reason was given, but Oliver didn't need one; he took my ring off straightaway. He had been forbidden to come here, and that is why he asked me to meet him in such an unlikely and secluded place. He wanted us to do as his father wished, at least in the meantime, and hoped to resume the match at a later date. I asked him to defy Papa for me, but he wouldn't, and I told him the betrothal was over, permanently. I won't be treated like that, not by Lord Fitzcharles, or by anyone else."

"Good for you!" Julia declared stoutly, but inwardly she was seething with rage. Lord Fitzcharles and his paltry son, the Dishonorable Oliver, had proved her only too right, but she wished with all her heart that she'd been wrong.

They continued along the path, for the sun had almost set now, and darkness was upon them. Soon the lake was behind them as they retraced their steps up toward the house, where lights had now begun to shine in some of the windows.

As they emerged from the woods, Sarah halted again. "It seems Lord Fitzcharles is in London at the moment. I can think only that he and my father have fallen out."

"Over what?"

"I don't know, but that's the only possibility that springs to mind. Heaven knows what they could have argued about, but given that Lord Fitzcharles is the person he is, I imagine he could pick a quarrel with the Archangel Gabriel if the circumstance arose!"

Julia smiled. "Well, at least your sense of humor hasn't been extinguished."

Sarah tried to return the smile. It was a brave but futile attempt, for suddenly her lips quivered and she could no longer stem the tears.

Julia held her close. "It will be all right, sweeting, I promise you it will. You are better out of that match."

In her heart of hearts Sarah now knew that Julia was right, but at the moment, with the devastation and pain so very fresh, it was hard to accept that her future would ever be happy.

4

DAYS passed, and there was no further word of any kind from Blackwell Park. Sarah didn't know whether or not she really expected Oliver to try to see her again, but she did know that she had absolutely no intention of communicating with him. It was over, and she wished to put it as far behind her as possible. She didn't mention him again to Julia, except on the day she wrote a letter to her father in London, explaining what had happened.

Two evenings after that, the friends were again seated in the library, and Julia was once more endeavoring to write to Thomas. As had happened before, she could not concentrate, and this time it was because she was still so angry about the shabbiness of Oliver's conduct. He wasn't a man; he was a mewling milksop without a will of his own!

The fierceness of her loyalty to Sarah made her smile a little, for it put her in mind of a time in the past when she had felt similarly indignant and defensive on her friend's behalf.

Sarah glanced across at the writing desk, where Julia's peach silk gown was brightened by the lighted candelabrum before her. "What are you smiling about?" she asked.

"I was recalling Lady Georgette Belvoir, *chienne* that she was."

"Was, and most probably still is," Sarah murmured.

Julia leaned back in her chair. Lady Georgette Belvoir had been the most beautiful and most spiteful girl at their school in Cheltenham. There had been no depth to which she would not sink in order to have her own way, and this unattractive side of her character had never been more clearly displayed than on the occasion when her brother, Geoffrey, the future Earl of Hayden, had visited the school and admired Sarah.

Georgette's jealous resentment had risen to such a pitch of fury that she'd resorted to scurrilous lies in order to blacken Sarah in Geoffrey's eyes. She'd succeeded, and the petty victory had given her enormous satisfaction, but the rest of the school had despised her for it. Georgette had remained unrepentant. She'd set out to vanquish Sarah, and that was all that mattered to her.

Sarah was remembering exactly the same incident. "It wasn't even as if I particularly liked her wretched brother. If the truth be known, I thought him as unspeakable as she. Even if she hadn't interfered, I wouldn't have welcomed his attentions."

"That wouldn't have made any difference; it was that he had a fancy for you that pricked her. She just couldn't bear to think that her brother liked someone she knew was far more popular than she was."

Sarah rose, her lilac taffeta gown rustling as she went to stand before the fire to hold her hands out to the warmth. "The whole Belvoir family is mean-spirited. Her sisters were just as disagreeable, and I've no doubt the earl and countess are relieved to have most of them off their hands now. Georgette is the only one left, isn't she?"

"Yes, even Geoffrey is married."

"I pity the man who takes Georgette to wife," Sarah observed uncharitably.

"So do I, especially as it's almost certain she'll have to accept someone from a lower level in society than she would like."

"Oh?" Sarah turned with interest.

"Marrying off his son and three other daughters has cost the earl dear, and after a number of unwise financial transactions, he no longer has the wherewithal to give her the sort of lavish dowry that would attract an eligible earl or someone from even further up the scale. According to Thomas, she doesn't lack suitors, but none of them are exactly exalted. It's my guess she'll have to accept a mere baron or baronet."

Sarah's eyes widened. "Surely not."

Julia gave a sleek smile that verged on the evil. "I fear

so, and when I think of all her airs and graces, and of how she swore one day to be a duchess at the very least."

They laughed, but then Sarah broke off to look toward the windows. "Listen! Isn't that a carriage?"

In the ensuing silence, they both distinctly heard the rattle of wheels on the gravel drive. Sarah hurried to look out, and saw the lamps swinging through the darkness as the coachman maneuvered the vehicle to a standstill in front of the house. For a moment she wondered who it could be, but then with a start recognized the carriage as her father's. But why had he returned a month early? He wasn't due back until some time late in November.

"It's my father," she said, turning quickly back into the room.

"But I thought he was staying in London until next month," Julia replied.

"So did I. Oh, dear, I hope he hasn't rushed home because of my letter." Gathering her skirts, Sarah hurried from the room, and after a moment Julia followed.

They waited together beneath the Ionic colonnade at the rear of the crimson-and-gold entrance hall as the butler, Bracklesham, crossed the echoing marble floor to open the main doors.

Mr. Howard came wearily in, his customary limp more pronounced because he was tired after the journey. He'd hurt his knee in a riding accident as a young man, and had never fully recovered. He was a tall man, and had become a little stout in recent years, but he was still quite handsome, with the same clear blue eyes as his daughter. Advancing years had not meant a balding head, however, and when he gave his tall hat to the butler, the light from the chandeliers fell upon his ample gray hair. He wore a caped brown woolen greatcoat that reached almost to his ankles, and beneath it an indigo coat and cream breeches.

The butler took his overcoat. "Welcome home, sir."

"Thank you, Bracklesham. Is all well here?"

"It is, sir," the butler replied, knowing that his master was referring to the running of the house and not to Sarah's private affairs.

Mr. Howard turned then and saw the two women waiting beneath the colonnade. He smiled at Julia, and then looked searchingly at his daughter before holding out his hands to her. "Sarah, my dear," he said, walking toward her.

She ran to meet him, flinging her arms around his neck and kissing him warmly on the cheek.

"How are you, my dear?" he asked, looking anxiously into her eyes.

"I'm all right."

"Are you quite sure?"

"I'm a little hurt about Oliver's weakness, but I'm certainly not in a decline. Julia has convinced me that I'm far better off without him."

He glanced past her toward Julia, and smiled. "You are a very wise young lady, Mrs. Thurlong."

Julia smiled.

He looked at Sarah again. "You will never know how glad I am that this match is over."

"Glad?" She was surprised. "But, I thought you welcomed it."

"I did, until I realized what a scoundrel Fitzcharles *père* is. The pursuance of self-interest is his motto, and his son appears to tremble at his every pronouncement. I'm relieved the betrothal was never officially announced, because, to be truthful with you, I've been agonizing as to how best to advise you against going on with things. I feared you were in love beyond redemption."

"I was, but am now in sound mind again." She smiled, but then became more serious. "Is it because of this that you've returned?"

"I had to be sure that you were coping with matters."

She searched his face. "Do you know why Lord Fitzcharles ended the match?"

"No."

The reply took her aback, for somehow she'd convinced herself that he would provide an explanation.

He smiled at her surprised expression. "What did you imagine, mm—a vile quarrel and pistols at dawn?"

"I did not think about pistols at dawn, but I certainly imagined a quarrel. It was all I could think of."

"Well, I fear that Fitzcharles's reason must remain a mystery, not that I am particularly concerned, since the ending of the match was the best thing that could have happened." He hesitated, and then looked at Julia for a moment. "How are you, my dear?" he asked.

"I'm very well," Julia replied, crossing toward them.

"I haven't seen anything of that dashing husband of yours, even though I know he's in London. How is he?"

"Thomas is also very well, sir."

"I believe he is being groomed for Downing Street," Mr. Howard murmured, his blue eyes twinkling.

"Lady Thurlong has ambitions in that direction," Julia replied.

"Ah, but what does Thomas himself think?"

"He isn't opposed to the notion."

"Which means that you will soon be toddling off to the capital, mm?"

"I fear so. To be truthful, I'd much rather stay in Cheltenham. I don't think I will ever be as diligent or devoted a political hostess as Lady Thurlong." Julia lowered her glance. "All I want is Thomas, and a family."

"An admirable ambition, my dear."

"At the moment I have neither."

He raised an eyebrow. "Soon you will have both, I'm sure."

"I hope so." Julia blushed a little, for it was a matter of keen disappointment to her that after two years of marriage she and Thomas were still childless. She wanted children more than anything else, and certainly wasn't looking forward to the hothouse atmosphere of Lady Thurlong's political world.

"Lady Thurlong will understand how you feel, you know," Mr. Howard said kindly. "She is a very amiable and considerate person, and a very old friend of mine. Actually, I once nearly married her."

Sarah was startled. "I never knew that!"

"I don't tell you everything." He glanced at Julia again. "My dear, I have a great favor to ask of you. I know that Sarah will be cross with me about this, but nevertheless my mind is made up. After what has happened she needs diversion, and since there is very little to divert here at Chalstones, I wondered if you and she could go to Cheltenham. I believe the season is in full swing there at the moment, but she will not suffer any embarrassment over the broken betrothal because it was never made public. I know that you don't intend to leave for London just yet, and so . . . ?" He allowed his voice to die away on a hopeful note.

"Yes, of course, provided Sarah doesn't mind," Julia answered without hesitation.

Sarah was as cross as he predicted. "There isn't any need, and besides, I can't leave you alone here," she protested.

"I won't be here; I'm going back to London almost immediately. I have various things to attend to."

She gave in reluctantly. "Then of course I will go to Cheltenham with Julia, if that is what you really wish."

"It's what I wish, and it will make me feel better. Mind you, I shall expect you to write regularly."

"You know I will."

"Address everything to my club."

She was surprised. "Your club? Not the Brook Street house?"

"Er, no. I am in the process of disposing of it."

Her surprise turned to astonishment. "But whatever for? I thought you liked it there."

"I did, until some dolt in the street behind chose to erect a monstrosity of an observatory on his roof. It's intolerable, for I swear that the fellow's interest is more earthly than heavenly, and that the scandalous goings-on in various Mayfair bedrooms are of more significance than the progress of the stars. I have therefore decided to sell the house and look elsewhere, and in the meantime I am enjoying the hospitality of my club—red mullet and the finest grouse from Scotland. What more could a man wish?" He laughed.

For a fleeting second, barely the space of a heartbeat, Sarah thought she saw a mask slip from his eyes. In that tiny moment she thought she perceived a dreadful anxiety he was trying to keep hidden, but then the mask slid back into place, and she saw only the laughing father she knew so well.

5

AS Mr. Howard was reunited with his daughter at Chalstones, Nicholas was drawing his yellow phaeton to an extremely hasty standstill outside Stephen's lodgings in lamplit Conduit Street, Mayfair. A quick glance up at his cousin's third-floor rooms informed him that someone was at home, for there were lights, and one of the windows was open, even this late on a cold October evening.

Alighting swiftly from the phaeton, he led the horses to the dark alley that led through into a small yard at the rear of the building. There he made the reins fast to a post and then retraced his steps out of the alley to the street, with its bright lamps and broad pavements.

He beckoned to a small boy he'd noticed on arriving. "Have you a mind to earn yourself a few pennies?" he asked.

The boy scampered toward him. "Yes, guv. Anything you ask."

"Just mind my horses." Nicholas nodded back toward the yard and then dropped some coins into the eager boy's outstretched hand. "Look after them well, and if I'm pleased on my return, I'll give you the same again."

The boy's eyes widened at his good fortune. "Oh, yes, guv! I'll look after 'em!" he promised fervently.

"And if you require me, I'll be at Mr. Mannering's lodgings here." Nicholas indicated the building.

The boy nodded, and then hurried through the alley into the yard, where he took up his station by the phaeton. Watching him, Nicholas wondered for a moment if even the yard was too public a place. He was certain Lady Georgette Belvoir had spotted him when he passed her carriage at Tyburn Corner. Knowing that if she had she would follow him, he had abandoned his original plans and endeavored to give her the slip by coming here instead. He'd used a very circuitous route, and been obliged to do some very nifty work with the ribbons, but he hoped he'd eluded her. Damn it, he felt positively haunted. He couldn't go anywhere at the moment without fearing that the tiresome creature would materialize at his side. He'd cried off two invitations today because at the last minute he'd discovered that she'd wormed her way on to the guest list. For an unmarried woman she was forward beyond belief, and if her parents knew the half of her recent activities, they would be shocked to the core. They'd certainly despair of ever marrying her off suitably, and the earl's choler would become positively explosive.

Nicholas looked warily along the street in both directions again, fearing that at any moment he would see her carriage. He wished he's been able to leave for Cheltenham before now, but legal problems had interfered. It was all settled now, though, and with luck he would definitely be able to leave the day after tomorrow.

He glanced up at the lodging house again. It was Mayfair, but not the best Mayfair, that was a fact. Still, for Stephen it was merely a place to stay until he inherited, at which point he would no doubt purchase an exceedingly extravagant residence. Tilting his tall hat back on his tousled black hair, Nicholas entered the house and went lightly up the stairs to his cousin's rooms.

Stephen was slumped disconsolately in an armchair. He'd lost again this evening, but for once had had the common sense to leave the table before he plunged in over his fool head. He recognized Nicholas's knock at the door.

"Come in, Coz," he called, smiling as Nicholas entered. "I thought you'd removed out of harm's way to Cheltenham."

"I've been detained by damned lawyers." Nicholas tossed his hat and gloves on to the table, and then went to hold his hands out to the fire, for the room was cold because of the open window. He looked up at the mantelshelf with its array of candlesticks, snuff boxes, pipe racks, and other paraphernalia always found in the rooms of fashionable young gentlemen. There were papers of all sorts wedged behind the candlesticks, and the chimney breast itself was hung with a collection of sporting prints, mostly of prize fighters. Sporting publications were scattered on a table, and a meal of bread and cheese lay waiting upon a plate bearing the Mannering family crest.

Stephen had a glass of whisky in his hand. "Some Scottish dew?" he inquired, nodding toward a decanter on a nearby table.

"I wouldn't decline." Nicholas went to pour himself some.

"What brings you here?" Stephen asked.

"Desperation."

"Really?"

"I'm running like a damned rabbit to avoid a certain female."

Stephen chuckled. "She is quite a problem, I grant you."

"I hope to see the last of her for some time when I leave the day after tomorrow for Cheltenham."

"Do you have a definite date for Naples?"

"Nothing firm. It's still set for a few weeks' time, at around the middle of November." He looked at his cousin. "I hope you don't mind me skulking in here like this?"

"Not at all, for you've livened up my otherwise excruciatingly dull evening."

"Believe me, excruciating dullness has its attractions. I vow sometimes that I even expect the wretched woman to appear beside me in the plunge bath!"

"She would if she could."

"I'm more than aware of that."

"Actually, I was under the impression that she had given up on you and was consoling herself with Sir Mason Thackeray," Stephen said.

"That, my dear fellow, is a ploy, and nothing more. The creature believes, or rather hopes, I will be so jealous that I will realize the error of my ways."

Stephen chuckled. "So that's how it is, eh? I must say I'm surprised that Thackeray has the time or inclination for the pursuit of the fair sex now that he has this tremendous tussle with Fitzcharles over that damned racehorse. What's it called? Icarus?"

"Thackeray *always* finds time for luxurious pursuits,"

Nicholas murmured. "As for the feud with Fitzcharles, it isn't even as if poor old Sir Gerald Pennyworth wants to sell to anyone at all. There's nothing he'd like more than to be left alone to race Icarus under his own colors, but Thackeray is like a gadfly on his hide, and Fitzcharles is in deadly earnest."

"Is it true that Pennyworth's bankruptcy is being helped along by Fitzcharles?"

"So the whispers have it."

Stephen drew a long breath. "Fitzcharles is a blot on society, and no mistake."

Nicholas sipped the whisky appreciatively. "The Scots know a thing or two about distilling," he murmured.

"I prefer it to cognac, if the truth be known, but cognac is the fashion." Stephen studied him. "By now you *must* have heard about the deep play at the club?"

"No, nor do I want to if it involves my father." Nicholas eyed him darkly. "Stephen, most people have the wit not to mention my sire to me, but you, it seems, do not learn."

"Oh, have it your own way, but I would have thought you'd like to know about the additions to your already substantial inheritance."

"I may not inherit anything at all, for he might feel disposed to disown me."

"He'll never cast you off, Nicholas."

"That remains to be seen." Nicholas looked at him. "Enough of my disreputable old man; what of you? Why are you in at this hour?"

"I saw wisdom for once. Every card I was dealt was appalling, and so I decided to beat a tactical retreat. Tomorrow is another day, as they say."

"Stay away altogether. You aren't like my father— Lady Luck seldom smiles upon you."

"So you keep warning me, but I just can't help it. As I said before, I've decided to mend my ways when I inherit. It's a target I've set myself."

Nicholas didn't reply. He knew his cousin far too well. With a sigh he finished the glass of whisky. "It should be safe to leave now, so I'll be on my way."

"Another glass first?"

"I think not, but thank you anyway. I've left my phaeton in the care of a boy who may or may not be up to the job, and I value my horses."

Stephen got up. "Have it your own way. This no doubt means we won't meet again until after your return from Naples. I wish you well, for November isn't exactly the best time of year to be crossing the Bay of Biscay. Just take care, eh?"

"I have one of Nelson's captains to guard my hide."

Stephen grinned. "Then nothing can possibly befall you," he murmured, seeing him to the door.

Nicholas tugged on his tall hat as he went down the staircase again, but as he emerged into the street a sixth sense brought him to a wary standstill. Glancing along the pavement, he saw a carriage he knew only too well. His heart sank. She had successfully followed the scent after all! But as he stood there, undecided what to do, he realized that she could not be in the vehicle, for by now she would have alighted and greeted him.

He turned instinctively toward the entrance of the alley. Had she driven past and seen the phaeton in the yard? Her eye was sharp, and the merest glimpse would have been sufficient. Cautiously he went the few steps to the corner, and peeped around. Sure enough, a lady in a cream velvet cloak was talking to the boy, who nodded and pointed toward the lodging house.

As Georgette turned, Nicholas drew sharply out of sight, hurrying a few yards farther on away from the lodging house, and hiding in a doorway. Glancing back with great care, he saw her emerge from the alley and pause for a moment by the door of the lodging house. As she looked up toward the third floor, her hood fell back, revealing her unrivalled golden hair and flawless, heart-shaped face. No one could dispute her incredible beauty. It was a pity her character was so unlovely.

He waited until she had entered the building, and then he hurried from his hiding place and into the yard, where her rose scent still lingered, almost as if she had returned unseen behind him. He quelled the urge to look over his shoulder, and handed the promised extra coins to the boy.

" 'Ere, mister, there was a lady just now, and—"

"I know, and I mean to be gone from here before she realizes she's missed me." Vaulting on to the phaeton,

Nicholas took up the reins and urged the team forward.
The light vehicle hurtled out of the alley into the street,
vanishing around a corner just as Georgette emerged,
furious.

Nicholas drove like the wind for Duke Street. Cheltenham could not come soon enough, nor Naples after that!

6

SARAH and Julia set off for Cheltenham on exactly the same day as Nicholas, and Sarah was destined to meet him before journey's end. It was not going to be an agreeable meeting.

But that was to come, and as the carriages were brought to the door at Chalstones, Sarah's thoughts were of her father. The mask she thought she had glimpsed had not been in evidence since, and she was more or less satisfied that she had imagined it. There was still a tiny niggling doubt, however, so much so that before leaving the house, she felt obliged to ask him outright if everything was all right. Without so much as a flicker, he assured her that it was, and her doubts evaporated completely.

They emerged into the morning sunshine to enter the waiting carriages. The first vehicle was to convey the two friends, the second their maids and luggage. Mr. Howard saw them off, and was in jovial mood as once again he made Sarah promise to write regularly. After she had elicited a similar promise from him, both vehicles commenced the forty-mile journey.

Julia wore a sage green merino pelisse and matching gown, with a wide-brimmed gypsy hat, and Sarah had chosen a shell pink gown and gray velvet spencer, with a gray jockey bonnet from which trailed a filmy pink gauze scarf. They were both decidedly *à la mode*, for Cheltenham was a very fashionable town, and when one went there, one had to wear the latest styles.

As the carriages bowled down the drive, Sarah looked back at Chalstones. The house and park had seldom looked more lovely than today. The trees were magnificent with the colors of fall, and the lake was a sheet of glass in the valley. Fallen leaves scuttered and whirled in the wake of the vehicles as they drew out past the lodge on to the main London turnpike, where the coachmen swiftly brought them up to a spanking pace toward Gloucestershire and the west.

The highway was busy, with stagecoaches, mails, and various private vehicles driving past those traveling more slowly, such as carts and wagons. There were also reminders of the war, with a column of infantry marching toward the capital, and a detachment of cavalry resting their horses by a crossroad. The carriages made good time throughout the morning, and it was not all that long before they were on the penultimate stage, which would bring them to the Frogmill Inn, an isolated hostelry on the western edge of the Cotswold escarpment.

Nicholas came up behind them on the same highway, tooling his bright yellow phaeton along at a spanking pace as the glossy black horses responded willingly to his light touch. He was glad to be free of the noise and smoke of the capital, and was looking forward to seeing his grandmother, Lady Worthington. He was also immeasurably relieved to have escaped from Georgette. His whip flicked and the team went faster, skimming past the two carriages from Chalstones. He didn't give them a second glance as he concentrated upon the road. He too was making for the Frogmill Inn, where he and Sarah were soon to meet.

The inn was famous for its hospitality, and was therefore always busy. Its yard was crowded with all kinds of vehicles as the two carriages from Chalstones arrived. Julia immediately noticed Lady Charterton's coat-of-arms on the door of a barouche, and since the lady was a relative of Thomas's, she decided to pay her respects. Sarah didn't know Lady Charterton at all, and elected instead to stay outside in the yard, where she could stroll in the fresh air after having been confined in the carriage for several hours.

Julia still hadn't returned by the time the new team had been harnessed, and so Sarah walked up and down a little longer. It was then that she noticed an archway leading to a meadow, and on impulse she walked toward it. On the way she barely noticed Nicholas's yellow phaeton drawn up in a corner nearby, in the care of a stableboy.

On the other side of the arch she discovered a beautiful view of the Cotswolds, with rolling hills, woods of every autumn shade, farms, dry stone walls, and flocks of sheep. Immediately to her right was a disused barn with a roof that at some time had been badly damaged by fire. The barn door stood ajar, revealing an uneven floor piled with old straw.

The meadow itself swept down toward a shallow stream that wended its way between a line of weeping willows. Nicholas was strolling along the bank, and Sarah watched him as he paused by one of the willows and leaned casually against it with his hands thrust deep into the pockets of his charcoal greatcoat. She knew by the quality and cut of his clothes that he was a man of means, and even at that distance she could see that he was very handsome indeed.

A light breeze stirred over the hillside, and he removed his tall hat to savor the coolness of the air through his hair. He was in a thoughtful mood, and it seemed to her that although physically he stood in a Cotswold meadow, mentally he was a thousand miles away.

Sarah didn't hear the step of a gentleman's boot behind her, and knew nothing of anyone else's presence until a hand was suddenly placed very improperly on her shoulder and a drawling voice addressed her in a forward and unpleasantly familiar manner.

" 'Pon me soul, I vow I've happened upon a vision of loveliness."

She whirled about, and saw a fop with a leering smile on his face. A surfeit of rouge shone on his cheeks and lips, and his golden hair was prinked into deliberate curls. His waistline was tightly laced to give him the latest look, and he was clad entirely in gray-and-white stripes. His grin and the lascivious glint in his pale eyes warned her that she was very much to his taste, and also very much at his mercy out here away from the busy yard.

" 'Pon me soul," he murmured again, his too warm gaze raking over her, and then lingering on the curve of her breasts. "May I know your name, sweet incognita?"

She tried to push past him toward the yard, but he forced her to stay by seizing her arm. "Your name, m'dear," he insisted, an edge entering his voice.

"Please let me go, sir," she said, more than a little alarmed.

"Politeness doesn't cost a farthing, sweetheart."

"I'm not your sweetheart, and I certainly see no reason to be polite to you! Unhand me now!" She hoped she sounded more self-possessed than she felt.

"How high and mighty you are, to be sure," he drawled, his fingers tightening cruelly around her arm. "Such a lack of civility needs punishment, I fancy." His glance moved toward the nearby barn, and its invitingly open entrance.

True fear rushed over her as she realized what was in his mind. She began to struggle frantically, and tried to scream, but he clamped his hand harshly over her mouth and started to drag her toward the barn. Then, just as he was about to thrust her inside and fling himself upon her, his hold was suddenly loosened. She heard him give a choked cry, and she turned swiftly in time to see the man she had seen in the meadow jerking him into the air by the scruff of his dandified neck.

The fop's face had drained of color, and his eyes were wide with terror as Nicholas shook him like a rat, before virtually hurling him into a nearby stone trough with a tremendous splash. Coughing and spluttering, her attacker floundered in the dirty water as he tried to scramble out, but then he saw the expression of intimidating fury on Nicholas's face and became still, terrified to do anything that might further provoke his fury.

Nicholas was contemptuous. "I think you should take me on instead, don't you? Or are defenseless women all you dare to prey on?"

The fop was frightened out of his wits. Take him on? Was the man serious?

Nicholas folded his arms. "Well, sir? What do you say? Shall we go a round or two? Or would you prefer to beg this lady's forgiveness for your unspeakable conduct?"

The latter course was infinitely more attractive. The fop's tongue passed nervously over his rouged lips, and he looked swiftly at Sarah. "I crave your forgiveness, madam," he mumbled.

Nicholas tutted disapprovingly. "That pathetic excuse for an apology won't do at all. Let's hear it properly."

"I crave your forgiveness, madam," the fop repeated.

"Louder!"

"I crave your forgiveness, madam!" the fop cried, trembling like a jelly.

Nicholas was scornful. "What a contemptible creature you are, so brave when it comes to forcing yourself upon a lady, but a cringing wheyface when confronted by anything more. Get out of here, and don't let me ever see your repugnant person again. Is that clear?"

"Yes, yes, very clear indeed!" Nodding his head busily, the fop clambered out of the trough, and without further ado took to his heels toward the yard, where his dripping appearance drew immediate guffaws of laughter from the grooms and coachmen.

As soon as he had gone, Nicholas turned abruptly to Sarah. "Are you all right?" The inquiry wasn't uttered solicitously, but on the contrary it was rather terse. His reaction was like that of a parent on discovering that a disobedient child was no longer missing or in danger; his anxiety dissolved into anger.

"Yes. Thank you." She was so grateful that she didn't notice his tone.

"Are you quite sure?"

"Yes." She was suddenly aware of his lack of warmth, and she met his gaze surprisedly. Close up he was even more handsome than she'd realized, but his memorable gray eyes were disconcertingly cool. His manner puzzled her. "I, er, don't know how to thank you for rescuing me, Mr . . . ?"

"Stanhope. Nicholas Stanhope." He inclined his head. "You now have the advantage of me, madam, for you know who I am, but I have no idea who you are."

"Sarah Howard, Miss Sarah Howard."

"Well, Miss Howard, you were exceedingly ill-advised to come out of the yard alone like this. An empty barn is only too convenient for those with base intentions, as I trust you now belatedly understand."

She felt herself bridling. Maybe she had been a little unwise, but that did not give him the right to lecture her like a naughty infant! "Oh, I understand the error of my foolish ways, Mr. Stanhope, and I would like to add that although you may be assured of my immense gratitude for your timely help, I think it best if we parted now, before your warmth and charm overwhelm me completely. Good day." With a toss of her head, she turned and stalked away into the yard.

Nicholas gazed after her in astonishment, for he hadn't realized how overbearing and supercilious he had been. For a moment he considered hurrying after her to apologize, but then thought better of it. She was justifiably angry and had already shown her spirit by verbally boxing his ears. He had no desire to suffer a second such boxing. He drew a regretful breath. Damn. He hadn't handled that at all well.

Sarah's cheeks were still very pink by the time she returned to the carriage, where Julia was waiting and wondering what had happened to her. "There you are! Where on earth have you been?"

Sarah took her seat, her eyes bright with anger. "I have been attacked by a despicable dragon, and rescued by an unspeakable Saint George," she replied.

Julia stared. "Would you care to explain?" she inquired as the carriage drew out of the yard.

Sarah told her what had happened, and Julia's eyes widened with horror. "Oh, no! How dreadful! You were actually being dragged into the barn?"

"I dread to think what would have happened if Mr. Nicholas Stanhope hadn't been there. He saw the dragon off in no uncertain terms, but then proceeded to berate the maiden for having been in distress! It was my fault for having been there, would you believe? I'm very grateful to him for coming to my aid when he did, but that does not prevent me from believing him to be the rudest and most arrogant man in creation!"

Her furious indignation took Julia slightly aback. "Well, I've never heard of this Nicholas Stanhope, and I trust I will never have the misfortune to meet him," she murmured.

As the Chalstone carriages neared the foot of the long hill down from the escarpment, Nicholas's bright yellow phaeton whisked past them again. As on the previous occasion, he didn't pay any attention to the other vehicles, and he certainly did not detect Sarah's incensed glare as he passed.

Noticing the attention she gave to the phaeton, Julia looked inquiringly at her. "I take it that that was the unspeakable Stanhope?"

"Yes," was the brief response.

"You neglected to say how handsome he is."

Sarah sniffed disparagingly. "His looks would seem to prove the veracity of the old adage."

"What old adage?"

"That you can't tell a book by its cover."

Julia decided that it would be tactful not to mention Mr. Stanhope again at this juncture, not when Sarah was so obviously seething over him. It certainly wasn't the moment to point out that if he was driving in the same direction as they, he was most probably bound for Cheltenham as well.

7

WITH several hours to go before night fall, the first houses on the outskirts of Cheltenham appeared by the wayside. Sarah was still a little shaken after what had so nearly happened to her, but she was also exceedingly wrathful about Nicholas's attitude. As she looked out at Cheltenham, however, she was determined to put the whole disagreeable business behind her and enjoy the diversions of the town's season. It was the place to be at this time of the year, with a social whirl that matched both Bath and Brighton, if not quite the capital itself.

Julia and Thomas's home, Thurlong Lodge, stood in the High Street, not far from the assembly rooms. It was an imposing new house fronting directly on to the broad pavement, but although it had no garden at the front, at the back it boasted three leafy terraces that descended directly to the banks of the River Chelt. The house was four stories high, with covered wrought iron balconies at the second-floor windows, and its front entrance was approached up a little flight of stone steps.

Julia had sent word ahead, and her butler was awaiting their arrival. Hemmings was a rather lanky personage with a long face and large nose, but if his appearance was unprepossessing, his manners and grace were exceptional as he opened the carriage door to greet his mistress. "Good afternoon, madam. Welcome home," he said, sweeping her a bow that would have done credit to any drawing room.

"Good afternoon, Hemmings," Julia replied, accepting his extended hand and alighting.

He then assisted Sarah down from the carriage, and she stood glancing around as Julia briefly inquired how things had been at the house in her absence.

The High Street was very busy, and the pavements

were thronged with fashionable ladies and gentlemen, including many army and naval officers. The clatter of hooves and rattle of wheels filled the air as elegant vehicles bowled to and fro, and suddenly Sarah's attention was drawn to one carriage in particular. It was a cerise landau drawn by a pair of cream horses, and at first the fact that the vehicle's hoods were lowered caught her eye, for the weather was hardly warm enough for that, but then it was the lady occupant who drew her gaze, for it was none other than Lady Georgette Belvoir.

Georgette was as heartstoppingly beautiful as ever, and was particularly eye-catching today because the clothes she wore were the same cerise color as the landau. Hence the lowered hoods, of course, for Georgette was always one to suffer nobly in the cause of fashion. She wore a closely fitted woolen pelisse with a gold-buckled belt around the waist high beneath her breasts and flouncy white plumes springing from her cerise velvet hat. The hat swept back from her face, the better to reveal every delightful feature, from her magnificent lilac eyes and rosebud lips, to her delicate bone structure and glorious golden hair. She caused a stir as she passed, and was enjoying every moment of attention, whether it was the admiration of the gentlemen, or the jealousy of the ladies. She and her parents had arrived in the spa only that afternoon, and this was her first excursion. It was going as excellently as she'd planned.

Sarah and Julia both observed her as the landau approached, and they didn't think Georgette had noticed them, but suddenly she looked in their direction. Her lips parted slightly and her lilac eyes sharpened, but she did not deign to acknowledge them as the landau drove on down the street.

Julia sniffed. "What a very vulgar display, to be sure," she observed crushingly. "Dear Lord, how I loathe that woman. I have only to look at her and my hackles rise."

"Vulgar display or not, it had the desired effect. Every male head in the street turned as if pulled by string," Sarah replied.

Julia gazed after the disappearing landau. "I wonder why she's here? The Haydens usually stay in London at this time of year because the countess has it in her head that Cheltenham is too damp."

"I only hope we don't encounter her anywhere," Sarah said with feeling.

"A vain hope, I fear. Cheltenham may be the height of fashion, but everyone moves in the same circle." Julia linked her arm. "Enough of that *chienne*; let's go in out of the cold."

They went quickly up the steps and into the house. The hall was white, with swags of glided plasterwork on the walls and ceiling, and the floor was elaborately patterned with red, black, and white tiles. There were two handsome doors, the one on the left leading to the drawing room, the one on the right to the dining room. A staircase rose from the far side of the dining-room door, and beyond it an archway concealed the way to the kitchens.

The servants had hastily assembled at the foot of the staircase, and Julia greeted them all with her customary kindness. Two footmen were delegated to unload the carriages, and Sarah was suddenly and disagreeably conscious of the surly look one of them was giving both Julia and her. He was tall, fair, and rather fleshy, and gave the impression of being exceedingly vain. She didn't particularly care for him.

When she and Julia had been relieved of their outdoor things by their personal maids, they adjourned to the drawing room, where Hemmings would soon serve a tray of tea. The drawing room was one of the most charming Sarah knew. It stretched from the front of the house to the back, where a large French window opened on to the first of the garden's terraces. The view down to the river and the meadows beyond was splendid, for the Cotswolds could be seen in the distance. The room was decorated in peach, with brocade on the walls and velvet on the sofas and chairs. Several gilt-framed mirrors gave the impression of more space, and when darkness fell two particularly handsome chandeliers gave all the light one could require. A fire had been lit, and the room was warm and welcoming as the two friends took their seats.

Sarah smiled as she looked around. "I think this is almost my favorite room in all the world," she declared.

"Almost? Oh, I suppose it trails miserably behind every closet and broom cupboard at your adored Chalstones," Julia replied dryly.

"Well, they're very superior closets and broom cupboards," Sarah answered with a grin.

"Indeed so. Worthy of royal receptions at the very least," Julia agreed with feigned seriousness.

At that moment a slight disturbance came from the hallway. Something fell to the floor with a thud, there was a curse, and then a brief but angry exchange between Hemmings and one of the footmen attending to the luggage. It was the butler who had the last word.

Sarah glanced at Julia. "What was that about, do you think?"

"Heaven knows, but it would seem that Hemmings has it all in hand. Now then, what was I about to say? Oh, yes, I was going to discuss all the things we might do in the coming days. We must go to the weekly subscription ball at the Royal Well, and visit the well itself, of course."

"To drink that dreadful water?" Sarah was appalled at the thought.

"Dreadful water? Miss Howard, I'll have you know that Cheltenham water has the finest curative properties in the whole of England."

"It tastes abominable."

"True, but one isn't supposed to say so." Julia smiled.

A knock came at the drawing-room door, and the footman Sarah had noticed earlier came in with the tray of tea. His face was ruddy with anger, and she guessed that he was the one who had just fallen foul of Hemmings. She was again conscious of his surly manner as he put the tray on a little table, but this time she realized that he was silently very resentful about something. But what? She watched him curiously as he bowed and withdrew, and then she felt a shock as she met his eyes, for the look he gave her was one of ill-concealed animosity. This time it wasn't directed at Julia, but solely at her.

When he had gone, she looked at Julia. "Has that footman been with you for long? I don't remember seeing him before."

"Andrew? A few months, I believe. Thomas engaged him. It was a case of army connections. Andrew's father was a sergeant-major in Thomas's father's regiment. Why do you ask?"

"I thought him a little, er, disagreeable."

Julia smiled and began to pour the tea. "No doubt he has fallen out with his latest ladylove. I understand from my maid that he is very much one for the fair sex. I have to admit that I don't much care for him, but he's Thomas's business, not mine, and if he steps out of line, I'll see to it that Thomas does what is required."

Sarah didn't say anything more, but made a mental note to be on her guard where he was concerned.

Andrew was at that moment returning to the kitchens, where most of the other servants were now seated around the scrubbed table, enjoying a moment of leisure before it was time to start preparing dinner. Hemmings sat regally apart from the others in his favorite chair by the fire, reading the newspaper that was still delivered to the house even though the master and mistress had both been away until today.

Instead of lifting a chair quietly in order to sit at the table with the others, Andrew dragged one over the stone-flagged floor before sitting down.

Hemmings was instantly irritated, and lowered the newspaper with an tut of exasperation. "You haven't got the time to be idle, my laddo, for you've a valise to get mended before Miss Howard finds out what you've done."

"But, Mr. Hemmings—"

The butler folded the newspaper and rose testily to his feet. "I don't want any of your whining. In your haste to try to finish and get away to that flibbertigibbet maid, you dropped the valise and broke its handle."

Everyone around the table was silent. All eyes were lowered, but all ears were very alert to the row that was brewing, for they all knew Andrew's capacity for getting himself into the butler's bad books.

"I wasn't rushing," Andrew replied with a scowl.

"Oh, yes you were, and now it's cost you your free time. I don't care how many hours you think you're due, or how obliging Lady Georgette's new maid would have been had you been able to meet her as planned. Your duties here come first, and you'll conduct yourself as *I* wish. That means behaving yourself, do I make myself clear?"

"Yes." Andrew could not have uttered the word more insolently had he tried.

Suddenly Hemmings strode across the stone-tiled floor and tipped the footman's chair over so that he was sent sprawling. The silence around the table became positively deafening.

The butler glowered down at Andrew. "I've had just about enough of you, so you'd better take note that unless you improve, I'll see to it that Mr. Thurlong gives you your marching orders next time he's back. Don't think your father's regimental connection will save your arrogant little neck, for Mr. Thurlong won't stand for any nonsense from the likes of you. As for Lady Georgette's maid, you're just going to have to hope she fancies you enough to wait until next time, because you're not going to see her today. Do you understand?"

Andrew struggled to his feet. His face was crimson, but when he replied this time, it was much more civilly. "Yes, Mr. Hemmings. I'm sorry, sir."

"Good. Then get that valise mended right now." The butler pointed to the damaged item, which stood in readiness by the back door.

"Yes, Mr. Hemmings." Andrew hastened to do as he was told.

As the door closed behind him, the butler resumed his fireside seat. "Cocksure young puppy," he breathed, shaking his newspaper open. At the table, everyone else still remained silent.

Andrew left Thurlong Lodge by the side entrance, and his face was dark and bitter as he strode down the street to the shop where he knew the damaged valise could be instantly repaired. If it hadn't been for Miss Howard's luggage, he'd have been making good progress with Tilly by now. It had been bad enough to have his departure delayed by the return of Mrs. Thurlong and her fancy friend, without having it canceled altogether because of a broken handle.

But there was more to his anger than temporary frustration. He had an ulterior motive for deciding to pursue Tilly, whom he had known for some time but had until that very morning found too plain and uninteresting to be worth bothering about. Tilly had always been flatteringly adoring, and now that she had so unexpectedly become

Lady Georgette Belvoir's maid, taken on suddenly because her predecessor had been summarily dismissed by her notoriously difficult mistress, it suited him to pay her the attention she had long been craving. He saw Tilly as an opportunity to advance himself. The Thurlongs were fine enough, but the Earl and Countess of Hayden were much higher up the scale.

Andrew Harrison was ambitious and unscrupulous, and was prepared to make endless love to Tilly for as long as she might be able to open aristocratic doors for him.

8

ACROSS the town in exclusive Cambridge Crescent, Nicholas was with his grandmother in the conservatory of the house she had taken for the season. Water splashed from a little fountain, and the humid air was heady with the scent of tropical flowers as Lady Worthington sipped a dish of chocolate while her grandson stood looking out at the garden, a glass of cognac swirling in his hand. She was almost seventy now, but still very elegant and handsome in a plum velvet gown that had rich blonde lace at the throat.

"Well, Nicholas, to what do I owe this honor?" she asked at last, for he had said very little since arriving.

"I have to go abroad soon."

A faint smile touched her lips. "And you thought you'd better come to see me in case I go to my Maker in your absence?"

He turned swiftly. "I wouldn't have put it quite like that."

"No, but that is the gist of it." She smiled again. "I'm pleased that you came."

"Are you? I'm not the best of company at the moment." He drained the cognac and went to pour himself another.

She watched him thoughtfully. "Are you allowed to tell me where you're going? I take it that it's on government business again?"

"It is. Naples."

"Ah. A place now thankfully free of that dreadful Lady Hamilton."

"Lord Nelson would not appear to think her dreadful," he replied.

"Lord Nelson is an appalling judge of women. His wife

is atrocious, and his mistress hideous. It's as well he is a better judge of sailing and warfare!"

Nicholas laughed. "I could not agree more, since one of his squadron will be conveying my elegant and precious hide."

"I wish you were not so fond of secret diplomatic errands, for I worry about you."

He smiled. "I do it well, for I am the quintessential diplomat. At least, I usually am." He glanced away, thinking of his conduct at the Frogmill.

She studied him for a moment, and then tactfully changed the subject. "When do you have to leave for Naples?"

"Within a few weeks, for it's vital that the Mediterranean is kept as free of French interference as possible. As soon as the despatches are ready, I'll be on my way."

His grandmother hesitated, wanting to choose her next words carefully. "Have you made it up with your father yet?"

"No."

"Oh, Nicholas—"

"I know that you think I should be the dutiful son and set aside all that he's said and done over the years, but I'm not prepared to forgive or forget, especially where my mother was concerned. He may be my father, but he's also a vile, manipulative blackguard who has long since forfeited any filial affection I may have felt for him. I'm sorry, but that is how it will remain."

She sighed. "I do understand, you know, for your mother was my daughter, and I saw how wretched she became at his hands. Enough of him. Who is handling your affairs during your absence?"

"Stephen."

"Oh, dear. Well, I trust he will show a little more wisdom with your business than he does with his own. It seems to me that he is always gambling himself into debt."

"He's handled my affairs for me before."

"You have more faith in him than I would. He may be my grandson, but I have to say I think he is irresponsible to say the least."

"I begin to wonder what criticisms you have for me behind my back," Nicholas murmured.

She gave him a tart look. "Nothing I would not say to your face, of that you may be sure. Which brings me to the matter of your wife."

"I don't have a wife."

"Precisely. The Stanhope line must be continued, you know."

"I am aware of that."

"What of these rumors about you and Lady Georgette Belvoir?"

He gave a long sigh. "What have you heard?"

"That you and she are quite the thing."

"We aren't the thing at all," he replied. "She has been doggedly pursuing me all this summer, even to the extent of trying to make me jealous over Sir Mason Thackeray of all men, and I'm heartily sick of the sound of her name."

"Oh, dear. Well, I'm afraid she's here in Cheltenham."

Nicholas lowered his glass in dismay. "Tell me this is a jest and you are merely trying to spoil my enjoyment of your cognac."

"I fear not. She really is here, and so are her parents. I confess that when you turned up, I expected you to tell me a betrothal was on the cards."

"No! You may take my word on it. I will *never* marry Lady Georgette Belvoir."

"So, if it isn't the Hayden wench, who is it?"

"There isn't anyone."

Lady Worthington raised a disbelieving eyebrow. "No one at all? Oh, come now, sirrah, you surely do not expect me to swallow that one. You are one of the most handsome men in society, with wealth, charm, and a title to inherit, and you tell me there isn't a lady in your life?"

"The only worthwhile women I've encountered of late have all been other men's wives, and I'm sure you wouldn't appreciate it if I caused a shockingly public divorce in order to acquire one of them."

"Hardly." She looked at him. "Is unrequited love the reason for your doldrums?"

"I have no idea why I'm feeling so low, but I promise it isn't due to unrequited love. The lady of my dreams will no doubt cross my path sooner or later."

"Just see that it isn't too much later," she replied.

"I'll do my best." He glanced out at the garden again. His best? he'd failed conspicuously to do that today.

"What is it, Nicholas?" his grandmother asked. "There is something on your mind, isn't there? Come on, out with it. A short while ago you made a mysterious remark about your diplomatic abilities. What did you mean?"

He exhaled slowly. "I was thinking of my conduct earlier today, when I was justifiably put in my place for my arrogance."

"Arrogance? You? Who accused you?"

"A young lady at the Frogmill Inn."

"What happened?"

"She ventured out of the yard into the meadow behind, and some damned dandy attempted to force himself on her. I sent him packing, and then proceeded to lecture her on her foolishness. I wasn't very gallant or considerate, for she had just suffered a frightening ordeal. She had been a little unwise, but did not deserve to be spoken to like that. It was inexcusable, and she rightly told me what she thought of me. I shouldn't have said what I did, but I was appalled to think what might have happened to her if I hadn't been there. It was reaction, I suppose. Anyway, I regret it now."

"Who was she?"

"A Miss Sarah Howard."

"Was she coming here to Cheltenham?"

"I have no idea," he answered.

"It's just that if she was, then maybe you will have a chance to make amends."

He gave a short laugh. "I rather fear that if I take one step in her direction, she'll add a poke on the nose to the box on the ears she's already dealt me."

Lady Worthington smiled shrewdly. "She's pretty, I take it?"

"I really didn't notice."

"Liar."

He gave her a roguish grin. "Is that any way to speak to your favorite grandson?"

"And who has misinformed you that you are my favorite?" she inquired archly.

"You did, in your last letter."

She sniffed. "I must have been unwell at the time."

He went over to her, bending to kiss her on the cheek. "Well, no matter how mean you are to me, you're still my favorite grandmother."

"I'm your *only* grandmother," she retorted with a smile.

It was almost sunset when Georgette at last deemed it too cold to continue her ostentatious drive around the streets of Cheltenham. She knew that Nicholas had arrived at his grandmother's now, but hadn't actually managed to catch a glimpse of him, even though she'd driven several times along Cambridge Crescent. Nothing deterred, she meant to persuade her mother to call upon Lady Worthington the next morning, and had every intention of being present during the visit.

Nicholas's presence here was her only reason for agreeing to leave London. Her father was arranging a match for her with someone she had no liking for at all, and in the meantime she meant to use every moment to finally win Nicholas around to wanting her as much as she wanted him. She was on thin ice where her father was concerned at that moment, for he did not approve of her conduct over Nicholas, and he had been appalled to learn of her brief dalliance with a womanizer as lacking in conscience or principle as Sir Mason Thackeray. To say that she was in Papa's bad books was to make a substantial understatement, and she had to take great care if she was to achieve what she really wanted before the wrong man's ring was on her finger.

After driving fruitlessly along Cambridge Crescent for a last time, she returned to the nearby avenue where her father had taken a house for the time being. When she reached her bedroom, she was greeted by the unmistakable sound of sniffling coming from the adjoining dressing room.

Her skirts swished irritably as she went toward the doorway, where she saw her new maid sitting on the windowsill, dabbing her eyes with a handkerchief. For a moment Georgette considered ticking her off, but then she had second thoughts. Tilly Brown might be plain and rustic, but she was very talented with coiffures, a fact that had been immediately evident. One did not find such cleverness all that often, and so perhaps a little patience might be wise.

"What is it? Why are you crying?" she asked, trying to sound concerned, but only succeeding in sounding impatient.

Tilly jumped as if scalded, for she hadn't heard her new mistress enter. She was thin and flat-chested, with lanky brown hair and a sallow complexion, and her crying had not done her looks any favors. She managed to bob a reasonably graceful curtsey. "Begging your pardon, m'lady," she said quickly, keeping her gaze lowered.

"I asked you what was wrong."

"It . . . it's nothing, m'lady."

"Are you in the habit of crying for no good reason?"

"No, m'lady."

"Then tell me what this is about."

"It's my young man, m'lady."

Georgette's eyes widened with surprise. The creature had a sweetheart? "What young man?" she demanded.

"Andrew Harrison, m'lady. He's a footman."

"Here?"

"No, m'lady. He's in the employ of Mr. and Mrs. Thurlong."

Georgette's lilac eyes became thoughtful. "Indeed?"

"Yes, m'lady."

"And why are you crying?"

"Because he didn't meet me like he said he would. I waited for over an hour, and he didn't come." Tilly mopped fresh tears from her eyes.

"Well, I'm sure there is an explanation. Have you been seeing him for long?"

"No, m'lady, today was the first time. Oh, not that we haven't known each other for some time, it's just that until today he hasn't shown any interest in me."

"Until today, you say?"

"Yes. I happened to see him, and I told him about my new position here. He was so pleased for me, m'lady, and asked me out with him there and then. He said he had a few hours off this afternoon, and I knew you would be out . . ."

A knowing glitter shone in Georgette's lilac eyes. It was obviously no coincidence that this Andrew person had changed his tune toward Tilly. He probably wanted a position in an aristocratic household. Yes, that had to be it. Well, it might be convenient to encourage him. A spy in the Thurlong household might, under the circumstances, be useful. "Wipe your eyes, Tilly, for I'm sure you will hear from him again," she said.

The maid's face brightened hopefully. "Do you really think so, m'lady?"

"I'm certain. And when you do, you may ask my permission to meet him."

Tilly stared, unable to believe her good fortune. "Oh, *thank you*, m'lady!"

Georgette said nothing more, but began to tease off her gloves. If things went as she wished, there wouldn't be any need to use the footman, but if things went against her, then a little inside knowledge about Sarah Howard might prove productive. It had surprised her to see Sarah here in Cheltenham, instead of hiding her face in the depths of Oxfordshire. Broken betrothals were always so humiliating, especially those broken for such devastating reasons.

Georgette's expression became more reflective as she remembered Sarah's manner outside Thurlong Lodge. She hadn't seemed unduly unhappy or even mildly distressed. Maybe there was a great deal she had yet to find out. Yes, that had to be it. She didn't know what her father had been up to in London.

9

SARAH'S first week in Cheltenham passed very agreeably. October gave way to November, and she and Julia indulged in all the things expected of them. They visited the theater, attended the Assembly Rooms, inspected the spa's excellent shops, and made plans for the weekly subscription ball at the Royal Well. The ball was always a grand occasion, and they had arrived in town on the day after the last one. They did not mean to miss the next.

With so much going on, the disaster of Sarah's broken betrothal faded so far into the background that it was almost as if it had never happened. So complete was her disenchantment with Oliver that he seldom crossed her mind at all. He was to return to haunt her, however, as were Lady Georgette Belvoir and Mr. Nicholas Stanhope. They were all to reenter her life on the same ill-fated day, although when Sarah awoke that morning, there was no hint of what was to come.

Annie aroused her mistress from her slumber when she brought the morning tea and the jug of hot water for the washstand. Sarah began to stir in the canopied bed as the maid drew back the yellow silk curtains at the windows, and sunshine streamed into the room.

"Good morning, Miss Sarah," Annie said.

"Good morning, Annie." Sarah stretched luxuriously between the lavender-scented sheets.

"Did you sleep well?"

"Excellently, thank you." Pushing her long, dark blonde curls back from her face, Sarah sat up and accepted the cup of tea the maid held out to her.

The room was on the second story at the rear of the house, facing toward the river. It was where she always slept when she stayed, and she was particularly fond of the yellow-and-white-striped Chinese silk on the walls and thick blue Wilton carpet on the floor. The furniture was mostly white and gold, and an elegant white marble fireplace held the fire that had burned low overnight. A bowl of sweet-smelling carnations stood on the table next to the bed. They had come from the garden, where there had yet to be a frost to wither them.

When she had finished the tea, Sarah got out of bed to go to the window. The Thurlong Lodge garden terraces descended to the riverbank, each one linked by a flight of balustraded stone steps. The level closest to the house was so sheltered that there were still grapes on the vines growing against the wall by the drawing room, and the second one was bright with roses and the carnations that had been picked for her room. Next to the river the last terrace was exposed to the weather, and as a consequence was much more seasonal in appearance, with tall purple Michaelmas daisies and bright bronze and yellow chrysanthemums.

A short distance to the left she could see the narrow lane that led from the High Street to the watermill and the river meadows, and to the right, at the other end of the town, was the splendid double avenue of elm trees that led up to the buildings of the Royal Well, where only fifteen years before King George had sampled the spring waters and made Cheltenham fashionable.

But her attention was drawn to the river meadows across the river, where it was the thing to be seen riding. Fashionable ladies and gentlemen were showing off their equestrian skills, and she realized that it had been some time since she last rode. Maybe she and Julia could go today. Yes, that would be very pleasant.

"Which gown will you wear this morning, Miss Sarah?" Annie asked.

"The primrose fustian, I think."

"Yes, miss."

The maid hurried to the wardrobe, and after looking out of the window for a little longer, Sarah went to the washstand to prepare to dress.

When she went down to breakfast, Julia was already seated at the dining-room table. She wore a jade dimity gown and matching ribbons in her dark hair. She was engrossed in the morning newspaper, and gave a guilty start as Sarah entered, for it was't done for ladies to read at the table.

Sarah smiled. "Caught you!"

"I know, but it's the local newspaper, and there is something very intriguing in the column of *on-dits*."

Sarah pretended to be shocked. "You are scouring for scandal, Mrs. Thurlong? I'm disappointed, for I expected better of you," she said, accepting the chair the footman drew out for her. It was Andrew, and once again she was unpleasantly conscious of him. He made her want to shudder.

"What may I serve you, madam?" he asked, his tone almost too polite.

"Just some scrambled eggs, if you please," she replied, not glancing up at him as she would have done normally.

A moment later he put the plate before her, and then withdrew to stand by the sideboard again, ready to serve anything more they might require from the array of silver-domed dishes waiting there.

Julia glanced up at him. "That will be all, Andrew. We'll serve ourselves from now on."

"Madam." He bowed and withdrew.

Julia waited until the door closed behind him. "That's better, for I don't want him listening while we discuss salacious rumors."

Sarah's eyes widened. "Salacious rumors? About anyone we know?"

"None other than Lady Georgette Belvoir."

"Really? Oh, do tell."

"Your eagerness to hear this mischievous item of journalism is very unbecoming, Miss Howard." But Julia cleared her throat and began to read aloud from the paper.

"Among the recent arrivals in Cheltenham from London are the Earl and Countess of Hayden, and their youngest daughter, Lady G. The latter is undoubtedly the most delightful prize as yet unclaimed on the Marriage Mart, but rumor hath it that this state of affairs will not continue for much longer. A betrothal announcement is said to be in the offing, although no one is telling who the lucky gentleman will be. No doubt all will soon be revealed."

Sarah raised an eyebrow. "How very mysterious."

"Mysterious and mischievous, for the implication is that there is something odd about the match." Julia gave a wicked grin. "This won't please the earl at all, for he knows that such an article will make Cheltenham teacups rattle with speculation and innuendo. All the old tabbies will be subjecting dear Georgette's character to a minute inspection."

"Do you think there is any truth in it? *Is* she here to be betrothed?"

"Oh, probably, for there is usually a sound base to these items."

"I wonder who the unfortunate gentleman is?"

"The Lord alone knows." Julia poured herself another cup of Turkish coffee from the elegant silver pot on the table. "There's something else of interest in the paper, but I don't think you'll like it very much."

Sarah lowered her knife and fork. "What is it?"

"Two names I spied among the list of arrivals. Lord Fitzcharles and the Dishonorable Oliver."

"Oh, no."

"I fear so. Which means, *ma chère*, that there are three odors in town for us to try to avoid."

"Four. Mr. Stanhope may be here as well."

"True. Ah, well, I have no doubt that we will endure such adversities with our customary stoicism."

"What customary stoicism?" Sarah murmured.

Julia sipped her coffee. "What shall we do today? You've been resisting my every endeavor to get you to the Royal Well, and so today I think I shall insist. It's a beautiful morning, and the walk there will do us good."

"Even if the dosage at the end doesn't," Sarah said with a sigh. "Oh, very well, the Royal Well it is, but only on condition that we go riding in the Chelt meadows this afternoon."

"Agreed. I'll have Hemmings send someone to hire suitable horses from the livery stables. Oh, by the way, there is a letter from your father." Julia picked it up from the dish on the table, and placed it next to Sarah's plate.

"Do you mind if I read it now?"

"When I've been indulging in a newspaper? Of course I won't mind."

Sarah broke the seal and eagerly unfolded the letter. It bore the St. James's address of her father's club, and was very cheerful. By the time she'd finished it she was assured that all was well with him, and that he had received the letter she'd written earlier in the week.

Julia had been right to guess that the atmosphere at the Earl and Countess of Hayden's residence was thunderous. The arrival of the newspaper and its scurrilous article had reduced the earl to such an apoplectic fury that the poor countess feared the physician would have to be sent for.

"That shameless publication should be closed down forthwith!" he fumed, thumping his fist so hard upon the breakfast table that the porcelain shook. He always had a ruddy complexion, but this morning his face was positively puce. Snatching his napkin from his throat, he rose to his feet and went to the window to look sourly out at the rear garden, which backed on to the gardens of nearby Cambridge Crescent.

The countess looked nervously at him. She was a timid woman with large doelike eyes that always made her seem startled, and she wore a salmon pink woolen gown. There was a lace day-bonnet on her powdered curls, and it trembled slightly as she waited for her husband's next words.

Opposite her, Georgette sat in circumspect silence, for now was not the time to gain her father's attention. Her plate of bacon and eggs lay untouched before her, and she toyed nervously with the frilled cuff of her long-sleeved turquoise muslin gown. Muslin was't really suitable for the time of year, but it was considered *à la mode*. She had been shivering before the arrival of the newspaper, but now she felt uncomfortably hot and bothered. Her lilac eyes were lowered to the table, and she resisted the temptation to adjust one of the pins in her golden hair in case the movement caught her father's eye.

The earl turned back from the window. "How did they find out about the match, that's what I want to know. Nothing has been settled, and yet this thrice-cursed news sheet has got wind of it." He gave his daughter a dark look. "If I had to guess, I'd say it had a great deal to do with a certain with Sir Mason Thackeray, for it smacks of his devious troublemaking."

Georgette's heart almost halted within her, for she had hoped her father had forgotten about Mason. She swallowed uneasily, and said nothing.

"Oh, well you may stay silent now, my girl. It's a pity you didn't show more sense earlier on in the proceedings. Thackeray, of all men! He is not only the sworn enemy of the family into which I'm trying to marry you, but he is also without a doubt the most shameless, unprincipled rakehell in London. And you have to allow him to compromise you!"

"I haven't been compromised!" Georgette protested defensively, and with complete untruthfulness.

"Whether or not you actually permitted any untoward advances, you were alone with him in circumstances that can only be described as improper."

"I conducted myself very correctly," she lied, for she had been the very opposite of virtuous.

The earl studied her, and chose to take her word for it. "Nevertheless, you associated with the very last man on earth I would wish to encourage, not only because of his reputation, but also because of the match I am arranging for you."

"I don't want the match, Father," she said.

"No, you want Stanhope. Well, he's made it abundantly clear that he doesn't want you, and so I've had enough of this shilly-shallying. While you've still got a reputation, I mean to see to it that you are safely married off."

"But, Father—"

"Provided I can come to satisfactory terms, satisfactory to my purse, that is, you are going to accept this match. Your sisters' marriages and my financial straits don't permit me to humor you any longer. Is that clear?"

"Yes, Father." Georgette met his eyes. Let him think she'd given in, let him think what he wished, but she had every intention of continuing her pursuit of Nicholas Stanhope. He'd been out when she and her mother had called at Lady Worthington's house, and now she'd have to think again about how to see him. One thing was certain, however; somehow or other she'd have what she wanted! The method by which she achieved her end was immaterial, for all was fair in love and war, and she was an expert at scheming and lying.

Lord Fitzcharles had rented a gentleman's residence on the outskirts of Cheltenham. It was an elegant property set in its own grounds, and was screened from the road to Tewkesbury by some particularly fine oak trees that were ablaze with color as Oliver strolled very slowly in the early morning sun. He was dressed to go into town, in a green coat and fawn breeches with a brown greatcoat tossed idly around his shoulders. He carried a cane with which he dashed some more leaves from the branches overhead. There wasn't a smile on his face, and he was pale and strained. His thoughts were of Sarah, and the bitter reproach in her blue eyes when they'd parted at the grotto.

A nerve flickered at the side of his mouth, and he swung the cane furiously at the branches above his head. Golden leaves cascaded to the ground, where he kicked them savagely. Why did things have to be this way? He and Sarah could have been happy together, and he certainly didn't want the future now being mapped out for him. But how could he defy his father? All his life he'd been ruled with a rod of iron, and that rod was as potent now as it had ever been. He would do as he was told.

"Master Oliver?" A footman came running over the grass toward him.

"Yes?"

"The carriage is ready to leave, sir, and his lordship is waiting."

Oliver nodded. "I'll come in a moment."

The footman was embarrassed. "Begging your pardon, sir, but his lordship said to tell you that you were to come immediately. He said there is much to be discussed, and he wishes it to be settled as quickly as possible."

With a sigh Oliver nodded once more, and then followed the footman back toward the house, where his father's carriage was drawn up in readiness by the door.

10

LADY Worthington teased on her blue fingerless mittens as she descended the stairs at the house in Cambridge Crescent. She wore a cream pelisse and matching gown, and a blue velvet hat.

Nicholas waited in the hall, and his glance swept approvingly over her. "You look positively radiant, and I will be the object of male envy when I escort you to tomorrow night's ball," he said, sketching her a bow.

She paused. "I am not supposed to be radiant, Nicholas, for I am in Cheltenham for my health."

"What a fib. The season is why you are here," he replied dryly.

"You, sirrah, are a wretch. I am required to take the waters, which is why, as I understand it, you are about to convey me to the Royal Well."

"So it is."

She surveyed him, taking in his superbly tailored maroon coat and cream cord breeches. "I still cannot believe that there is no young lady in your life, Nicholas. I vow that if I were young again, and my eye fell upon someone like you, I'd give chase until I'd cornered you."

"You sound ominously like Lady Georgette Belvoir," he observed with feeling.

His grandmother could not resist twitting him a little. "Ah, yes, the beautiful Lady Georgette. How fortunate that you were out when she and her dithery mother called the other day. I almost gave them a time to call back, so that they could be sure of seeing you, but I took pity on you."

"I'd never have forgiven you."

"Come now, admit that you are Lady Georgette's mysterious match, as mentioned in this morning's scurrilous broadsheet."

"I will not dignify that inquiry with an answer, but I will make the observation that whoever he is, he has my sincere condolences. Now then, shall we go?" He offered her his arm, and together they emerged into the morning sunshine, where his phaeton awaited.

As soon as he had assisted his grandmother up onto the high seat, Nicholas climbed up as well and took the reins. A moment later he had stirred the team into action, and the vehicle skimmed away along the crescent, bound for the Royal Well.

About five minutes earlier Sarah and Julia had set off for the same destination. Wearing bonnets and spencers with their morning gowns, they walked at a leisurely pace along the busy pavement, pausing now and then to examine the more fashionable shops.

The Plough Inn stood in the High Street, and just beyond it was a print shop where something on display in the bow window was causing a stir. A small crowd had gathered, and several arguments were in progress. As the two friends drew near, they saw that the furore was caused by some satirical engravings of the royal family. The prints were far from flattering, much to the rage of the royalists in the crowd, and the amusement of those of a more radical disposition.

As Sarah and Julia stood on tiptoe to look over the shoulders of those in front, Sarah became aware of someone watching her. It wasn't a pleasant feeling, and she glanced uneasily around. With something of a shock she found herself looking at Lord Fitzcharles, who stood nearby with Oliver.

Oliver was engrossed in the controversial prints, and hadn't noticed her as yet, but his father had perceived her from the moment she approached. Lord Fitzcharles was a short, fat man, with jowls that bulged over his neckcloth, and his girth needed a great deal of lacing in order for him to squeeze into the latest tight fashions. He wore a coat that was brick in color, and his tall hat was pulled low over his forehead, casting his face in shadow from the bright autumn sun, but his eyes glinted brightly as he stared without acknowledging her at all. It was a calculated snub.

Suddenly Oliver turned and saw her. A mixture of

emotions crossed his face, and for a moment she thought he would speak, but then his father caught his arm and ushered him away across the street. Oliver didn't look back at her, but once again did as his father bid.

Mortified color drenched Sarah's cheeks. She had never been cut before, and felt both hurt and humiliated. How could Oliver have neglected to even incline his head to her? She felt as if everyone in the High Street had observed, and suddenly she wanted to run all the way back to Thurlong Lodge to hide away, but Julia, who knew what had happened, quickly linked her arm.

"Don't pay any attention to them, Sarah, for the Fitz-charles family are all boors. Just remind yourself that you very nearly married that spineless oaf."

Julia's pithy tone brought a reluctant smile to Sarah's lips. "I still can't believe how blind I was, where you saw through him straightaway."

"We all make mistakes. Come on, let's continue our walk."

Arm in arm, they made their way past the print shop and then on along the pavement, but within a minute something occurred to further disturb Sarah's composure. It happened when they reached the corner where the new colonnade was being erected. Everything was in the usual chaos of building, and pedestrians had to walk in the road. Thus Sarah and Julia were about to step off the curb at the precise moment Nicholas's phaeton drove around the same corner.

At the last second Sarah became aware of the vehicle's approach, but Julia's attention was on something across the street, and unthinkingly she stepped out. With a cry Sarah dragged her back to safety just as the phaeton swept by.

Nicholas was hard put to bring the nervous team under control, and the phaeton had traveled a number of yards on around the corner before he was able to bring it to a halt at the side of the road. After ascertaining that his grandmother was all right, he quickly alighted to hurry back. He hadn't as yet recognized Sarah.

Julia was quite confused for she really hadn't noticed the phaeton, and it wasn't until she'd been snatched back to the pavement that she realized how close she had come to being knocked down.

Sarah looked anxiously at her. "Are you sure you're all right?"

"I . . . I think so. To be honest, I don't quite know what happened."

"That idiot with the phaeton nearly drove over you, that's what happened," Sarah replied angrily, turning as she heard the same gentleman hurrying up to them.

Nicholas's attention was on Julia. "I'm truly sorry, madam. I trust I did not harm you in any way."

Startled, Sarah stared at him.

Julia was beginning to recover from the shock, and having only briefly seen him drive past when they'd left the Frogmill Inn, she didn't recognize him. "Sir, I think I should be the one apologizing, for I stepped out without thinking."

"I was a little close to the corner."

His conduct at the Frogmill still rankled with Sarah, and her blue eyes flashed angrily. "Yes, Mr. Stanhope, you were indeed somewhat remiss, were you not?" she said, her tone as disapproving as his had been on that previous occasion.

He turned swiftly. "Miss Howard?" he murmured, inclining his head.

"No doubt you think we are ill-advised to venture out on to the street where we are at the mercy of every atrocious driver."

A light passed through his eyes. "You are entitled to your opinion of my driving, Miss Howard, incorrect as that opinion may be."

"On your own admission you were too close to the curb," she replied, unable to resist the urge to get her own back. It was very childish, but the exercise made her feel much better.

"One miscalculation does not add up to complete incompetence, Miss Howard," he said stiffly.

"No? You surprise me, sir, for you certainly gave me the impression that that was *precisely* what one miscalculation added up to." She held his gaze, her chin raised defiantly.

"Miss Howard, if anything I have said, either now or in the past, has offended you, then I apologize, but I have no intention of standing here laboring the point *ad yawnum*. Good day to you."

Inclining his head again, he turned and walked back to the phaeton, where his intrigued grandmother had observed the exchange with interest. Lady Worthington was intensely curious, but on seeing how stormy he looked as he resumed his seat, she wisely refrained from saying anything—for the moment at least.

As the phaeton drove swiftly away, Julia looked quizzically at Sarah. "That was quite a performance, Sarah Howard, indeed I don't think I've seen its like since—"

"The schoolroom? No, you're probably right, but, oh, I feel vastly improved now." Sarah smiled at her. "It was very gratifying to give him a little of his own insufferable medicine."

"He did have the last word," Julia pointed out.

"It was the last word of a defeated man," Sarah replied with relish.

Julia raised an eyebrow, but let the subject rest. "Come on, let's complete this wretched walk."

"We can go back if you want," Sarah offered.

"No, I'd like to go on."

After glancing carefully in both directions, they set off across the corner and then on toward the open undeveloped land that extended to the Chelt. A rustic bridge spanned the water, and on the other side began the famous double avenue of elm trees that flanked the walk leading up toward the even more famous well.

Crisp leaves lay underfoot as they began the long but gentle climb. It was the custom for the waters to be taken in the morning, and so a number of other ladies and gentlemen strolled up and down the walk. Those who were too elderly or infirm to accomplish the climb used the nearby carriage road, which approached the well by a more circuitous route from the road to the nearby village of Hatherley.

It had not yet occurred to either Sarah or Julia that Nicholas and his elderly lady companion might be making for the same destination, but they were soon to find out.

Nor had it occurred to Nicholas and Lady Worthington that Lady Georgette Belvoir might that very same morning be accompanying her parents and a party of acquaintances to sample the waters, but she was.

11

THE spring that had brought fame and fortune to Cheltenham was now enclosed by a small well building that boasted inappropriately grand wrought iron gates between tall brick posts. On either side of the well house were two much larger buildings, one housing various superior shops, the other the sumptuous ballroom where the following night everyone in society would attend the subscription ball.

It was considered beneficial to listen to soothing melodies while sipping the rather unpleasant-tasting water, and so music was playing in the ballroom. This morning the orchestra was playing Bach, and the gentle notes were just audible above the babble of refined voices.

Georgette was conscious of being the subject of sly whispers because of the newspaper, but her thoughts were all of Nicholas, and how best to go about snaring him. He was proving unexpectedly difficult to keep an eye on, and she suspected that he was doing all he could to avoid her. She didn't know his haunts here in Cheltenham as she did those in London, nor did she know the mutual friends he might call upon, which all made it immensely frustrating. There was the ball the next night, of course. He and Lady Worthington were almost bound to be there.

In the meantime there was always the hope of a chance meeting, and with that in mind she had been careful to look her very best each time she went out. Today she wore a lavender corded silk pelisse and matching hat, for the hat showed off her lovely golden curls, and the color emphasized the lilac of her eyes. She was confident that her appearance was all any woman's could be, and it did not occur to her that nothing she did would ever win him, for he not only disliked her personally, but he was also indifferent to her charms.

She and her party had lingered in the ballroom for some time, when suddenly Nicholas and his grandmother entered. Georgette's breath caught, and she quickly put down her glass of water. She had no intention of allowing him to slip through her net this time, and so kept out of sight as she made her way around the edge of the room in order to approach him from behind.

Lady Worthington noticed her at the last moment, but had no opportunity to warn Nicholas before suddenly Georgette was there, with a winning shine in her eyes and a gushing warmth in her voice as she greeted them both.

"Why, Lady Worthington, Mr. Stanhope, what an unexpected pleasure this is," she cried, treating him to one of her most disarming smiles.

Nicholas's heart sank, and his own smile was rather fixed as he returned the greeting with a lack of enthusiasm that would have deterred any other woman. "Good morning, Lady Georgette."

Lady Worthington inclined her head. "Good morning, my dear."

"I do hope that you will take a glass of the water with me," Georgette said quickly, determined not to allow them any chance to get away.

As Nicholas desperately sought of an excuse to decline, his grandmother came to his rescue.

"I fear we cannot, my dear, for we were just about to leave."

Georgette's sweet smile slipped for a moment. "But you've only just arrived!"

"I know, but I fear I have developed a dreadful headache, and I really cannot endure the babble in here. I have just this moment informed Nicholas that he must take me home again."

Nicholas resisted the urge to glance gratefully heavenward. Thank God for his grandmother's quick wits!

Georgette was inwardly furious. "I . . . I do hope you are soon recovered, Lady Worthington," she replied insincerely. Plague take the old biddy for having a headache! May it give her agony for the rest of the day! Her thoughts were moving apace, however, and she smiled agreeably. "I do trust that you will be recovered in time for the ball tomorrow night."

"Thank you, my dear, I'm sure I will."

Georgette was a little mollified, for at least she now knew for certain they would be attending, as it was highly unlikely that Nicholas would allow his grandmother to come alone.

Lady Worthington turned to him. "My headache is really quite bad, Nicholas. Could we leave now?"

As he was about to draw her hand over his arm, Georgette spoke again.

"Lady Worthington, before you go make I ask a favor of you?"

"A favor?"

"I would like to call upon you to discuss something important."

Nicholas held his breath, willing his grandmother to come up trumps again.

Only too conscious of his silent pleas, Lady Worthington couldn't completely disguise her discomfort. "I cannot imagine what you would wish to see me about, Lady Georgette."

"I have a notion to organize a grand ball to raise funds for our wounded soldiers and sailors, and since I know that you have done such things yourself in the past, I hope I may take the liberty of pressing you for information on how to go about it." Georgette uttered this monstrous fib without a flicker of conscience. Charitable works had never figured in her philosophy, and she had no more thought of organizing such a ball than she had of flying to the moon.

Nicholas's heart sank like a stone, for he knew his grandmother would not be able to wriggle out this time.

Lady Worthington gave a weak smile. "Why, yes, my dear, of course you may call upon me."

"Thank you *so* much."

Fearing that Georgette would think of something else, Nicholas was determined to leave without further ado. Quickly he offered his grandmother his arm. "Let me take you home," he said, inclining his head to Georgette as civilly as he could. "Good day to you, Lady Georgette."

"Mr. Stanhope." Georgette's voice was soft and caressing, and her eyes fluttered prettily as she gave him a parting smile that was meant to breach every defense he possessed.

Lady Worthington gave a polite parting smile, and then she and Nicholas made good their getaway. As they emerged into the sunshine, she glanced at her grandson.

"I begin to see what you mean about her persistence."

"She's like a wasp after the jam. I have no intention of being present at her next visitation."

"You can always leave by the back way."

"I mean to. As for the ball. . . ."

"I take it you no longer wish to attend?"

"Crying off seems suddenly very attractive."

"As you wish. Balls are no longer the be-all and end-all of my social existence. Two country dances and I'm done for these days." She smiled at him, and they walked on toward the line of carriages and other vehicles drawn up at the curb nearby.

As they reached his phaeton, Lady Worthington's attention was drawn to the avenue. "Aren't those the young ladies you spoke to earlier?"

He followed her glance and saw Sarah and Julia emerging from the trees to cross toward the well house. "Yes," he replied shortly.

Lady Worthington's earlier curiosity was aroused once more. "Who are they?"

"I, er, don't recall their names."

"Come now, Nicholas, if you are going to fib, at least do it well. Who are they?"

He sighed. "The one on the right is Miss Howard, but in the heat of the moment she neglected to introduce me to her friend.

"*The* Miss Howard. Of Frogmill fame?"

"Yes."

Lady Worthington studied Sarah. "A pretty gel, and no mistake."

"With a tongue that would put a cat-o'-nine-tails to shame."

"Ah, so the lady had her revenge, did she?" Lady Worthington couldn't help a smile.

"Revenge? You might say so."

"It would seem that your former contrition has been replaced by indignation at having to swallow your own medicine," she observed accurately.

"Yes, as it happens it has," he said, looking at Sarah.

"Introduce me," his grandmother said suddenly.

"I would rather not."

"Introduce me," she insisted.

"Are you absolutely set upon it?"

"I am."

With another sigh he gave in, and they began to walk toward the well house.

At that moment Julia turned and saw them. She swiftly nudged Sarah. "Look who's coming to speak to us!" she whispered. "It's Mr. Stanhope and his lady companion."

"Oh, no . . ." Dismayed, Sarah followed her glance. "Let's pretend we haven't noticed them," she said quickly, trying to walk on through the wrought iron gates, but Julia shook her head.

"It's too late; they know I've seen them. Please be courteous this time, for I could not endure another fireworks display."

With great reluctance Sarah turned and waited, managing a smile of sorts as Nicholas and his grandmother came up to them both. "Mr. Stanhope," she murmured, inclining her head civilly.

"Miss Howard." His gray eyes were expressionless. "May I present my grandmother, Lady Worthington? Grandmother, this is Miss Howard."

Sarah inclined her head. "Lady Worthington."

"I'm pleased to meet you, my dear," Lady Worthington replied, her approving glance taking in every inch of Sarah's appearance.

Sarah introduced Julia. "May I present Mrs. Thurlong? Julia, this is Mr. Stanhope. I, er, fear I omitted to introduce you a little earlier." Dull color flushed to her cheeks, and for a brief moment she met Nicholas's eyes, before looking quickly away again.

Julia smiled and nodded to Nicholas and Lady Worthington. "I'm delighted to make your acquaintance," she said.

Lady Worthington's attention returned to Sarah. "Tell me, my dear, will you both be attending the ball here tomorrow night?"

"Yes, we will."

"Then I trust I will see you again then. I'm usually to be found holding court at one of the sofas. I am a little old to gallop around the floor these days, but I do still like to watch." Lady Worthington steadfastly ignored Nicholas's silent rebuke.

Sarah smiled, liking the old lady's humor. "I look forward to speaking to you again, Lady Worthington."

"Perhaps you will honor my grandson with a dance?"

Unable to believe his ears, Nicholas gazed fixedly at a point somewhere beyond the avenue.

Sarah didn't quite know how to respond, for it was clear to her that the last thing he wished to do was dance with her. Throttle her, maybe, but not dance! After a tiny hesitation she gave a weak smile. "That would be most agreeable, Lady Worthington."

"We will leave you now, my dears," Lady Worthington glanced surreptitiously at her grandson's thunderous visage. "Am I in your bad books now?"

"Just a little," he replied in a falsely cordial tone.

"I changed my mind."

"So I noticed."

"How very prickly you are, to be sure. Lady Georgette Belvoir may be appalling, but Miss Howard is quite charming."

"Charming? She is impossible."

"And you aren't?"

He didn't reply.

"Come now, Nicholas, you know as well as I do that she isn't at all impossible. You are just being a sulky bear. I like Miss Howard, and I've decided to go to the ball after all. I trust you do not mean to let me go alone?"

"I'm sorely tempted," he replied with feeling.

"You don't mean that." She gave him a winning smile as he helped her up on to the phaeton. "Besides, just think how well you will be able to mend bridges if you dance with her."

"Are you by any chance matchmaking for me?" he asked.

"Me? As if I would do anything like that!"

"I don't need any assistance in that direction."

"You haven't been doing all that well until now," she observed lightly, arranging herself comfortably on the seat.

"I'll do my own pursuing, thank you, and when I do, Miss Howard will not be the object of my attentions!"

"No?"

"No!" Taking up the reins, he urged the horses away.

Sarah and Julia proceeded into the well house to purchase their glasses of the water, and from there they went into the ballroom, where to their unutterable dismay, they were confronted by Georgette, who was in a foul mood after her latest disappointment over Nicholas.

The sight of her old school adversaries brought out the very worst in the Earl of Hayden's daughter, and she descended upon them determined to be as unpleasant as possible.

"Why, if it isn't Miss Howard and Mrs. Thurlong. What a very happy coincidence," she purred.

Julia sighed and refrained from replying, but Sarah managed to give a cool response. "Good morning, Lady Georgette,"

"My dear, you are looking far too thin, but then I suppose it is hardly surprising, given your unfortunate circumstances," Georgette went on, her eyes like gimlets.

"Circumstances? What do you mean?"

"Don't you know?"

"If I did, I wouldn't ask," Sarah replied.

"Oh, well, I'm afraid it isn't my place to explain. Suffice it that I know why Lord Fitzcharles felt obliged to terminate your betrothal to his son."

Sarah stared at her, and Julia swiftly intervened. "Georgette, you do not improve with the passing of time, indeed you have become even more obnoxious."

Georgette's lilac eyes flickered. "And you, my dear Julia, become of less and less consequence. If you think that I am merely taunting dear Sarah without any foundation, let me assure you that that is not the case. I know only too well why Lord Fitzcharles no longer regards her as a suitable bride for his son and heir. Dear little Sarah is being kept in the dark, and will soon receive a quite horrid shock."

Julia was at her vitriolic best. "I'll warrant that the shock will not compare with the one you experienced this morning on opening the newspaper," she said smoothly. "You must be quite wretched over all the whispering and speculation. Do you know, I have actually heard it being said that you are having to be married in haste because you, er, anticipated your vows?"

Fury flashed in Georgette's eyes, and without another word she turned and walked away.

Julia gazed darkly after her. *"Chienne,"* she murmured.

Sarah was uneasy. "What do you think she meant?"

"Nothing at all. Just think about it, Sarah, La Belle Belvoir has always thrived on being as malicious as she can, and she has never forgiven you for having won her brother's heart, albeit briefly."

"But how does she know about my betrothal?"

"Because Fitzcharles *père et fils* are in town."

"Yes, but—"

"There aren't any buts, Sarah. Ignore them, and ignore her, too. She wanted to wind you up to a pitch, and it seems she's succeeded. Don't give her the satisfaction."

"That is easier said than done."

Sarah tried to put the incident from her thoughts, but couldn't, and when she and Julia were walking home, she brought it up again.

"Julia, about what Georgette said—"

"Just forget the wretched creature; she's a viper through and through and isn't to be trusted about anything," Julia interrupted quietly but firmly.

"I can't help dwelling on it. She really did seem to know something, as I think even you cannot really deny."

"She is mistress of her beastly art, Sarah. Of course she sounded convincing, for that is what she set out to be."

Sarah halted. "Do you remember when my father came back from London so unexpectedly? And he said he was selling our town house and moving to his club?

"Yes, of course I remember."

"I thought it a little odd at the time, and for a moment I was certain he was hiding something important from me."

Julia gave her a very stern look. "Why, then, are his letters so cheerful?"

Sarah looked at her. "I . . . I don't know."

"Well, I do. His letters are cheerful because everything is all right. Do stop this, Sarah. Georgette would be hugging herself with delight if she knew how well she'd managed to upset you with just a few well chosen words."

Sarah ruefully conceded the point. "You are right, of course. I'm being silly."

"Never more so," Julia replied reprovingly.

"I promise not to mention it again."

"Good, for there are other much more agreeable things to discuss, such as our ride this afternoon, and what gowns we will wear to the ball tomorrow night."

They walked on, and by the time they reached Thurlong Lodge, Sarah had managed to put Lady Georgette Belvoir completely from her mind.

12

NOTHING would have gone wrong during the ride that afternoon had not Hemmings chosen to send Andrew to engage two saddle horses at the livery stables.

Tilly's gratifying availability may have removed the footman's initial reason for disliking Sarah, but now he had another. Ever since the business with the broken valise, Hemmings had kept an eye on him, picking fault with everything he did, and as far as Andrew was concerned, this too was because of Miss Sarah Howard. All his recent problems had stemmed from her arrival, and he was more than ready to do her an ill turn should the chance present itself.

The opportunity arose when he was sent to order two horses, and he didn't hesitate to advise the livery stable that although Mrs. Thurlong required a steady mount, Miss Howard was an excellent horsewoman who would not be pleased unless her horse was spirited and difficult. He covered his tracks by saying that Miss Howard had given him the instruction very privately, in order not to offend Mrs. Thurlong, who would be mortified to learn that her her riding skills were held in such low esteem. The livery stable was renowned for its discretion, and gave a solemn assurance that under no circumstances would Mrs. Thurlong ever learn, and Andrew returned to the house slyly content that Miss Sarah Howard would experience a very difficult time of it on her ride.

It was still bright and sunny when the two friends set off early in the afternoon. Julia wore a rose merino riding habit and gray beaver hat, and was mounted on a pretty chestnut mare that had to be coaxed into anything other than a sedate trot. Sarah wore purple velvet and a black hat with a black net veil that covered most of her face, and her horse was a large, mettlesome roan that very swiftly proved to be more than a handful.

They rode down the narrow lane from the High Street to the watermill by the Chelt, and it was all Sarah could do to keep the roan in check. The horse fought against the bit, and capered willfully along the path toward the stone bridge spanning the river. Julia was soon dissatisfied with the mare, which trotted at the same slow pace, no matter how much she urged it to greater effort, but by the time they rode through the copse of tall sycamore trees that stood between the river and the meadows, Sarah was beginning to wonder if she would be able to maintain control.

She soon discovered she could not, for just as Andrew had hoped, the troublesome roan set off unbidden at a spanking pace. Unfortunately for Sarah, Julia did not realize that the headlong gallop wasn't of her friend's choosing, and so paused to talk to some acquaintances she saw among the other riders.

The roan gelding galloped along with its tail high and ear pricked, feeling immensely pleased at being master of the situation. It had the better of its rider, and intended to make the most of things. The bit was between its teeth, and there was nothing Sarah could do except hold to her seat as best she could. Several other riders turned in astonishment as she flew past, and at last she decided that the only way to get the horse back under control was to let it run on until it ran out of energy.

This proved less fun for the gelding, which gradually began to slow down until at last Sarah was able to get it in hand again. She reined in as tightly as she could, and to her relief the horse came to a standstill.

She slipped thankfully from the saddle. "You loathsome beast," she muttered beneath her breath, wondering if it would be preferable to risk riding back again, or suffer the ignominy and discomfort of walking in her riding boots. Neither prospect filled her with joy. She began to wish she'd stayed in bed that morning, for this day was going from bad to worse.

"Are you all right?" a voice called behind her.

It was a voice she knew, and she turned unwillingly to see Nicholas riding swiftly up on a tall bay thoroughbred.

He had seen the difficulty she was in, but as yet did not realize who she was because of the veil over her face.

"Are you all right?" he asked again, reining in close by and dismounting. He wore a pine green riding coat, and his white cord breeches were like a second skin. A diamond pin sparkled on the knot of his starched neck-cloth, and his top boots shone so that one could almost see one's face in them.

He was the picture of sartorial excellence, and still one of the most infuriatingly attractive men she had ever encountered. As she slowly raised her veil to reply, she reminded herself that Mr. Nicholas Stanhope's handsome book cover concealed disagreeable pages within. "Yes, thank you, Mr. Stanhope, I'm quite all right," she said.

"Miss Howard again? We seem destined to keep meeting," he said resignedly.

"So it seems."

He glanced at the horse. "He seems a difficult brute."

"He is." She raised her chin a little defiantly, determined not to suffer an other ticking-off. "You may be sure that I have already realized that the horse is beyond my capabilities, sir, so please do not wag your disapproving finger at me again."

A faint smile touched his lips as he removed his tall hat. "Miss Howard, I assure you I have learned the error of my ways where you are concerned. A finger wagged in your direction is liable to be bitten off. Not a single reproving word will cross my lips, I promise you. Now then, is there any way in which I may be of assistance?"

"Unless you can wave a wand to rid me of this horrible creature, and replace it with something more sedate, then I fear not."

"Magic is not one of my accomplishments, but I am more than prepared to see you safely home."

"Thank you, but there is no need."

"There is every need, Miss Howard. I may not have been the soul of gallantry on our first meeting, but I would like the opportunity to redeem myself. Besides, the walk would no doubt do me good, so please permit me to see you home."

She wanted to decline, but knew that to do so would be churlish. "Thank you, Mr. Stanhope, I accept your offer."

He took the reins of both horses and offered her his

arm, and they walked in silence for a minute or so. Then he spoke again. "I am sorry if my grandmother caused you any embarrassment this morning, Miss Howard."

"Embarrassment?"

"By suggesting that you and I might share a dance at the ball tomorrow night."

"I wasn't embarrassed, sir."

"No? Then perhaps I misread your reserved response at the time."

She colored a little.

Faint humor touched his lips. "I am sure that we can manage to be civil to each other for the duration of a polonaise or cotillion, Miss Howard."

"I trust you are right, sir."

"It is settled then. You are to save a measure for me tomorrow night." He hid a wry smile as he pondered his grandmother's expression, were she present right now.

"If that is your wish . . ." Sarah began uncertainly, wishing that she didn't find him as disconcerting when he was being courteous as when he was being insufferable.

"It is, Miss Howard. My manners may be defective here and there, but I swear that my dancing prowess is second to none."

"I'm sure it is, sir." She gave him a shy smile, realizing that his charm was winning her over. Suddenly the incidents at the Frogmill and on the corner of the High Street no longer seemed of particular consequence.

At that moment Julia came riding belatedly toward them, still urging the lazy mare for all she was worth and achieving nothing more than the usual slow trot. "Sarah? I'm sorry to have been so long, but this wretched arm-chair of a creature is quite impossible." She reined in, her curious glance moving to Nicholas. "Mr. Stanhope," she murmured, inclining her head.

"Mrs. Thurlong," he replied. "Forgive me for asking, but is your husband related to Lady Thurlong?"

"He is her nephew, sir."

"I thought there had to be a connection, for it isn't a very common surname." So, she was the wife of the much-favored Thomas Thurlong.

"You are acquainted with Lady Thurlong, sir?" Julia inquired.

"I have that honor." He glanced at Sarah. "Miss Howard, now that Mrs. Thurlong is here, there is no need for me to impose my company upon you any longer. I trust, however, that you will still reserve that measure for me tomorrow night?"

"I will, sir, and thank you for coming to my rescue again."

"Good day to you, Miss Howard," he said, handing her the reins of her horse.

"Good day, Mr. Stanhope," she replied.

He inclined his head at Julia. "Mrs. Thurlong," he said, mounting his own horse and putting on his tall hat.

"Good day, Mr. Stanhope," Julia answered, glancing after him as he rode away. Then she looked quizzically at Sarah. "A measure tomorrow night? And by his expression he appeared to be genuinely looking forward to the moment. Things would seem to have improved since this morning."

"A little."

"More than a little, I would say." Julia dismounted. "What happened? I saw you galloping off like the wind itself, and—"

"You saw my horse getting the better of me," Sarah corrected.

Julia was appalled. "It bolted?"

"More or less."

"I had no idea! I thought you were enjoying a good gallop."

"My wretched mount was enjoying it, but I certainly wasn't. In the end I let him have his head until he ran out of energy. That was when Mr. Stanhope came to see if I was all right."

"Has his armor become shining and white after all?"

"Possibly."

Julia smiled. "I confess I wouldn't be averse to a measure or two with him."

"Please feel free to take my place."

Julia raised a wry eyebrow. "You wouldn't like it if I did, Sarah Howard, for if I am not mistaken, your so-called indifference is a sham."

Sarah halted. "What do you mean?"

"I think you are drawn to him, unwillingly maybe, but drawn all the same."

"That is nonsense," Sarah replied, but knew her cheeks were on fire.

"Is it?"

"Yes."

Sarah knew the denial was futile. She *was* drawn to him, and far too much for her peace of mind. It was too soon after Oliver, and Nicholas Stanhope's present charm was merely an endeavor to rectify past failings. She'd be foolish to believe otherwise.

At evening Georgette sat before the dressing table in her bedroom. Candlelight swayed gently over the elegant furnishings and flashed upon the diamond earrings as she took them from her jewelry box. She put them on, and then turned her head from side to side, examining her reflection in the mirror. Yes, they were her favorites and suited her well, indeed they suited her to perfection. She would wear them tomorrow night at the ball with her silver tissue gown, and she would dazzle Nicholas into submission.

Her smile of anticipation faded, and she replaced the earrings in the box, for she had suddenly thought of the betrothal being negotiated for her whether she wanted it or not. She closed the box, and then ran her fingertips over its beautiful polished marquetry surface. Damn Sarah Howard's father, damn him to Hades itself. If it were not for him . . .

Taking a deep breath, Georgette rose from the dressing table and then went to the window. Holding the velvet curtain aside, she looked out into the night. Her room at the back of the house faced toward the Cambridge Crescent. She knew every room and light of Lady Worthington's house. Was Nicholas at home now? Or was he out somewhere? Maybe he wasn't alone, maybe his real reason for being here in Cheltenham was to pursue someone . . .

Georgette turned sharply from the window as a surge of jealousy washed over her. The thought of someone else winning his heart was too much to endure. She desired him so intensely that sometimes she could hardly bear it, and in that moment she knew that if she ever found out he had given his heart, she would move heaven and earth to destroy whoever held it.

The torrent of jealous frustration rushing through her was so powerful it made her tremble. She would never allow anyone else to have him—never.

13

THE Royal Well ball was a crush, and therefore a resounding success. Carriages thronged the approach road, and countless little lanterns twinkled in the trees. Much music and laughter rang out, and the air in the ballroom itself was fragrant with the scent of the flowers that were regarded as de rigueur for balls; the more blooms there were, the more grand the occasion, which meant that the proprietors of the well had spent a great deal of money upon the baskets, bouquets, garlands, and sprays that decked every wall, column, and corner.

It was hot inside, so hot that the chill of the November evening outside meant little as minuet gave way to polonaise, and *ländler* to country dance. There wasn't any ventilation, and the heavy crimson velvet curtains were drawn firmly across the tall French windows that lined one side of the room. Fans fluttered everywhere, and many ladies constantly resorted to glasses of iced fruit drink, or even to the more drastic remedy of the vial of *sal volatile*.

Both Sarah and Julia had elected to be just a little daring for the occasion. Sarah's gown of dusty pink satin boasted a very low square neckline and little puffed sleeves. A thin golden belt adorned the high waistline beneath her breasts, and her arms were encased in long white gloves. A three-string pearl choker necklace glowed at her throat, and more pearls trembled from her ears. She carried a little evening reticule and an ivory fan, and there was a delicate white-and-gold shawl over her arms. She was filled with nervous anticipation about the hours ahead, and it was all due to the prospect of dancing with Nicholas Stanhope.

Julia was no less striking for the occasion. She wore an oyster silk tunic gown over a clinging white silk slip, and her dark hair was almost hidden beneath an ice blue satin silk turban. Aquamarines shone at her throat and encircled her white-gloved wrist. A pale blue feather boa trailed carelessly along the floor behind her, and the same plumes adorned her fan.

The two friends alighted from their carriage and entered the brilliantly illuminated building, but as two small boys dressed as Ottoman emperors relieved them of their evening cloaks, their lightheartedness was marred almost immediately by an uncomfortable incident involving Oliver Fitzcharles.

It happened as they turned to go toward the ballroom entrance. Oliver was just emerging. He wore the obligatory formal evening black worn by all the other gentlemen, except those in the forces or the clergy, and he paused in the entrance, glancing around as if looking for someone.

He looked handsome and distinguished, but Sarah felt nothing as she watched him, nothing, that is, except a keen desire to deny him the opportunity to cut her as he had done outside the print shop the day before. But even as she caught Julia's arm to try to steer her away, he saw them. He gave a visible start, and stared at Sarah for a few moments before turning and hurrying back into the ballroom, where he soon disappeared in the crush.

For Sarah it was the same humiliation as before, and the only satisfaction she gained from the incident was that his manner could only be described as ashamed. Yes, that was it—ashamed.

To her relief on this occasion Julia did not appear to have noticed what happened, and so nothing was said as they entered the crowded ballroom, where a *contredanse* was now in progress, and where they soon found themselves claimed as partners, Sarah by a dashing naval captain, and Julia by an old friend of Thomas's. Of Nicholas Stanhope and his grandmother there was as yet no apparent sign. Perhaps, Sarah reflected rather wryly, they had elected not to come after all. If so, it would serve her right for being so foolish as to go back on her first impression of him! It would certainly serve her right for being so attracted to him.

After two more dances, Sarah saw Oliver again, and this time he wasn't alone, but was dancing with none other than Georgette, who was wearing a silver tissue gown that plunged so low over her bosom she seemed in danger of revealing all to the world. There were tall plumes springing from her golden hair, and she shimmered with diamonds. Her attention wasn't on the dance, and certainly wasn't on Oliver, who attracted not a single glance as they danced. Her lilac eyes constantly scanned the ballroom, and a disappointed pout came to her lips as each long look failed to reveal the face she evidently sought.

For the next hour or more Sarah and Julia took part in every dance, but still there was no sign of Nicholas. So much activity was quite tiring, and after a while they elected to sit out the next dance, but deciding upon such a course and actually being able to find somewhere to sit were two different things. There wasn't a chair or sofa to be had in the ballroom itself, and so their quest took them out into a passageway that led to smaller rooms at the rear of the building.

As the door into the passage closed upon the noise of the ball, they both became aware of voices coming from the nearest of the other room. The door was very slightly ajar, and the two gentlemen inside did not realize they could be heard.

Sarah recognized one as Lord Fitzcharles, for his guttural tone was very distinctive, and she automatically turned back toward the ballroom, but Julia overheard something the two men were saying that made her catch Sarah's arm urgently.

"Wait!" she hissed, taking a cautious step even closer to the doorway and craning her neck to hear.

As luck would have it at that moment, with a lull in the music and noise from the ballroom, the two voices became even more audible. Lord Fitzcharles was in an unusually expansive mood. "Well, my lord earl, things are certainly going well for me at the moment, eh? Sir Gerald Pennyworth's financial misfortunes have at last forced him to consider selling Icarus, and I have a fancy that I will easily outbid that damned maggot Thackeray, Dear God, how I abhor the fellow! If I could exterminate him without getting caught, I swear I would."

The other man in the room shifted uncomfortably.

"Thackeray, d'you say? I don't know him all that well personally."

Julia tugged at Sarah's arm. "It's the Earl of Hayden!" she whispered, being very careful indeed to speak so that only Sarah would hear.

Lord Fitzcharles gave a humorless laugh. "Thackeray is a thorn in the side of humanity itself, and of no practical use to anyone, except perhaps his legion of mistresses. God above, I sometimes marvel at the foolishness of women."

"Er, yes." The earl's response was still more uncomfortable.

"Well, that's by the by, and we have far more important matters to finalize, eh?"

"We do indeed, sir."

Lord Fitzcharles gave a throaty chuckle. "Dame Fortune is to be congratulated for her timely intervention at the card table. I might so easily have been saddled with a millstone for a daughter-in-law."

Sarah stiffened angrily. A millstone? How *dared* he refer to her in such a disparaging way!

The earl concurred. "Yes, indeed. As it is, we have been able to sort matters out to our mutual satisfaction, and instead of a millstone, you now have a lady of impeccable lineage. A thoroughbred, in fact." This last amused him, and he began to laugh.

Lord Fitzcharles was less disposed to humor on the point. "A thoroughbred in need of a wealthy owner," he pointed out tersely.

There was a moment of silence, and then the earl cleared his throat again. "Forgive me, I did not mean to imply anything untoward, and of course the match is ideal for both parties. I am more than cognizant of your son's fine qualities."

Lord Fitzcharles was a little placated. "Yes, well, I suppose my only real regret is losing the estate which would have come with the other match."

"A pretty enough plot, I grant you," the earl conceded. "Maybe Cranham can be persuaded to part with it."

Sarah and Julia exchanged mystified glances, for until that moment they'd both been convinced that the 'other match' had been Sarah. Now it seemed that that couldn't be so, for who was 'Cranham'?

Lord Fitzcharles was less than hopeful. "Cranham won't be parted from anything once it's his."

"He doesn't want another estate, not when he already has vast acres in Kent and Sussex. You may stand a chance, particularly if you offer a good price." The earl's tone became sly then. "I trust, of course, that any such offer would not be subtracted from the marriage settlement?"

Lord Fitzcharles's lack of humor was again to the fore. "An agreement is an agreement, sir. The details have been made final, and my word is my bond."

"Forgive me for pointing this out, my lord, but your word was not your bond where the previous match was concerned."

"Nor will it be this time if your financial affairs plunge into the pit. I am a man of honor, sir, but not a complete fool. I will not take on a bride who brings nothing to the match, not even a titled bride."

"The point is taken, sir, and you may be sure that my finances are as steady as yours, if at a somewhat lower level. Come now, don't let's fall out at this juncture, for if we do, we'll be throwing away a truly excellent arrangement. A toast, my lord. To Georgette and Oliver."

Glasses clinked, and Lord Fitzcharles responded. "To Oliver and Georgette," he said, pointedly reversing the order of the names.

Then the two men put the matter of the match aside and returned to discussing Lord Fitzcharles's obsession with acquiring the racehorse, Icarus.

The door from the ballroom opened suddenly as a noisy party of ladies and gentlemen emerged into the passage, and Sarah and Julia drew guiltily away from their eavesdropping. They hurried past the other guests, and returned to the noise and crush of the ballroom, where they sought as thinly occupied a corner as they could to discuss what they'd overheard.

Julia's fan wafted busily to and fro as she raised her voice to be heard. "What did you make of that?"

"The same as you, I should imagine. Oliver is now to marry dearest Georgette."

"They deserve each other." Julia's dark eyes searched Sarah's face. "I was thinking more of the mysterious 'Cranham'. Right up until he was mentioned, I really thought they were referring to the severed match with you."

"So did I."

"Do you know, I believe that that wretched Lord Fitzcharles had negotiated yet another match for dear Ollie, besides the one with you."

"Not even he would do that."

"What other explanation is there? Besides, I wouldn't put anything past him. I'll warrant that even now he has yet another bride in mind, just in case Georgette's dowry doesn't come up to scratch."

"Julia, I know that Lord Fitzcharles is unscrupulous, but that's going a little far, even for him."

"Then who is this Cranham person?"

"I have no idea," Sarah replied.

"The only Cranham I know of is Lord Cranham. Thomas's aunt, Lady Thurlong, cannot abide him. He's her vintage, and very unpleasant. Not a man to cross."

Sarah shrugged. "Maybe it's him, maybe it isn't. All I know is that I really don't care. Oliver and Georgette richly deserve each other."

"She'll eat him alive," Julia observed. "Still, the little weasel hasn't earned my pity, that's for certain." Her gaze moved to the dancing, where, as luck would have it, Oliver and Georgette were again partnering each other.

Sarah studied them. "Actually, it seems to me that neither of them is particularly enthusiastic, especially Georgette. She keeps looking around, and whenever Oliver speaks to her, she has to ask him to repeat himself because she wasn't listening the first time. Look, it's just happened again!"

At that moment Thomas Thurlong's friend came to claim Julia for another dance, a *ländler*, and as Sarah turned to see if there was anywhere she could sit and watch, she saw Nicholas coming toward her.

He smiled, and the noise of the ballroom faded all around her, leaving only the sudden thundering of her heart.

14

FORMAL evening wear suited him. His tight-fitting black coat was made of corded silk, and an amethyst pin reposed in the ample folds of his lace-edged neckcloth. He wore a white satin waistcoat, and his white silk breeches were superbly tailored. His dark hair was a little tousled, and his gray eyes were clear and steady as he bowed to her.

"Miss Howard."

"Mr. Stanhope."

"I trust you will forgive my belated arrival. My grandmother sends her apologies, but one of her friends is unwell, and she has gone to sit with her."

"I hope Lady Worthington's friend is not too indisposed?"

"I am uncharitable enough to believe she is suffering from a surfeit of rich food," he replied, smiling.

The smile reached past her fast diminishing defenses. She found him disturbing and wished that she hadn't suddenly become so vulnerable to his considerable charm.

The *ländler* for which Julia had been claimed had still not commenced, and Nicholas glanced at the dance floor, which was fast filling up. Then he smiled inquiringly at her. "Will you entrust yourself to me for this dance, Miss Howard?"

"Yes, sir, I will," she replied, accepting his arm.

The *ländler* was an almost private measure, involving couples facing each other with their arms entwined. It was neither fast nor slow, allowing ample opportunity to talk, and its intimacy confronted Sarah more and more with the spell he was weaving around her.

If he realized the effect he was having upon her, he gave no sign. "I have been somewhat remiss, Miss Howard, for I have neglected to tell you how very lovely you look tonight."

She blushed. "It is kind of you to say so, sir."

"You think I am paying an idle compliment?"

"I . . . I didn't say that."

"Not in so many words, but I assure you that I mean every word."

"I confess I never expected to hear you praise me, sir."

"And I certainly never expected to dance with you like this, Miss Howard." He smiled. "I recall that when I nearly knocked Mrs. Thurlong down, I thought you would prefer to shoot me rather than ever consider treading a friendly measure. It was a novel experience for me to be torn off such a strip."

"I fear I was rude," she murmured, lowering her eyes.

"No more than I had already been." He smiled. "Do I bring out the worst in you, Miss Howard?"

"You did."

"Did? Past tense?"

Slowly she met his gaze again. "Yes, sir, past tense."

"I'm very glad to hear it, for I find it much more agreeable to be on friendly terms with you. In fact, I would go so far as to say I find it very agreeable indeed."

She didn't know what to say. The color on her cheeks become positively fiery, and she was sure he could read her every thought. Oh, why was she suddenly such a dunce at concealing her feelings? Everything she did, every glance or word, told tales upon her. She had to change the subject. "Are . . . are you in Cheltenham for long, Mr. Stanhope?"

"I fear not. I came to see my grandmother before going abroad."

Disappointment rushed over her. "Where are you going?"

"From time to time I'm called upon to be a glorified errand boy for the government, and on this occasion I am required to take some important documents to Naples."

"Isn't that a little dangerous?" she asked, immediately thinking of the war.

"Not when I have Lord Nelson and his frigates to look after me." He smiled again. "Besides, the French haven't had command of the high seas for some time now."

"I know, but—"

"Are you concerned for my safety, Miss Howard?"

"I . . . I would be concerned for anyone traveling out of this country when we are at war, Mr. Stanhope." Oh, why wouldn't the color go from her cheeks? She strove to shake off her silly confusion. "You, er, said you are sent abroad from time to time, Mr. Stanhope. Where have you been?"

"Washington and Vienna." His gaze moved past her suddenly. "Oh, no, I have just seen a lady whose attention I do not wish to attract. Miss Howard, would you mind very much if we sat out the rest of this dance? Perhaps we could adjourn to the supper room for a glass of champagne?"

"Yes, of course." As he led her quickly from the floor, she stole a backward glance to see whom he was referring to, but there were so many ladies it could have been almost anyone.

They entered the supper room, which lay beyond a colonnade, and he spoke apologetically to her. "I trust you will forgive this hasty exit, Miss Howard, only I have been the subject of this lady's attentions for some time, and now I avoid her at all costs. I do not mean to sound ungallant toward her, but there is no polite way of saying it."

"You should be flattered that she is so smitten."

"I wish with all my heart that she'd never noticed me, for she appears to be the most singleminded and purposeful creature on this earth. I came to Cheltenham confident that she was still in London, but my grandmother soon disabused me of that notion. It may appear vain on my part, but I suspect the lady's arrival is no coincidence and that somehow she found out what my plans were. However, enough of that, for I see a blessedly vacant sofa in that far corner over there." He ushered her toward it. "Would you care for some supper as well a glass of champagne?" he asked when she was seated.

She shook her head. "The champagne is sufficient, Mr. Stanhope."

He beckoned to a footman to bring them two glasses, and then he sat down next to her. "Now then, Miss Howard, we have spoken about me, but have yet to discuss you."

"Me? There is nothing to discuss."

"I cannot believe that. For instance, is there a particular gentleman in your life?"

She lowered her eyes. "There was, but there isn't now."

"Was?"

"The betrothal was called off." She didn't wish to speak of Oliver, and since the brief engagement had never become public knowledge, except perhaps to Georgette, she saw no reason to ever mention it again. It was a part of her past she wished to forget had ever happened.

He saw how she suddenly lowered her eyes. The betrothal was evidently a sensitive point, and he wondered what had happened. "Whoever he was, he has lost a prize, Miss Howard," he said quietly.

She raised her eyes again. "More flattery, sir?" she murmured.

"A mere observation of fact." He was more intrigued than he'd expected, and, he had to admit, a little pricked to know that someone had been that close to her. Both realizations took him by surprise. "May I be impertinent enough to ask if you still carry a torch for this gentleman?" he asked, unable to curb his curiosity. He wanted to know more about her, perhaps he even wanted to know everything about her . . .

"The torch has been extinguished in no uncertain terms," she replied.

The answer satisfied something deep inside him. Dear God, what manner of lunacy had descended upon him tonight? He was about to ask her something more when he happened to glance through into the ballroom. To his chagrin he saw Julia looking around, obviously wondering where she was. "I, er, believe Mrs. Thurlong is searching for you, and so perhaps I should return you to her."

Sarah smiled at him. "I'm glad we've put our differences behind us, Mr. Stanhope."

"And so am I." He placed their almost finished glasses to one side, and then rose, extending a hand to her.

He wanted to say more to her as his fingers enclosed hers. For a moment he held her hand as the unspoken words slipped dangerously close to his lips, but then he drew back from the brink. He didn't know what had come over him tonight, but cool common sense must be allowed a place in the proceedings.

As he led her back to Julia, Sarah was not unaffected by his brief moment of hesitation. The minutes she had spent alone with him had woven more of a spell over her than she wished. Something about him drew her as she had never been drawn before, and with great disappointment she smiled and inclined her head to him as he took his leave of her.

Neither of them knew they had been secretly observed from the moment of Nicholas's arrival at the ball. A figure in silver tissue and diamonds had watched from the shadows by the colonnade, and her bitterly jealous gaze had followed them as they went up to Julia.

Georgette had been seized by an almost uncontrollable rage as she'd seen how he had immediately sought Sarah. Sarah Howard, of all women! Her fan moved busily to and fro before her hot face. He was too honorable to be guilty of hiding the truth, which meant that he didn't know anything, and if it were not that the little Howard was so painfully naive, one might suspect her of ulterior motives. For with things as they were, who better could she seduce than Nicholas Stanhope? But yesterday at the well it had been clear that Sarah knew nothing of recent events involving her father, which meant that her sudden acquaintance with Nicholas must have come about purely by chance.

A nerve flickered at Georgette's temple. How could fate have been so unkind as to deny her the man she wanted, and present her instead with a milksop like Oliver Fitzcharles? And how could it be fair that Sarah Howard should succeed with Nicholas? Georgette's fan moved furiously for a moment, but then it became still as a malevolent smile began to play upon her lips. She had succeeded in interfering in Sarah's life before, and she would do it again. The little Howard wasn't going to have Nicholas Stanhope, not while Georgette Belvoir lived and breathed!

She was so lost in her jealous spite that she gave a guilty start when her father put a hand on her arm. "Georgette, m'dear, at last it is all agreed to the last detail, and we've decided that there is no time like the present for announcing the match."

She stared at him in dismay, and then looked desperately at her mother, who stood at his side. "Mother? Please don't—"

But the countess, who was dressed in vermilion silk, halted her words with a nervous shake of her head. "You must do as your father wishes, Georgette," she said.

"But must it be announced tonight?"

The earl was implacable. "Yes. All society is here, and it seems appropriate."

"No! Please, Father—"

His face hardened. "You have already given your consent, madam, and now you must stand by it. You have only yourself to blame for your name being associated with Thackeray and for there to be whispers about your interest in Stanhope, and now I'm left with no option but to marry you off as swiftly and suitably as possible. I don't intend to have you on my hands forever more because your reputation has been ruined. Now then, either you do as I wish, or—"

Her yearning gaze swung toward Nicholas, who was standing in conversation with some gentlemen.

The earl followed the gaze. "Don't keep deluding yourself that Stanhope will ever want anything to do with you."

Georgette looked away.

The earl looked at her. "Who was the little piece in pink he was with earlier? I may be mistaken, but I thought it was—"

"Sarah Howard? Yes, it was." Georgette spoke through clenched teeth.

"Well, well. that's quite a turn-up, eh?"

Georgette didn't reply.

"Do you think she knows who he is?"

"No, but even if she did, she wouldn't have the wit to be that clever. Besides, I am almost certain she has no idea about her father. And before you ask, no, I do not for a single moment believe Nicholas would be dishonorable enough to court her company if he knew about it all. If he was aware of anything at all, he'd be sure to tell her. It's clear neither of them knows."

The earl shrugged. "It's immaterial to me; all I'm concerned with is marrying you off, and you're going to have to make the best of it. The Fitzcharles match is quite advantageous for you, you know. Not only will it provide you with wealth, but also with a husband who hasn't the courage to stand up for himself. He'll be putty in your hands, provided, that is, you don't make the mistake of going against his father. Fitzcharles senior is a very different kettle of fish. Cross him, and you'll regret it. Which brings me back to matter in hand. The betrothal is about to be announced. Do you understand?"

"Yes."

"Good. Now then, your hand on my arm, if you please."

Several minutes later the ball was brought to a standstill by the peremptory rapping of the master-of-ceremonies's cane. An expectant murmur rippled through the gathering as the earl and countess accompanied Georgette onto the orchestra's stage, followed by Lord Fitzcharles and Oliver. The contents of the previous morning's newspaper were immediately called to numerous minds, and hands and fans were raised to conceal whispers.

Georgette suppressed a shudder of distaste as the betrothal ring was slipped on her finger.

15

HAD Georgette but known it, the ring that sealed her loathed engagement was the same one that sealed Oliver's previous betrothal.

Sarah was close enough to recognize it, but there was no trace of regret in her heart. She reflected wryly that the Fitzcharles family was evidently very thrifty in such matters, and had no intention of wasting a perfectly good ring! How furious Georgette would be if she knew! Sarah studied Oliver as he and his new bride-to-be accepted the polite applause greeting their announcement. The weakness of his character was evident in his face, and if she had married him, it would indeed have been the disaster Julia had predicted.

For a moment her thoughts returned to the puzzling conversation she and Julia had overheard earlier in the evening. A great deal was now confirmed, but not everything was clear. For instance, who was the mysterious Cranham? And who was the 'millstone' referred to?

Nicholas paid scant attention to the brief betrothal ceremony, except to hope that it would free him from Georgette's continuous and unwanted attentions. His thoughts were still of Sarah, and his unexpected reaction to being with her. He wanted to see her again, and common sense was having less and less to do with his thoughts where she was concerned.

He looked toward her. She was alone again for a moment, because Julia's attention had been called away by old friends. Suddenly he decided to dispense with convention. Maybe she would give him his *congé*, but that was a chance he was prepared to take.

He made his way back to her. "Miss Howard?"

Her breath caught at the sound of his voice, and she turned with quick surprise. "Mr. Stanhope?"

He paused, gazing into the endless blue of her eyes. Endless blue? Dear God, he was like a gauche schoolboy! "Miss Howard, I must speak to you again."

"Speak to me? By all means, sir. What is it you wish to say?"

"I know that I am being too forward by far, and that I'm most definitely presuming upon what is a very new acquaintance, but unless I do . . ." He couldn't finish the sentence. He hadn't felt like this in a very long time, and suddenly he really didn't know what to say without making it sound like the opening gambit in a disreputable seduction.

"Whatever is it, Mr. Stanhope?" His obvious quandary aroused her concern.

"Miss Howard, please do not misunderstand what I am about to say, for my intentions are not base. When I say that I wish to speak to you again, what I really mean is that I would regard it as a great honor if we could perhaps meet again."

She stared at him.

"There is a great deal I wish to say to you, things I would not dream of saying so swiftly were it not for the circumstances of my imminent departure for Naples. Rules are rules, whether they are written down or not, but sometimes they must be broken, or at least bent a little, in the interests of the heart."

Her own heart almost stopped within her. "The . . . heart?" she repeated slowly, a myriad of confusing thoughts swirling richly through her. Was she imagining these moments? Or maybe misinterpreting? Yes, that was what it must be. . . . She was understanding what she wished to understand, not what he was really saying.

"I will understand if you despatch me to the devil for such forwardness, Miss Howard, and I will also understand if you decline to favor me in any way whatsoever, but nevertheless I will be at the bridge by the watermill at two o'clock tomorrow in the hope that you will chance to walk that way with your maid."

Taking her hand, he drew it swiftly to his lips, then he turned and walked away again.

She stared after him, so at sixes and sevens that she could hardly think. She felt certain that everyone in the ballroom must have seen what had happened, and possibly even heard what he'd said. Her cheeks flamed with a heady mixture of embarrassment and excitement as she tried to collect herself.

She toyed with the delicate spines of her fan, and her fingers trembled visibly. Everything she had ever been taught about what was proper and improper told her that she should not keep such an assignation, but she knew that she would walk by the bridge at two the following day.

When the ball was over at dawn, and the guests departed to their beds, Georgette returned home in a bitter mood. Still wearing her ballgown, she paced restlessly up and down in her bedroom, where the curtains were drawn and everything was lit by the flicker of firelight.

The scenes she had witnessed at the ball were all around her, taunting and mocking. She could still see Nicholas smiling into Sarah Howard's eyes, both before the betrothal, and then, more humiliatingly still, immediately after it. What had he said to her when he'd sought her out again? Whatever it was, there had been no misinterpreting the way he'd kissed the creature's hand, or the blush the gesture had left on her cheeks. Oh, how much honeyed tenderness would there be if they knew about each other's identity?

Tilly waited uncomfortably by the dressing table. She was always nervous when her unpredictable mistress was in such a mood. Suddenly Georgette stopped pacing. It was time to make use of Tilly's friendship with Julia Thurlong's footman, of whose character so much more had been learned after some careful quizzing.

"Tilly, does your young man still dislike Miss Howard as much as he did?"

"Yes, m'lady, for she has caused trouble for him."

"How open is he to a bribe?"

Tilly stared at such a question. "I . . . I beg your pardon, m'lady?"

Georgette was irritated. "I spoke plainly enough. How disposed would your footman be to render paid assistance?"

"I don't know, m'lady." But Tilly lowered her eyes unhappily. She was infatuated with Andrew, but was far from blind to his failings. She wasn't fool enough to believe that he was pursuing her for herself, and knew that ambition was his motive. He would be only too open to bribery. . . .

Georgette studied her shrewdly. "I can see by your face that he can be bought."

Tilly nodded reluctantly. "Yes, m'lady."

"Good, for I wish him to do something for me. I need to know Miss Sarah Howard's every movement, and if she has plans, I wish to know of them in advance. Do I make myself clear?"

"Yes, m'lady."

"I am particularly interested in learning of any dealings she may have with Mr. Nicholas Stanhope. Is that also clear?"

"Yes, m'lady.."

"I wish you to speak to him without delay, for I must know everything immediately. He will be paid handsomely for his services. You may go."

"Yes, m'lady." Tilly bobbed a curtsy and hurried from the room.

As the door closed behind her, Georgette remained where she was. Her reflection gazed back at her from the tall cheval glass in the corner. She knew how beautiful she was, and how glorious she had looked tonight, but *still* he had had eyes only for Sarah Howard!

As she looked, the firelight caught the new betrothal ring on her finger. With a grimace of distaste she removed it and hurled it across the room, where it rolled into a corner.

Across the town at the Fitzcharles residence, Oliver was slumped in a leather armchair in the darkened library after his return from the ball. The fire had burned low, and it was time for the parlormaid to come and tend it, for outside the sun was now above the horizon.

His evening coat was undone, and he had loosened his neckcloth. He leaned his head wearily back, wishing he were even more drunk than he was. There was a half-empty decanter of cognac on the table beside him. It had been full to the brim when he'd first picked it up an hour before. Seeing Sarah again at the ball had reminded him of the mistake he'd made, a mistake he'd compounded when he'd gone through with the betrothal to Georgette.

It was Sarah he wanted, not the Earl of Hayden's detestable daughter.

A nerve flickered at his temple, and he stretched over to pour himself another large measure of the cognac. His head was swimming, and his hand swayed so much that he poured as much of the liquid over the table as into the glass. His gaze moved to the mantel shelf, where a drawing of the racehorse Icarus had been propped up behind a candlestick. His father had commissioned a painting of the thoroughbred, and the drawing was the artist's initial sketch. It had been greeted with wholehearted approval by the man who was convinced that his devious scheming and machinations would soon result in Icarus being installed at this stables at Blackwell Park.

Oliver raised his glass to the drawing. "May Thackeray outbid you, Father, for it would give me great pleasure to see you denied something for a change." His voice was thick and slurred, and he spilled more of the cognac as he drank deeply from the glass.

The door opened and the parlormaid entered carrying the heavy scuttle of coal. She halted immediately as she realized he was totally in his cups, and then she hastily withdrew again.

Oliver wasn't even aware that she'd been there. He was fast losing consciousness, and his eyes closed, the glass slipped from his fingers, shattering on the floor. The sound was very loud in the silence of the room.

16

SARAH didn't tell Julia about the assignation with Nicholas because she was only too aware that she was flouting convention, but she took Annie with her, informing her that they were merely going for an airing on what was another beautiful autumn afternoon. There was no risk of Julia choosing to come because she wanted to write a letter to Thomas. The sun shone from a clear blue sky as she and Annie set off, but the light breeze was cooler than of late. Sarah wore a daffodil yellow merino pelisse over a white gown, and her hair was pinned up beneath a stylish gray silk bonnet that was tied on with flouncy white ribbons.

The sound of rushing water soon drifted along the narrow lane as they walked toward the mill and the river, and Sarah's courage began to falter. What if he wasn't there? What if she was the subject of a prank—maybe even a wager? As each successive dire possibility occurred to her, so the inclination to draw back increased.

She almost turned away, but then the bend in the lane brought the bridge into view, and she saw him. He was leaning on the parapet, his cane swinging in his gloved hands as he looked down at the river. He wore a maroon double-breasted coat and cream breeches, and his tall hat was tilted back on his head so that the sunlight fell across his face.

In those few moments before he realized she was there, she knew beyond all doubt that common sense no longer had any place in her actions. She was attracted to him like a moth to a flame, and for the moment it did not matter that she might be burned. All her apprehension evaporated, and there was only the rightness of what she was doing.

Suddenly he saw her and straightened to come to meet

her. A warm smile grew on his lips, and Annie suddenly realized there was nothing accidental about this encounter. For a moment the maid didn't quite know what to do, but then she fell discreetly back, lingering several yards behind her mistress. She was close enough to still be with Sarah, but far enough away not to overhear anything that might be said.

Nicholas's gray eyes were warm and steady as he halted and removed his hat. "I'm glad that you decided to come, but if you have any doubts at all, and would prefer it if I walked on by now, then you have only to say."

"I don't want you to walk on by," she replied, feeling warm as she met his gaze.

"Then let this appear to be a chance meeting that results in us choosing to stroll together," he said, offering her his arm.

She accepted, and they crossed the river to the sycamores copse, beyond which riders could be seen in the meadows. There was no one else in the copse, and they were alone except for Annie, who was now the soul of tact as she followed.

The maid was completely astonished that her usually proper mistress was keeping a tryst with a gentleman she hardly knew. It was completely out of character, so much so that Annie knew there was nothing trivial about today's decision to go against the accepted way. The maid hoped that the meeting appeared innocent to others, and she glanced around in case someone else was near, but there didn't seem to be anyone else close by.

There was someone else, however, for Georgette was watching secretly from a deserted corner by the mill, her orange taffeta clothes blending with the rich autumn colors all around. Her decision to bribe Andrew had borne swift fruit, for the footman had discovered through Annie that Sarah intended to go for a walk by the river at this particular time, and had sent word through Tilly. Georgette's already suspicious mind was alert to any possibility, especially after the intimate moments she'd witnessed at the ball. The walk by the river might be just that, a walk. But on the other hand, it might be so much more. And so she had gone to the mill well before two o'clock, and to her fury had seen the meeting she knew full well had been prearranged.

Unaware that they were under such vigilant and resentful scrutiny, Nicholas placed his hand briefly over Sarah's as they walked. "I'm so very glad that you came," he said softly.

She was conscious of his hand, for his touch was so affecting that it was as if neither of them wore gloves. . . .

He smiled a little. "I wish I weren't leaving for Naples, for there is so little time, and that is why I've taken the liberty of asking you to meet me like this. I may not have known you for long, Miss Howard, but in that brief time you've made a very deep and favorable impression upon me. Dare I hope that you have kept this meeting because I have made a similar impression upon you?"

She nodded, for she saw no point in being coy.

He smiled. "If it were not that I am to leave so soon, I would have conducted things much more properly, I promise you, but if I dilly-dally with all the usual conventions, I will not have progressed beyond the first politenesses before I'm on my way to the Mediterranean. The last thing I want is to be kicking my heels in Naples, wishing with all my heart that I'd been bolder before I left, and I certainly couldn't endure the thought of someone else winning your favor in my absence. I wish to know you much, much better Miss Howard, and that is the absolute truth." He glanced at her. "Have I shocked you by coming so swiftly to the point?"

"Shocked me? No. Indeed, Mr. Stanhope, your frankness deserves the same from me. Nothing would please me more than to know you better." She was intoxicated by the warmth in his eyes, and she floated on air, weightless and free as never before. It was as if she'd waited for this moment, when nothing else on earth mattered except being with this man.

He put his hand briefly to her cheek. "Fate has appalling timing, does it not? In another two weeks or so I shall have to leave," he murmured.

She closed her eyes, savoring the gentle caress of his fingers. "Will you be away long?" she whispered.

"I fear it will be months, possibly even as long as a year if the balance of the war at sea should change."

A year? It seemed a lifetime. She looked away to hide her dismay.

"May I call you Sarah?" he asked softly.

"Yes."

"Sarah, last night you mentioned a broken betrothal . . ."

"It is well and truly over," she replied truthfully. "I feel nothing for the gentleman concerned." She searched his face then. "You haven't mentioned your private life, except to tell me about the lady who has been unsuccessfully pursuing you."

"I am unattached, and there has never been anyone who has had cause to hope. Oh, I've made love to many women, and I admit to having had several mistresses in the past, but I've never been *in* love, nor have I offered for anyone's hand. There is no wife hidden away anywhere, and no secret inamorata." He held her gaze. "I have never been more serious about anything in my life than I am about this now. I hardly know you, but I love you, Sarah Howard, and I wish everything to be placed on a proper footing before I leave. May I call formally upon you this evening?"

His eyes were compelling, and her heart seemed to have stopped within her. She was oblivious to everything but him. All she could do was whisper his name. "Nicholas . . ."

He took her by both hands. "I love you, Sarah," he said again, his voice so soft it was as if he stroked her. He'd hardly known the confession was on his lips; indeed he'd hardly known that that was how strong and unerring his feelings had become.

"And . . . I love you, too," she whispered, knowing that it was true. She was in love, hopelessly so, and nothing had ever been more certain.

He didn't say anything more, but pulled her into his arms, kissing her fiercely on the lips. It was a hungry kiss, urgent and intense, and she gave herself willingly, her body yielding against him as if she had been fashioned solely for him. Caution flew away on the autumn breeze, and a rich desire took its place, aching exquisitely through her. It was a sweet pain, urging her to surrender, robbing her of any will to resist, and turning her blood to fire. Luxurious sensations she had never felt before surged irresistibly over her now as his lips teased and aroused, and she was alive to the hardness of his body against hers.

Annie stared, dumbfounded, and then glanced uneasily around again, still afraid that someone might see her mistress's indiscretions, but once more there did not seem to be anyone else nearby.

Georgette was still there, however, and her face was like stone as she watched the two lovers among the sycamore trees. There was no mistaking the intensity of the kiss, or that Nicholas had instigated it. His feelings for Sarah were written large on his face, and the way he held her, oh, the way he held her. . . . Georgette's heart twisted with fury, and her jealousy tightened so fiercely that she had to pull back so that she couldn't look any more. She was trembling from head to toe, her lilac eyes bright with malice and resentment. She wouldn't let this happen, she wouldn't!

In the copse, Nicholas's face was flushed as he drew slowly back from the kiss. Sarah's eyes remained closed with ecstasy. The spell still coiled around her, beguiling her senses and quickening her pulse so that it raced almost unbearably.

His lips brushed softly against her forehead, and then he released her completely. "I think we should walk back now, for we have already risked too much if your reputation is to be protected. Are you staying with Mrs. Thurlong?"

She struggled to return to reality. "Yes, at Thurlong Lodge."

"I will accompany you, and as we agreed earlier, it will be as if we happened to meet and chose to stroll together. I will then ask if I may call upon you tonight."

She nodded, and then smiled up into his eyes again. "Just kiss me once more before we go," she whispered.

He did not deny the request, and she closed her eyes again as his lips moved warmly over hers. There was no restraint in the way she linked her arms around his neck and pressed close. For just a few moments more there was no nod in the direction of caution or wisdom, just a sensuous disregard for anything but their new and overwhelming love. Never in her wildest imaginings would she have dreamed it possible that she would behave like this, but then she had never felt like this before. Now she tingled with emotions that had slumbered until today, and might have slumbered forever more had she not met Nicholas Stanhope.

Suddenly Sarah remembered Annie, and pulled guiltily away as she turned to look at the maid. Annie prudently averted her gaze, as if nothing untoward had taken place during the past half an hour or so.

As they began to walk back toward the bridge, Georgette remained out of sight, but she watched them cross the river and enter the lane that led to the High Street. Her beautiful face was ugly with spite. Sarah Howard wasn't going to have him! Nothing in the world was more certain than that!

Nicholas's hand was warm over Sarah's until they reached the High Street. There they became the picture of etiquette and decorum as he walked her to Thurlong Lodge. Neither of them observed Georgette's cerise landau drawn up much farther along the thoroughfare, in the opposite direction from Julia's house. If they had, their suspicions might have been aroused.

At Thurlong Lodge, Nicholas removed his hat and bowed to Sarah as Hemmings opened the door. "With your permission I will call this evening, Miss Howard," he said politely.

"That will be most agreeable, Mr. Stanhope," she replied, and then went into the house.

The door closed behind her, and Nicholas replaced his hat before strolling along the pavement in the direction of Cambridge Crescent.

Georgette had followed them to the corner of the lane and watched their leave-taking. She guessed he was now returning to his grandmother's house, and she meant to be there before him, paying the call for which she had already sought Lady Worthington's permission. She hurried to her carriage, and soon drove swiftly past him en route for Cambridge Crescent. She already knew that Lady Worthington was out, but that was all to the good, for she intended to time her arrival to coincide with his. He would have little option but to admit her and then show her every courtesy while she was there.

In Thurlong Lodge Julia had finished her letter to Thomas, and had overheard the brief exchange by the front door. She raised a quizzical eyebrow as Sarah entered. "Mr. Stanhope is calling tonight?"

"Yes. I hope you do not mind." Sarah felt her cheeks warming with telltale color.

"Mind? No, of course not, although I *do* mind being fibbed to."

"Fibbed to?"

"About going out for a mere walk. You were keeping a tryst, weren't you, Sarah Howard?"

"I wasn't!"

"Fibber." Julia smiled. "What a sly boots you are, to be sure. Making assignations with the most wickedly handsome gentleman in town! I'm shocked, madam, shocked beyond all redemption."

Sarah's cheeks were fiery. "I know I shouldn't have done it, but I simply couldn't help myself . . ."

Julia went to her and hugged her. "Don't feel wretched about it, for there is no need, least of all with me. How do you think I first became properly acquainted with Thomas? His family didn't approve of me at all, because my family is as staunchly Whig as they are Tory. We prevailed, however, and now we're as happy as it's possible to be, at least as happy as we can be without the family we both long for so much."

"You'll have all the family you wish, I know you will," Sarah replied reassuringly, but then gave a shy smile. "Julia, do you believe it is possible to fall in love so swiftly?"

"Yes, of course I do. My dearest Sarah, from the moment I saw your Mr. Stanhope drive past us on the road from the Frogmill, I knew there was more to your indignation with him than you realized, and on each occasion after that it became increasingly clear to me that you were drawn to him. Then, at the ball, I knew beyond all shadow of doubt that you and he had formed a considerable tendresse for each other. I will not mind at all if he calls upon you here tonight; indeed I will welcome it, for I am sure he is perfect for you."

Georgette timed her arrival in Cambridge Crescent to the very second, waiting around the corner and then seeing to it that her landau drew up at the curb outside Lady Worthington's house at exactly the same moment

Nicholas walked along the pavement. She alighted directly in front of him, her orange taffeta skirts rustling, and she gave him the brightest and most innocent of smiles.

"Why, good afternoon, Mr. Stanhope," she said, looking as engaging and innocent as she could.

Nicholas's heart had sunk the moment he saw her, but somehow he managed to return the smile and greeting without appearing concerned. "Good afternoon, Lady Georgette," he replied, bowing civilly.

"I was about to call upon Lady Worthington concerning the ball I wish to arrange."

"Indeed? I fear my grandmother isn't at home."

She feigned dismay. "No? But I sent word that I would call now. No doubt she means to return at any moment. May I wait?"

There was little he could say to such a request, and so he made the best of it by smiling and nodding. "Yes, of course, Lady Georgette," he murmured, reluctantly offering her his arm.

Together they entered the house.

17

GEORGETTE'S little black shoes tapped upon the elegant marble floor of the entrance hall, and her taffeta skirts whispered as she turned to face Nicholas. "I do hope that you will honor me with your company while I wait, Mr. Stanhope?"

"I, er . . ."

"Please, sir, for I am only too aware that my conduct of late hasn't been all that it should have been." Never had Georgette's wide-eyed remorse seemed more sincere.

After the success of his assignation with Sarah, Nicholas was loath to be ungracious. Besides, if Georgette really did wish to smooth matters over, he was willing to meet her halfway, and so he smiled and nodded. "I will gladly join you, Lady Georgette," he said, allowing the butler to relieve him of his outdoor things.

Placing the items on a small table, the butler bowed to him. "Shall I serve tea, sir?"

"Yes, Hart, if you please."

"Sir." The butler bowed and withdrew toward the kitchens.

Nicholas indicated the drawing room. "Shall we?" he murmured to Georgette, who stepped exultantly through the doorway ahead of him.

Lady Worthington's drawing room was sumptuously furnished, although not to her own taste, the house having been leased fully furnished. Nicholas's grandmother preferred pastel colors on the walls, but this room was hung with heavy crimson brocade. Georgette was immediately conscious that the surroundings clashed with her orange taffeta but she wasn't deterred.

"Do sit down," Nicholas said, gesturing toward a velvet sofa.

The taffeta whispered sensuously again as Georgette

obeyed. She arranged herself very carefully, making certain that when he sat down opposite, he was treated to her best side. He had to be charmed as never before, and no one could be more charming than she when she chose.

She smiled at him. "You seem in excellent spirits, if I may say so, sir."

"I am."

"Would it be impertinent of me to inquire the reason?"

He decided to be blunt. She had expressed a wish to put her recent conduct behind her, and he would take her at her word. "I believe that I have found the lady with whom I wish to spend the rest of my life, Lady Georgette," he said, meeting her eyes squarely.

She didn't flinch on the outside, but inside she was cut to the very quick with dismay and disbelief. Surely it couldn't have progressed that far already? Her smile remained steady. "May I know the lady's name, sir?" she asked, struggling to sound politely interested.

"It would be ungentlemanly of me to divulge that information, Lady Georgette, for I have yet to call formally upon her."

"I do understand, for a lady's reputation is all important, is it not? Not that I think for a moment that her reputation has been compromised," she added quickly. "Whoever she is, the lady is very fortunate indeed."

"It is flattering of you to say so, Lady Georgette."

She feigned pretty embarrassment. "Mr. Stanhope, I must ask your forgiveness for my conduct in recent months. I have been less than sensible, and I beg you to forget all about it."

"It is forgotten already, Lady Georgette. Besides, you now have your betrothal, and I am sure the future augurs well for both you and your husband-to-be."

For a fleeting moment her smile became fixed, for the last thing she wished to talk of was her betrothal to Oliver Fitzcharles! "I hope you are right, sir, but I fear that few arranged marriages ever equal true love matches, such as I hope you and your mystery lady will one day enjoy. It must be very frustrating for you to meet her so suddenly, and then have to leave the country."

"I didn't realize you knew I was leaving, Lady Georgette."

She hesitated, wondering if she'd spoken out of turn.

She'd found out about his journey to Naples through her usual method, that of bribing servants, this time one of his London footmen. "Oh dear, is it supposed to be a secret?" she asked with pretty confusion.

"Only from the French, though I'm curious to know how you happened upon the information."

She was a little flustered. "I, er, really can't remember. I believe I overheard it in London before I left. Yes, I'm sure that was it. I attended a dinner party at Lansdowne House and someone mentioned it."

He smiled. "It isn't of any real consequence, provided there were no revolutionary Frenchmen at the table."

She gave a trill of laughter. "Oh, I promise you there weren't any such low insects present, sir. La, sir, what a thought!" Her smile faded with calculated sympathy. "I am so sorry that you and your lady are to be parted so soon, sir," she said, determined to return the conversation to the matter of Sarah Howard.

"It will not be forever, Lady Georgette."

She treated him to the full force of her beauty, her lilac eyes large and soft with emotion. "How very romantic, Mr. Stanhope. You are putting your life at risk for your country, and your love waits anxiously for your safe return."

"You make it sound like something from a novel, Lady Georgette," he murmured.

The dryness of his tone pricked her, as did his stony indifference to her wiles. She was employing every feminine artifice in order to catch his attention, but he was apparently immune, just as he had been immune to her flirtation with Sir Mason Thackeray. Nothing seemed to arouse his interest, nothing at all.

Suddenly she wanted to hurt him as much as he was hurting her, but above all she wanted to punish Sarah Howard for winning him so effortlessly. Dangerous resentment surged through her, but still she managed to hold it in check as she wondered spitefully how it would be if Sarah knew who he was, or indeed if he knew about what had been happening to Sarah's father in London. So far everything pointed to their continued ignorance, but Sarah would soon learn some devastating facts, facts that might even make her wonder about Nicholas Stanhope's honor.

Georgette smiled. "Did you say you have yet to pay a formal call upon your lady?"

"Yes, but I mean to rectify the omission this evening."

"I trust that all will go as you wish, sir."

"Thank you. I trust, too, that all will go well for you in your betrothal, Lady Georgette."

Again the unwelcome reminder. She lowered her eyes as if blushing, but in reality it was to hide her anger. When she looked up, she was again mistress of herself. "When do you expect to leave for Naples, Mr. Stanhope?" she asked, thinking it best to change the subject for the time being.

"In a few weeks. Which reminds me, I must write to my cousin Stephen. He's handling my affairs while I'm away, and there are several matters I neglected to mention when last I saw him."

"Stephen? Would that be Stephen Mannering?" she asked, her interest quickening sharply.

"Yes. Are you acquainted with him?"

"A little." She masked the keen anticipation that was now coursing through her. She knew a great deal about Stephen Mannering, even if she wasn't all that well acquainted with him personally. She knew, for instance, that her brother Geoffrey held a number of his promissory notes that were not intended to be called in until the following year, when Stephen inherited a considerable fortune. Would it be a wise move to purchase those notes at the first possible moment? If Stephen was to be Nicholas's agent during his absence, it might prove very useful indeed to have him under her thumb. The threat of jail for someone like Stephen, with his dread of being enclosed, would be a very potent weapon indeed.

At that moment the door opened and the butler brought the tea. When he had served them both and withdrawn once more, Georgette promptly returned the conversation to the matter of Nicholas's unnamed love, as if that had been what they'd been discussing before the tea arrived. "I believe I know the identity of your secret sweetheart, Mr. Stanhope," she announced conspiratorially.

"I hardly think so, Lady Georgette."

"Well, let me put two and two together. Last night at

the ball I noticed you and Miss Howard sitting in the supper room for some time."

His lips parted slightly as he was caught off guard.

Georgette was triumphant. "Your face gives you away, sir. So, it is my old friend Sarah who has captured your heart!"

"You are, er, acquainted with Miss Howard?"

"Very well indeed, sir. We attended school together right here in Cheltenham. Oh, there is so much I can tell you about her." My powers of invention are second to none! By the time I've finished, you will be forced to doubt dear little Sarah's virtue, as well as her sincerity in welcoming your overtures now. You won't be able to trust her motives.

But before Georgette could launch upon her vengeful mission, a travel-stained carriage drew up at the curb outside. Georgette looked up swiftly, fearing that it would be Lady Worthington returning, but instead she saw an elderly gentleman alighting. She recognized Sir William Ballenby, an under-secretary at the Foreign Office, and she looked swiftly at Nicholas.

"I fear your journey to Naples may be upon you a little earlier than expected, sir. Sir William Ballenby has just arrived."

Nicholas rose quickly and went to the window. Yes, it was Sir William, and that meant that Georgette was probably right about Naples. He turned to the door as his visitor was shown in.

The under-secretary was a thin, stooping man of very aristocratic and refined appearance. He was a little wizened now, but his eyes were as brown and sparrow-bright as ever. He wore a formal, rather old-fashioned blue coat and white silk breeches, and a powdered wig covered his receding hair.

As he entered, his gaze went straight to Nicholas by the window, and he didn't notice Georgette on the sofa, nor did she do anything to draw attention to herself, for there was always the chance of overhearing a useful snippet of information.

Nicholas went to him. "Good afternoon, Sir William," he said, taking the older man warmly by the hands.

"Good afternoon, m'boy. I'm glad to have found you in."

"You have news for me?"

Sir William nodded. "I fear so. Things have developed, and now you'll have to leave immediately. Within the hour, in fact."

Georgette's eyes glittered thoughtfully as she remained mouselike upon the sofa.

Nicholas was appalled. "Within the hour? But surely there is no need to be quite so hasty?"

"It can't be helped. The frigate *Joyous* is standing by to leave Bristol on tonight's tide, and that means getting yourself down there as quickly as possible. These despatches must reach Naples without delay, for it is imperative that none of the Mediterranean territories are lured over to the French. I wish I could give you more notice, but it's a fait accompli. An hour is all I dare give you, and I'll have to brief you about it all as we drive to Bristol."

Nicholas nodded resignedly. "As you wish, sir. I'll instruct my man to pack what he deems necessary." He left the room and shouted for his valet.

Sir William turned then, and suddenly noticed Georgette sitting so demurely upon the sofa. "Why, Lady Georgette, I had no idea you were there."

"Oh dear, have I been privy to state secrets, Sir William?" she inquired, her eyes wide and innocent.

Ever susceptible to a pretty face, Sir William was at pains to reassure her. "Do not concern yourself, my dear, for you haven't heard anything you should not." Then, knowing of her keen pursuit of Nicholas, and misconstruing the reason for her presence, he smiled apologetically. "I fear I must crave your forgiveness for taking Mr. Stanhope away from you."

She lowered her eyes becomingly. "I believe I may eventually be able to forgive you, sir," she murmured, but her mind was racing. Surely there was something in all this she could turn to her own advantage? But what?

Nicholas returned. "I should be ready soon, Sir William, but I must crave your indulgence to the extent of writing two letters before we leave. First of all I must advise my cousin Stephen on certain matters, since he is acting for me while I'm away, and—"

Sir William looked sadly at him. "You haven't mended the rift with your father?"

"No, nor am I likely to. Too much has passed between us."

"He hasn't disinherited you," Sir William reminded him.

"No, but only because he loathes my cousins even more than he loathes me," Nicholas replied trenchantly.

"You said there were two letters you wished to write?"

"Yes. The other is to someone who expects me to call this evening."

Georgette was on her feet in a moment. "I will deliver that second letter for you, Mr. Stanhope. It was my intention to call upon Sarah soon anyway, and if I go there without delay I will be able to explain to her that you really have had to leave without notice."

"I, er . . ." Nicholas didn't like being put on such a spot. Georgette may have given every impression of being a reformed character, but would it be all that wise to accept her at face value?

Georgette was at her most persuasive. "You may have faith in me, sir, for I am a very old friend of hers, and besides, I really do wish to make amends."

On impulse Nicholas decided to trust her. "You are very kind, Lady Georgette."

"Not at all, sir, for it is the least I can do when you are employed upon such a vital patriotic duty."

As he went to the writing desk in the corner, she concealed the feline gleam in her eyes. Sarah Howard wasn't going to receive any letter; on the contrary, she was going to be left wondering why her new love hadn't bothered to send any word to her at all. Nor would she receive any future missives from Nicholas, because the ambitious and unscrupulous footman at Thurlong Lodge could be relied upon to purloin any such letters. Oh, how sublimely useful servants could be. From Tilly she now knew that more than anything Andrew wanted a post at Hayden House in London, and so this was the carrot to be dangled before him from now on.

It wasn't going to be long before the burgeoning romance between Nicholas and Sarah Howard was at an end, and Sarah's heart was broken for the second time. How sad. And how sad, too, that Nicholas would think himself ignored by his sweet little lady love. It would serve him right for spurning a Belvoir in favor of a mousy nonentity from the depths of Oxfordshire!

Georgette stood by the window, looking out at Sir William's travel-stained carriage. Knowing of Nicholas's deep loathing for his father, and of his unwillingness to hear anything about that gentleman's activities, it was only too likely that he didn't know the significance of the name Howard, but one still had to wonder a little about Sarah herself. It didn't seem possible that she was completely unaware of Nicholas's real identity, but that was how it appeared. It was tempting to consider divulging certain information to her, but that might prove unwise just yet. Innocent and naive the creature might be at the moment, but would she remain so once she learned the truth? It was hard to say what she might do if the Devil held the reins. A cap set determinedly at Nicholas, who was so very honorable, might prove to be the trump that would overturn all the recent play at a certain green baize table in London, and that wouldn't do at all. No, far better to wait and see, and in the meantime Stephen Mannering's IOU's would be acquired from Geoffrey. One thing was certain, whatever the future held, if it was in her power to do anything about it, she was going to make both Sarah Howard and Nicholas Stanhope suffer for loving each other.

In under an hour Nicholas had left Cambridge Crescent with Sir William. There hadn't even been an opportunity to say good-bye to his grandmother.

Georgette had already departed with the letter for Sarah in her reticule, and as soon as her carriage had drawn away from the curb, she had broken the seal to see what he'd written. With each loving word she read, her face became more and more ugly with hatred and bitterness, and when she'd finished, she tore the letter savagely into tiny pieces before tossing them out of the carriage. They fluttered like snow along the street, scattering beyond all retrieval on the cobbles and in the gutters.

As Georgette's carriage drove on, Nicholas's letter to Sarah was lost forever.

18

SARAH waited in vain that evening, but Nicholas did not call as promised. Nor did he call the next day, or the day after that, and with each hour that passed, the pain of disillusionment increased.

Discreet inquiries elicited the information that he was no longer at Lady Worthington's house, but had left Cheltenham. She did not learn that he had had to leave for Naples with barely an hour's notice, or that he hadn't even had the chance to say good-bye to his grandmother. All she knew was that he had gone without sending any word at all to Thurlong Lodge, and as far as she was concerned this eloquent silence signified an end to their fleeting liaison.

The only unpainful excuse she could think of was that he had been called away on his duty to Naples much more swiftly than expected, but if that had happened, surely he would at least have sent her an explanatory note? There hadn't been any such note, nor even a verbal message through a footman, and she was forced to acknowledge that she'd been foolish not to abide by her unfavorable first impression of Nicholas Stanhope. She'd been even more foolish to so far abandon rules of conduct as to keep the tryst by the bridge.

Yet again Julia was upset on her friend's behalf, and did what she could to offer comfort. She knew that the brevity of the affair did not make the blow any easier to bear, for this time Sarah had fallen completely and utterly in love. Julia was angry to hear Sarah sobbing into her pillow at night, and her anger was reserved entirely for Nicholas, whom she regarded as a toad of the lowest order. What possible purpose had been served by what he'd done? Why make so many promises when he had no intention of keeping them? He was unspeakable, and

Julia wished him in perdition, along with Lord Fitzcharles and his son. May all three roast together!

Four days after Nicholas's departure from Cheltenham, the letter carrier called as usual at Thurlong Lodge. It was Andrew's allotted task to accept the mail, and so he went to the door with the purse of coins that was always kept in readiness. The moment the letter carrier had gone, the footman glanced carefully through the assortment of letters and immediately took out one addressed to Sarah. It was from Nicholas, and had been written in Padstow, Cornwall.

Placing the other letters in the silver dish on the hall table, Andrew took the one for Sarah into the deserted drawing room. There he broke the seal and began to read.

Padstow. Friday.

My dearest Sarah,

I am on board the frigate *Joyous* which has been forced to put into this port to replenish supplies which were unfortunately lost overboard last night. The pilot has promised to send this letter for me, and as he is waiting for me at this very moment, I must be very brief.

I trust you received my previous letter from Lady Georgette. I had so little time to do anything before I left that I could not call in person to take my leave of you. Forgive me, my dearest, for I did not willingly fail you.

If there is one thing I now regret about those moments by the river, it is that I neglected to ask the most important question of all. I love you with all my heart, Sarah, and do not need any more time in which to be certain that I wish you to be my wife. No other woman has ever reached my soul, let alone stolen it, but you have. Marry me, Sarah, for you are all that I want in the world, and I know that you return my feelings. We were meant to be together.

The pilot grows impatient. I will write again from Gibraltar.

I am forever yours,
Nicholas

A thin smile curled Andrew's lips as he slowly ripped the letter into fragments and cast them into the eager fire, where they shriveled and curled, and soon were no more.

He whistled to himself as he left the drawing room. He would report to Tilly, who would in turn report to Lady Georgette. Soon that position at Hayden House would be his!

Nicholas's voyage was storm-tossed. The *Joyous* heaved on mountainous seas, her timbers straining and her pennants fluttering like things possessed. The gimbal-mounted candlestick in his tiny cabin at the stern creaked to the motion of the ship, and beyond the boarded window the gale shrieked as it gusted demonically across the notorious Bay of Biscay.

He lay wide awake on his narrow bed, wishing the elements would relent a little and permit at least one day of calm weather. When they'd set sail from Bristol, there had only been a light breeze, but the moment the *Joyous* rounded Land's End, the gales had struck.

A wry smile played upon his lips as he watched the candlestick swing against the heaving wall. How far away now the Royal Well ball, and the *ländler* when he'd first realized how he felt about Sarah. And how far that magical moment by the Chelt when he'd taken her in his arms and kissed her on the lips. He recalled the unbelievable joy he'd felt when he knew she returned his love, and the sensuous delight of her pliant body cleaving close to his.

For a moment a shadow passed through his eyes. Had he been foolish to entrust that letter to Georgette? He wished now that he'd declined her offer, no matter how kindly meant, and chosen instead to send his message by a footman, but it was too late for regrets. He could only hope that Georgette's new leaf was sincere. Besides, by now Sarah would have received the letter from Padstow. The shadow left his eyes. Yes, by now she would know that he wished her to be his bride.

Lord Fitzcharles was exultant. He and Oliver were in the library at their house on the edge of Cheltenham,

and he was pouring them both a liberal glass of the finest
cognac with which to toast the drawing of Icarus.

Beaming with delight, he pressed the glass into his
son's hand. "A job well done, eh? Old Pennyworth's nag
is mine at last!"

Oliver looked sourly at the drawing on the mantel
shelf. "The horse is only yours because you sank to even
lower depths than usual," he observed, swirling the glass
without drinking.

His father's smile faded into a snarl. "That's enough
from you, my laddo. How I go about my business is
nothing to do with it. The end always justifies the means.
Besides, what better feeling can there be than to rub
one's enemy's nose in the dirt?"

"Sir Gerald Pennyworth was hardly your enemy."

"I was referring to Thackeray, you dolt." Lord Fitzcharles looked sourly at him, and then read his mood
correctly. "Dear God above, I sometimes despair of your
intelligence, boy! How can you possibly moon over that
worthless Howard creature when you have someone like
Lady Georgette?"

Oliver took his courage in both hands. "I don't want
this match, Father, in fact, I wish to be released from
it."

Lord Fitzcharles blinked. "Eh?"

"I wish to withdraw from the match, and—"

"I heard you!" his father snapped. "No, sir, you may
not withdraw from the match. It's a good contract and
will bring excellent blood into the family."

"But hardly a fine dowry!"

"Fine enough. Hayden's providing as handsomely as
he can. Be sensible, boy. You wouldn't get an earl's
daughter if it were not that said earl is finding moths in
his purse these days!"

"Father, I—"

"No! The match goes ahead." Lord Fitzcharles's eyes
became small and hard. "We go to London shortly, and
once there you will dance attendance upon your bride-
to-be, do you understand? She is to be kept satisfied that
you are eager for her, is that also understood?"

"Yes, Father."

"Good, then let that be the last I hear of withdrawing
from anything." Lord Fitzcharles drained his glass and

then slammed it upon the table before marching from the room.

Oliver closed his eyes. All he could hear was Sarah's voice, and all he could see was her face. He opened his eyes again, and then tossed his untouched cognac into the fire. The flames roared and leapt for a moment, before dying away again.

Nicholas was relieved when at dawn on the seventeenth day out from Land's End, the *Joyous* dropped anchor in Gibraltar's Rosia Bay. The great rock fortress loomed out of the mist as the frigate swayed on the full tide, and as he stood on the quarterdeck he could see the guns bristling from the battlements that towered out of the water.

A sailor approached him. "Begging your pardon, sir, but the longboat is waiting to take you ashore."

"Thank you." Nicholas felt inside his greatcoat, to be certain the precious despatches were safe, and then he followed the sailor to the rope ladder that had been lowered over the frigate's port side.

The longboat was rowed steadily toward the harbor, where the British flag flew with brave defiance from every vantage point. It was odd to step ashore and have solid ground beneath his feet instead of swaying timbers, but he didn't take long to regain his balance and find someone willing to conduct him to the governor's residence, where he had to deliver a personal message from Sir William Ballenby to the governor himself, General O'Hara.

He was received with great courtesy. General O'Hara was an elderly but bantam-tough soldier from County Sligo, known universally as 'The Cock of the Rock' because of his courage. He was pleased to be given the message from his old friend, Sir William.

"Well, will you return the compliments to him on your return?" he said in his pronounced Irish accent.

"I will," Nicholas replied, nodding as the other picked up a decanter of Irish whisky and looked inquiringly at him. "A measure would be very welcome, early hour or not," he added, smiling.

"A man after my own heart. Tell me, Mr. Stanhope,

what is your business here? I can't imagine that it's simply to deliver impudent messages from my old friends."

"I'm on my way to Naples, to deliver despatches to the British ambassador there."

General O'Hara's face changed. "Well, by all that's holy! What a happy coincidence!"

"Coincidence?"

"The ambassador is here in Gibraltar at this very moment. His wife's uncle is here and the ambassador came to see him about urgent family matters. You'll be able to hand over your despatches without going a league farther. Come, I'll take you to him, for he's staying in this very house."

Unable to believe his luck, Nicholas drank the whisky and then followed the governor from the room.

Two hours later, with his business accomplished in full, he was at liberty to return to the harbor to seek what passage he could on the first available vessel going back to England. He soon found a berth on the sloop *Hecuba,* which was set to leave on the evening tide. She was much smaller than the *Joyous,* and the return voyage promised to be even less enjoyable than the outward, but the three-masted vessel looked superb to his glad eyes as he transferred his belongings from the frigate, which would now sail on to Naples without him.

The weather was fair as the *Hecuba* slipped her moorings that evening, and soon her sails filled as she caught the favorable winds that would carry her swiftly to Portsmouth.

19

NICHOLAS had yet to arrive back in England when Sarah's next ordeal began. November had surrendered to December, and the beauty of the autumn had been lost in the ice cold frosts of winter, and in the middle of a particularly cold night, when the sky was bright with stars, an urgent message arrived for Julia from her husband in London.

Everyone at Thurlong Lodge was aroused by the loud hammering at the door, and at first it was thought that something must have happened to Lady Thurlong, but that was not the case. The hastily written note requested Julia to break the news to Sarah that her father had been taken gravely ill at his club with a seizure of the heart, and was now at Thurlong House. Sarah's presence was required as swiftly as possible, as his life was despaired of.

The house was immediately thrown into confusion, as the two traveling carriages were ordered for the journey to London, and Julia and Sarah's maids were instructed to pack as quickly as possible. They set off well before dawn. It was so cold that the horses' hooves rang upon the iron-hard road.

Frost glinted on the fields and hedgerows as the carriages toiled up the long incline toward the Cotswold Hills. Sarah shivered as she gazed out of the misty window, but the cold she felt was as much due to anxiety as to the temperature. Please let her father not be so ill as it was feared. Her hands twisted nervously together in her fur muff, and she huddled deeper into her blue merino cloak. Never had London seemed farther away than it did now.

They changed teams at the Frogmill. The yard was almost quiet, with only one other coach waiting to de-

part. Her glance crept briefly to the shadowy outline of
the archway, and then she looked away again. She didn't
want to remember her first fateful meeting with Nicholas;
she didn't want to remember him at all.

With a fresh team in harness the carriages set off again.
The roads were clear and the moon still up. They would
make good speed and reach the capital by the next
afternoon.

As Sarah and Julia drove with all haste through the
night, the Earl and the Countess of Hayden's Cheltenham house was in darkness. Packed trunks and valises
waited in the entrance hall because the family's stay in
Cheltenham was at an end, and they, too, were going to
London.

Georgette was asleep, her golden hair catching on the
rich lace trimming of her pillows. Her bedroom was
warm and firelit, and she didn't stir as Tilly crept quietly
in with a candle.

"M'lady?" the maid whispered, hesitating before putting a timid hand on her mistress's arm to arouse her.

Georgette's eyes fluttered and then opened. For a moment she was still sleepy, but then she sat up irritably.
"What on earth is it?" she snapped.

Tilly drew warily back, for Lady Georgette Belvoir's
anger was a fearsome thing, as her unfortunate predecessor had discovered to her cost. "I . . . I have word of
Miss Howard, m'lady."

Georgette's lilac eyes sharpened. "What word?"

"Andrew has just come from Thurlong Lodge, m'lady.
It seems Miss Howard's father is dangerously ill, and she
has left for London. You . . . you said you wanted to be
told anything as soon as I heard it."

"Yes, fool, but I didn't expect to be woken in the
middle of the night!" Georgette cried furiously, reaching
over to seize a book from the table by the bed to hurl
at the unfortunate maid.

With a cry of dismay Tilly scuttled from the room,
shielding the candle flame with her hand. In the passage
outside she was just in time to see Andrew slipping
stealthily out of Georgette's adjoining dressing room.

The maid gasped and glanced around nervously, but
the house remained silent. She caught his arm urgently.

"Are you mad?" she breathed. "You shouldn't be up here at all, but should have stayed down in the kitchens."

"No one even knows I'm still in the house."

"Why did you go into the dressing room?" she demanded, keeping her voice very low.

He grinned, and held out his hand. The shivering light from the candle flashed upon the diamonds in Georgette's favorite earrings.

Tilly was horrified. "No! You must put them back!" she whispered, trying to take them from him.

His hand closed firmly over the jewels, and he shook his head. "Not likely, Tilly. She's got more earrings than she knows what to do with, and won't miss these."

"But she will! They're her favorites!"

"She'll think they were lost in the packing, or somewhere between here and London. Besides, they're of more value to us than to her, because they'll fetch a pretty penny for our future together," he said slyly, aware that he was more important to her than anything else.

Tilly's lips parted, and her eyes shone with happiness in the wavering light. "Our future?" she breathed.

He bent his head to kiss her on the lips. "Don't you ever doubt it, sweetheart," he murmured, pocketing the earrings.

Tilly didn't protest any more as he pulled her close, but as his embrace became more urgent, she drew warily back. "We can't—"

"Come on, Tilly. You're off to London in the morning, and I don't know when her ladyship will choose to send for me. Let's just have one more before you go." His voice was silky and persuasive.

She weakened. "All right, but not here," she whispered, taking his hand and leading him along the sumptuously decorated passageway toward the back stairs, which led down to the deserted kitchens.

Unaware of what had transpired just outside her room, Georgette lay in her vast four-poster bed, staring up at the dove gray brocade hangings and reflecting upon how exquisitely well her stratagem against Sarah and Nicholas had been working. Andrew had kept close watch upon everything at Thurlong Lodge, and had told Tilly, so that

Sarah's heartbreak over Nicholas's apparent indifference had reached her enemy's delighted ears.

It was all going well, and Georgette knew she could rest content, and that in the hope of a post at Hayden House, Julia's perfidious footman would continue to do her work for her. Any further letter Nicholas might write would meet the same fate as its predecessors. When everything had been satisfactorily accomplished, Andrew would be granted the position he desired. Crafty, willing creatures such as he were always useful when something underhanded or devious was required.

Thinking about London brought something else to Georgette's mind, and she sat up suddenly to open the drawer of the table beside the bed. She took out a note that had been secretly delivered to her several days before. It was from Sir Mason Thackeray and expressed a hot desire to resume their brief relationship. She had been astonished to receive it, for she hadn't expected to hear from Mason again after he'd realized she'd only used him in an attempt to make Nicholas jealous. The note's tone was flattering in the extreme, conveying the intense passion she'd aroused, and she smiled as she read it again by the light from the fire. Mason wanted to see her as soon as she arrived in London. She would oblige him, for what ever else he might be, he was an exciting lover, and he would be compensation for her humiliating failure with Nicholas. He would also be a welcome distraction from Oliver, whom she loathed more each time they met. Her father had advised her that Oliver's spinelessness might be advantageous for a woman as strong and determined as she, and maybe that would indeed be the case, but such weak-willed subservience to Lord Fitzcharles's every whim could only earn her increasing contempt.

She put the note back in the drawer, and then snuggled down in the bed again. It would be good to amuse herself with Mason. She'd have to be careful, of course, for his name was anathema to her father because of his feud with Lord Fitzcharles over that wretched racehorse, but the risk would make such an affair all the more exciting. Besides, Lord Fitzcharles had won, and that surely made a difference.

An affair with Mason wouldn't be the same as one

with Nicholas, of course, but that couldn't be helped. Nicholas. Her pleasure faded for a moment. She'd never forgive him for remaining indifferent to her, and even though she would soon take Mason as her lover, she wouldn't relent in her campaign of revenge. She wouldn't be satisfied until she knew beyond all doubt that her deliberate and systemmatic destruction of Nicholas Stanhope's affair with Sarah Howard had succeeded completely.

20

THE light of the short winter afternoon was beginning to fade, and the weather had changed dramatically when the two carriages from Cheltenham arrived in London after traveling all day. A bitterly cold wind blew as they drove along Piccadilly, past inns, private houses, coach ticket offices, and all manner of fashionable shops with glistening panes and bow windows. London's noise and bustle was all around, with the ringing of church bells and the clatter of hooves and wheels.

The wind blustered strongly, tugging at ladies' skirts and obliging the gentlemen to hold on tightly to their tall hats, and the smell of coal smoke was in the air from the capital's thousands of chimneys. There were street calls and a barrel organ playing on a corner, and a disturbance outside the Gloucester Coffee House, an inn and stagecoach ticket office, as a pickpocket was chased by scarlet-waistcoated Bow Street Runners.

Not long before the carriages turned south at the corner of St. James's Street, they passed a particularly large mansion on the left, facing over Green Park. It stood behind a high brick wall and wrought iron gates, a gloomy place made more so because every curtain was tightly drawn, and black funeral hatchments were fixed to the doors, signifying a death. A wagon from a fabric warehouse stood in the courtyard, and men with black ribbons tied to their arms carried numerous bolts of black cloth into the house to drape the rooms.

Sarah caught a glimpse of the hatchments, with their armorial bearings set in lozenge-shaped frames. The deceased was evidently a person of noble birth, and certainly a person of wealth and influence.

Julia looked out as well. "That's Cranham House," she said. "It belongs to the Lord Cranham to whom Lord

Fitzcharles and the Earl of Hayden may have been referring at the Royal Well ball."

"It would seem likely that his lordship is no longer
with us," Sarah murmured, suppressing a shiver. *Please
let this not be an omen . . .*

Julia understood. "I'm sure all will be well with your
father, Sarah. Lord Cranham was a great deal older than
he, and he certainly won't be missed, for he was very
disagreeable indeed. There were few who liked him, and
I believe he was even estranged from his only son, although I don't know much about it."

The carriages drove down St. James's Street and then
along Pall Mall, passing the Prince of Wales's sumptuous
residence, Carlton House, with its magnificent gardens
overlooking St. James's Park from the north. Lady
Thurlong's house in Queen Square, Westminster, faced
the park from the south.

Queen Square was named after Queen Anne, and
dated from the time of her reign. The houses surrounded
a plain cobbled courtyard in the center, and those that
backed on to the park boasted fine raised gardens and
elegant rear facades intended to be admired by those
strolling or riding in the fashionable Mall. Access to the
park from the square was gained down a wide flight of
stone steps that gave on to the royal carriageway of Birdcage Walk, and thence to a gate in the fence enclosing
the park itself.

Thurlong House, the largest property, with three floors
and an attic story with nine small dormer windows, was
built of brown brick with stone facings, and the canopied
front door was approached up three rounded steps. The
sound of the carriages echoed around the square as they
at last came to a standstill at journey's end.

Sarah alighted swiftly, not waiting for the coachman
to climb down from his perch, or even for any servants
to emerge from the house. But as she hurried up the
steps to the door, it was opened by Lady Thurlong's butler, a tall man with a rather grand manner, who bowed
politely as she hastened into the white-painted paneled
hallway.

Julia's husband was just coming down the staircase at
the far end, and he came quickly toward her to take her
hands. Thomas Thurlong was of medium height with fair

hair and gray-green eyes. He wasn't handsome, but possessed an engaging charm, and even though he was a brilliant politician who would obviously go far, he was nevertheless genuinely warm and kind. He wore the almost obligatory black coat, white breeches, and powdered wig expected of those with Whitehall connections.

His hands closed solicitously over hers. "It's all right, Sarah, for I have good news. Your father has shown definite signs of improvement since I sent word to you."

Relief surged through her. "Are you sure?"

"Quite sure. His physicians have confirmed it. He isn't yet entirely out of danger, but there is reason to be encouraged."

Tears filled her eyes, and she clung gratefully to his hands. "I . . . I've been so anxious. . . ."

"I can imagine." His glance moved past her to Julia, and he smiled, his eyes softening with love. "It's good to see you again at last, my darling."

Sarah quickly stood aside so that he could go to his wife, and she smiled through her tears as she watched, for theirs was a love match of the highest order. If only their marriage could be blessed with the children they yearned for so much.

Julia savored his embrace for a moment or so, but then drew back. "Sarah has many questions to ask, Thomas," she said gently.

"Yes, of course." He waited until the two women had been divested of their outdoor garments, and then nodded toward the tall door into the drawing room. "Shall we?" he said, ushering them both inside, just as the first of the luggage was brought in from the carriages.

The drawing room was a large chamber, paneled like the hall and the rest of the house. There was an immense chimney piece carved with shelves and pillars, and numerous portraits adorned the walls. The furniture was upholstered with tapestry, and there were a number of fine tables.

Thomas conducted the two women to a sofa near the fire, where it was warm after their journey, and then he stood with his back to the flames, waiting for any questions Sarah might wish to ask.

She wasted no time. "Do you know what happened?

I mean, he was taken ill at his club, but I don't know whether he had been ill for a few days, or—"

"He hadn't been ill, exactly, but he had certainly been in very low spirits for some time."

She was surprised. "But how can that be? His letters to me were always so cheerful."

Thomas shifted uncomfortably, catching his wife's eyes for a moment and then looking at Sarah. "Cheerful was the last thing he was, Sarah, for I have learned that he has been under a considerable strain since before he went briefly to Chalstones to see you both."

Sarah glanced away for a moment, remembering that moment at Chalstones when she'd felt her father's mask had slipped. Maybe she hadn't been mistaken after all.

Thomas continued. "Sarah, it seems that things have been going on here, things I only learned myself over the last day or so. I fear that being so immersed in government business has kept me aloof from gossip."

"Gossip?"

"Your father has apparently been losing very heavily indeed at the gaming tables at his club."

Her breath caught. "But he seldom gambles!"

"I know, but on this occasion he has been doing so to a very great degree. At least, that is what I've been told by those who were present night after night when he insisted upon resuming his place at the table. Sarah, I'm afraid that after an initial win that led him into temptation, your father fell victim to the old mistake of being certain his subsequent run of bad luck would suddenly change. It didn't, and he continued to lose. I don't know exactly what he has lost, but I do know that he has been obliged to sell your house in Brook Street."

Sarah was shaken. "But he told me he was selling the house because of an observatory that had been built on a property at the rear!"

"Go there and see for yourself, Sarah. There is no observatory," Thomas said quietly.

Slowly she rose to her feet. "I . . . I find this difficult to take in," she said at last.

"As I did when I first heard," he said gently, "but this afternoon he admitted to me himself that he'd lost very heavily indeed. If it hadn't been for the letter he received this morning from Lord Cranham, I fear he would not have begun to recover."

Sarah's eyes flew to meet his. "Lord Cranham? What has he to do with it?"

"He was the man your father was playing, and to whom he lost."

Sarah turned to Julia, whose lips had parted with shock.

Thomas drew a long breath. "The letter must have been the last Cranham ever wrote, for he passed away at noon today after tripping over a loose carpet rod on the staircase at Cranham House. A somewhat unnecessary end, I think."

Sarah's mind was reeling. The conversation at the ball returned to her again, and suddenly it all seemed so clear. Had she after all been the "millstone" to whom Lord Fitzcharles had referred? And was Chalstones the property he wanted to acquire? Chalstones. She closed her eyes for a moment, not wanting to contemplate the possibility now facing her. Had her father lost Chalstones itself to Lord Cranham?

Julia got up from the sofa. "Thomas, do you know what the letter said?"

"No. All I know is that it was the source of immeasurable relief to Sarah's father, and from the moment he read it he began to show signs of rallying. His physicians examined him this afternoon and said that he was definitely better than he had been yesterday. I can only imagine that Lord Cranham had agreed to some sort of settlement. His sudden death may delay any action, for his son Nicholas has now inherited, and he is away in Naples on government business."

Sarah had to steady herself by holding on to the back of a chair. "Nicholas? Nicholas Stanhope?" she asked faintly.

"Yes. Do you know him?"

She nodded. "Oh, yes, I know him," she murmured.

Thomas was curious about her reaction, but as he was about to question her, Julia shook her head warningly. He remained silent.

Sarah collected her scattered wits. "I, er, I think I would like to go to my father now."

"Yes, of course. My aunt is sitting with him." Thomas went with her to the door, and then beckoned to a footman waiting outside. "Please conduct Miss Howard to her father," he said.

"Sir." The footman bowed and led her toward the staircase.

Thomas went back into the drawing room and looked inquiringly at his wife. "Is there something I should know?"

Julia nodded and sighed. "Oh, yes, Thomas, there is indeed." She told him all about Sarah's unhappy experience at Nicholas Stanhope's uncaring hands.

Sarah herself was still numb with shock about all she had heard, and she was hardly conscious of the route she took as she followed the footman up through the house to the bedroom where her father lay asleep in an immense, heavily carved four-poster bed richly canopied with gold-fringed crimson velvet.

The room was warm and candlelit, for the curtains had been drawn to keep out the cold winter air. Lady Thurlong was seated at the bedside, an open volume of poems on her lap, but she set the book aside the moment Sarah was shown in.

Thomas Thurlong's widowed aunt was not at all what one would have expected of one of London's most fearsome political hostesses, for the scourge of the Whigs was a diminutive lady of deceptively fragile appearance. Her face was dainty and her eyes very dark, and her hair was white with powder. She wore a bluebell taffeta gown, and there was a warm, white woolen shawl around her shoulders. She smiled hesitantly.

"Miss Howard, I presume?"

"Lady Thurlong?" Sarah gave a respectful curtsy.

"There is no need for that, my dear. My, my, how very like your mother you are."

"You knew her?"

Lady Thurlong smiled again. "Knew her? I fear I was her most determined rival for your father's affections. I lost the battle, but I have never stopped being very fond indeed of him." Her dark eyes went warmly to the bed, where Mr. Howard still slept, unaware of his daughter's arrival.

Sarah smiled as well. "I know that you and he were once close, Lady Thurlong, for he mentioned it only a short while ago."

"It is because we go back such a long way that I would

not countenance his remaining at his club. I insisted that Thomas bring him straight here."

"It's very kind of you, Lady Thurlong."

"Kindness has nothing to do with it, my dear. When one reaches my age, one's oldest and dearest friends are too precious to desert."

Again Lady Thurlong's eyes moved to the sleeping man, and it was clear that she felt more than just affection for him. If Sarah had had to guess, she would have said that Thomas's aunt had never stopped loving her former sweetheart. "It is still very good of you to look after him like this, Lady Thurlong," she said.

"You and he will be welcome beneath my roof for as long as is necessary, my dear. I know that you no longer have a house here in London, and it is out of the question that he should return to his club, or that you should seek lodgings or some other accommodation. Please regard Thurlong House as your home."

"Thank you."

"Not at all."

Mr. Howard began to stir.

Lady Thurlong touched Sarah's arm gently. "I will leave you now, my dear." She left in a rustle of taffeta, closing the door gently behind her.

Mr. Howard's eyes flickered and opened. For a moment he seemed confused as he looked up at the bed's ornate canopy, but then he remembered.

Sarah moved closer, leaning to put her hand over his. "Father?"

His watery eyes turned toward her. "Sarah, my dear . . ."

She bent to kiss him on the forehead, and then sat on the edge of the bed, still holding his hand.

"They shouldn't have sent for you, for I'm quite all right," he said.

"You aren't all right at all, and my place is with you."

He looked away for a moment. "You may not think that once you know how much I've failed you. I've been very foolhardy, my dear, and I came very close to losing everything. As it is, I've still lost a great deal, but I've saved what really matters."

"Chalstones?"

He met her eyes again. "You know?"

"I know that you've been losing at the gaming tables, and I've put two and two together."

His eyes filled with sudden tears. "Forgive me, my dear, for I don't know what demon drove me. Gambling has never been one of my vices, but on this occasion . . ." His voice broke for a moment, and he struggled to regain his composure. "I seldom take my place at those tables, and yet this time I decided to play a hand or two. I won, handsomely, and like a fool played on. I didn't win again, but I lost, oh, how I lost."

"To Lord Cranham."

He nodded. "Which is still more evidence of my foolishness, for he is—was—a very hard man. I feared he would stand firm about Chalstones, but in the end he was persuaded to consider my properties in the Indies. He had property there himself and was interested in extending his holdings. I heard early this morning that he was prepared to exchange Chalstones for my Caribbean estates." He paused for a moment. "By midday, of course, he was dead," he added in a murmur.

Sarah squeezed his hand. "When you are better, we will return to Chalstones."

"Yes, but our circumstances will be severely reduced, my dear. I have some money left, enough to live in comfort, but not in luxury." Fresh tears filled his eyes. "Can you ever forgive me, my dear?"

She was close to tears herself. "I love you, Father, so of course I forgive you," she whispered, bending to kiss his forehead again.

"I have let you down."

"No, of course you haven't."

"It was because of my foolishness that Lord Fitzcharles saw to the ending of your betrothal."

"Yes, I know."

"Do you promise me that you no longer love Oliver Fitzcharles? I couldn't bear it if I thought you did."

"I feel nothing for Oliver."

He searched her eyes, and was satisfied she told the truth. "I do not deserve you, my dear."

She continued to hold his hand, and after a few minutes he drifted into sleep again. She sat on the bed for a little longer, and then left the room.

21

LORD Cranham's sudden death had placed a heavy burden upon Stephen Mannering, who had immediately been called to Cranham House to act in his capacity as Nicholas's representative. He wasn't related by blood to the late lord, being Nicholas's maternal cousin, and thus was very conscious indeed of perhaps appearing to interfere in Stanhope family affairs, for there were other cousins, uncles, and so on, but as he had been nominated by the new Lord Cranham, he was obliged to carry out his duties.

There had been a great deal to do, and at the end of the day he returned wearily to his lodgings in Conduit Street, his head aching from all the papers he'd had to go through and decisions he'd had to make.

Entering his rooms, Stephen went straight to the window to raise it and allow the cold night air in. It was still very windy outside, and the curtains billowed as the draft swept into the room. A newspaper on the table rustled and flapped, and the flames drew in the hearth. Taking a deep breath, he turned to pour himself a glass of whisky, and then he sat by the fire, his legs stretched out before him. He wore a suitably somber black coat and dark gray breeches, and beneath the coat a black weeper was tied around the upper arm of his shirt.

Swirling the golden liquid, he contemplated his position. Nicholas was expected to be away for months, and that meant much responsibility for his reluctant cousin. When Nicholas had been absent on previous occasions, nothing in particular had ever arisen. This time it was very different. Stephen sipped the whisky and then grimaced as the fiery spirit stung his throat. He loathed responsibility, and with hindsight wished that he'd declined when Nicholas had approached him. But it was too late now, and he was obligated to see to it all.

· With a sigh he leaned his head back. "Plague take you, Coz. Please don't languish for too long in the sunny Mediterranean, there's a good fellow," he murmured.

As Stephen reflected upon his unwanted duties, Georgette and her parents were just arriving at Hayden House, their elegant balconied residence in windswept Park Lane. The earl did not usually elect to travel through the hours of darkness, but on this occasion he wished to be in London in time for the annual general meeting of his club. He had a number of complaints to raise, and intended to be very vocal indeed about his disapproval of the club's running in recent months.

Hayden House was bright with lights because Georgette's brother, Geoffrey, was in town for the time being, having left his wife and family on the earl's Scottish estates. It did not take much for Geoffrey to leave his wife, for he found her tiresome, and had a taste for actresses, preferably buxom and saucy. He had installed one such obliging minx in a villa on Primrose Hill, and was about to depart to sample her charms when his family returned.

The future Earl of Hayden was a pale image of his beautiful youngest sister, with the same golden hair and lilac eyes, but there the similarity ended, for where Georgette was gloriously attractive, Geoffrey was plain. It was his rank and wealth that drew favors from actresses, not his person.

In the confusion of the family's return, Geoffrey drew his sister aside into the library, where the wind outside sucked down the chimney and made the fire glow very brightly. He quickly closed the door and turned to face her. "Cranham's dead," he said bluntly.

Georgette's lips parted. "When?"

"At about noon today. I believe he took a tumble down the staircase and broke his unpleasant neck."

"Is Nicholas his successor?"

"Yes, the old boy didn't cut him out, and knowing your, er, interest, I thought I'd tell you straight away."

"My interest in dear Nicholas has changed somewhat."

"Oh? In what way."

"I now despise him."

Geoffrey raised an eyebrow. "A woman scorned, eh?"

"You could say so." Georgette turned away. "Stephen Mannering is acting for him, I believe."

"Eh? Er, yes, I think so. He was called to Cranham House today, anyway, so I imagine Nicholas appointed him."

She faced her brother again. "I want Stephen's promissory notes, Geoffrey."

He drew back slightly. "Why?"

"I just do, that's all."

"Look, Sis, many a thing I'll do for you, but it ain't the thing to hand over a fellow's notes."

"I want them, Geoffrey, and I intend to have them." She smiled coolly. "You wouldn't want your wife to find out about that *belle de nuit* you keep at Primrose Hill, would you?"

His face changed. "You wouldn't do that!"

"Try me."

He inhaled slowly. "Very well, you can have Mannering's notes."

Georgette smiled. "I rather thought you'd come around," she murmured.

"What do you intend to do with them?"

"That's my business."

"Just don't involve me."

"I won't. By the way, how do matters stand concerning old Lord Cranham's acquisition of the property belonging to Mr. Howard?"

"The notorious gambling gains? Why do you want to know."

"You surely remember dear little Sarah Howard, don't you—the creature you had a brief penchant for long ago in Cheltenham?"

"Yes, but—" He broke off, his eyes clearing. "She's Howard's daughter?"

"Yes, and I still hold a grudge."

"When don't you?" he replied dryly. "Well, Sis, if you have a notion to interfere in that particular area, let me advise you as to a strong rumor circulating that Cranham was considering exchanging property he'd won from Howard here in England for some estates in the Indies. Maybe he'd already agreed to such a transaction."

"And maybe he hadn't put pen to paper before he so

obligingly fell down the stairs," she replied. "I hope he hadn't made anything final, but even if he has, with Nicholas abroad, I can make things as difficult and awkward as possible for the Howards."

"Through Stephen Mannering?"

"He can be leaned on."

"He's honorable."

"And afraid of enclosed spaces. The calling in of his IOU's would mean jail, for it is some time yet before he inherits."

Geoffrey gave a disbelieving laugh. "Dear God, I never cease to be amazed at how poisonous you can be. So, you have it in for both Nicholas Stanhope and Sarah Howard, do you?"

Angry color stained her cheeks, and she said nothing. Suddenly she could see the Chelt again and the two lovers standing in a passionate embrace among the golden sycamores.

Geoffrey studied her, and suddenly he guessed the truth. "Good God! Stanhope and Sarah Howard!"

"By the time I've finished, they'll despise the mere sound of each other's names," she whispered. "I will visit Stephen Mannering first thing tomorrow and find out exactly where everything stands. Then I will decide what to do."

"Stanhope isn't a man to trifle with, Sis. If he returns and finds out you've been interfering—"

"He'll be away for months yet." She went to the door, and then paused. "By the way, I take it that Mason is still at Cavendish Square?"

Geoffrey's breath caught. "Thackeray? Are you mad? Sis, just leave well alone, eh? You're betrothed to Fitzcharles now, and you *know* how much loathing there is between Thackeray and your future father-in-law! It was always bad, but ever since Fitzcharles senior succeeded in laying hands upon that damned racehorse—"

Georgette's glance swept briefly over him from the doorway. "I despise my betrothal, Geoffrey, and I shudder at the thought of Oliver Fitzcharles ever laying a hand upon me. I have been forced into accepting this match, but I don't intend to be the obedient daughter in everything. Mason wants to see me again, and I want to enjoy his attentions."

"Thackeray never does anything without good reason, and he won't have forgiven you for encouraging him simply in order to make Stanhope jealous. The world and his wife knew that was what you were up to."

"That is in the past," she answered swiftly. She had thought she'd been discreet in her previous dealings with Mason, but it seemed she hadn't, for everyone in creation appeared to know about it!

"In the past it may be, but I suspect Thackeray's motives."

"Motives such as?"

"I don't know, Sis, but just be careful. If you've any sense at all, you'll forget about Thackeray. If you must take a lover, choose someone less dangerous."

"I want Mason," she replied.

"Don't say I didn't warn you."

The door closed behind her, and within an hour, protected by a trustworthy footman, Tilly had been despatched with a note to Sir Mason Thackeray's elegant residence in Cavendish Square. The December wind was still blowing across the capital, and the maid huddled in her cape, which flapped around her ankles like a thing possessed. It seemed to take an age to reach Sir Mason's residence, where she gained immediate admittance.

She waited in the entrance hall, where a portrait of Georgette's lover gazed down at her from a huge canvas on the half-landing of the double staircase. Sir Mason was handsome in a very refined but almost vulpine way, with chestnut hair and brown eyes. He dressed with extravagant attention to fashion, and was particularly fond of embroidery upon the cuffs and lapels of his coats. In the portrait he wore a golden coat with silver embroidery.

The painting seemed to be intent upon her, and Tilly shivered a little, hoping that the required reply would soon be forthcoming. Her wish was granted, and soon she was on her way back to Park Lane. An assignation was arranged for the following night at Cavendish Square, with Georgette advised to show circumspection by leaving her carriage in the mews lane behind and entering the house through the garden.

As the maid departed, Sir Mason watched from an upstairs window. The satisfied smile on his lips wasn't pleasant to see—no, not in the least pleasant. Georgette would have been alarmed had she seen it, for her brother's warning had been well founded. Sir Mason Thackeray's purpose was to cause trouble, and that was something at which he excelled.

Georgette would also have been alarmed to know that instead of being hundreds of miles away in Naples, Nicholas was at that morning coming ashore from the *Hecuba*. The sloop had dropped anchor at Spithead, which was protected from the full force of the winter wind by the mass of the Isle of Wight to the southwest. Many other vessels lay in the anchorage, and the roar of the wind and waves was all around as the longboat labored its way from the rocking sloop toward the haven of Portsmouth.

His lips tasted of salt, and his hair felt sticky from the voyage. Dear God, it was cold here after the milder temperatures of the south. It didn't take one long to become accustomed to more agreeable climes. He pulled his greatcoat closer and turned the collar up against the gale. The welcome lights of Portsmouth were close through the spray now, and he knew that in a few minutes he would be on English soil again.

The sailors strained to row as swiftly as they could, and at last the longboat slid into the relatively calm waters of the harbor. A moment or so later the bow nudged the wooden wharf steps, and one of the men made the line secure as Nicholas stepped relievedly ashore. One of the sailors carried his luggage up behind him.

A coach rattled past over the wet cobbles, and the church bells in the town sounded midnight. The wind gusted slightly, and he was forced to hold on to his hat or risk having it whisked away into the harbor. What he required was a posting inn, somewhere he could eat, wash, and rest for an hour before hiring a chaise to drive to Cheltenham, and Sarah. He knew that he should go to Whitehall first, to report upon the safe delivery of the despatches, but a day or so more would make no difference, especially as he wasn't expected back for a long time yet.

Glancing around, at last he saw what he wanted. The Red Lion hostelry appeared to be the very thing, and he hastened toward its swaying sign. The landlord was anxious to be as obliging as possible, and promised him a suitable chaise within two hours, by which time he would have eaten a good meal, washed and changed, and had a few minutes in which to lie down. He was given an excellent chamber overlooking the harbor, and was served a robust roast beef dinner that went down very well indeed after the indifferent fare on board the *Hecuba*.

It was with some pleasure that he enjoyed the first good shave he'd had since leaving Gibraltar. The warm water and blade felt good against his skin, and he began to feel restored. In the mirror he could see the reflection of the room behind him, and he paused in his shaving to look at the large tester bed. Sarah would be asleep now, not knowing that he would be with her again soon. How he wished he were lying beside her, with her perfume all around him. He had thought of little else but her in the weeks since he'd left England, and now he meant to be with her as quickly as he possibly could.

The post-chaise was ready as promised, and in the small hours of the morning Nicholas set off for Cheltenham. The chaise was driven with all speed by the two yellow-jacketed postboys who rode postillion and who were sufficiently reckless to warrant the usual nickname of their kind, yellow bounders. Chances were taken, and bridges feather-edged as they kicked each successive team through the night toward the dawn.

As first light appeared in the east, the travel-stained chaise was making its way across the Cotswold Hills, and as the milkmaids went about their business, it began the long descent from the escarpment toward the sleeping spa. The first vendors were calling in the High Street as Nicholas at last arrived at the door of Thurlong Lodge.

It was well before the fashionable hour for breakfast, but he didn't care about the time. All that mattered was Sarah, and he alighted from the chaise to hammer loudly upon the door. At first there was no sound from within, but then Hemmings's grumbling voice could be heard as he hurriedly put on his coat and came from the kitchens, where he and the other servants had been been enjoying their first cup of tea of the day

Then, suspicious of some villainous intent, he called

from the other side of the door. "Who is it? What do you want?"

Nicholas came straight to the point. "This is Mr. Nicholas Stanhope. Will you please inform Miss Howard that I am here?"

The name was not lost upon Hemmings, who immediately opened the door. "Mr. Stanhope? I fear Miss Howard isn't here, nor is Mrs. Thurlong. They've gone to London."

Nicholas was dismayed. "London?"

"I fear so, sir. Miss Howard's father has been taken gravely ill, and she was sent for."

"Where are they in London?"

"At Lady Thurlong's residence, sir."

Nicholas removed his hat and ran his tired fingers through his hair. "Mr. Howard is gravely ill, you say?"

"Yes, sir. A message arrived here the night before last, and they left immediately."

Nicholas nodded. "Thank you, er, Hemmings, is it not?"

"It is, sir."

Nicholas was about to turn away, when something occurred to him. "Hemmings, do you happen to know if Miss Howard received a letter from me that was posted in Padstow?"

Although it was Andrew's duty to accept mail at the door, it was the butler's responsibility to take it to the recipients, and he knew there hadn't been any letters at all for Miss Howard. "There was no such letter, sir."

"Are you quite sure?"

"Absolutely certain, sir."

"Very well. Thank you."

"I'm sorry not to have been of more service, sir."

Hemmings closed the door and Nicholas returned to the waiting chaise. London. He couldn't face the thought of more traveling just yet. He needed a little rest.

The nearest postboy looked inquiringly at him. "Where to now, sir?"

"Cambridge Crescent. I'll direct you," Nicholas replied wearily, climbing back into the vehicle. As he sat back once more, he prayed his grandmother would be pleased to receive him at such an ungodly hour.

22

LONDON was still very blustery and cold as Georgette prepared to make her call upon the unfortunate Stephen Mannering, who would have left town had he known what lay in store for him over the breakfast table.

Georgette was in excellent spirits. Not only was she about to embark upon the next and even more vindictive stage of her campaign against Nicholas and Sarah, but she was also to see Mason that night. As she dressed in the same cerise pelisse and gown she'd worn in Cheltenham when first Sarah and Julia had seen her, she pondered the pleasant problem of what to wear for her tryst. The primrose silk? Or maybe the gold tissue, for that was infinitely more daring and alluring. Yes, that was what she'd wear. With the diamond earrings.

She turned to Tilly. "I've decided upon the silver satin tonight, Tilly, and I want you to make sure my diamond earrings are unpacked from whichever box they are in."

Tilly swallowed, for this was the moment she'd been dreading, when Georgette thought of wearing the stolen jewels. "The diamond earrings, m'lady?"

"Yes." Georgette turned her head from side to side to admire her reflection in the cheval glass.

"Very well, m'lady." The maid felt suddenly sick, and Andrew's promises about the future seemed less persuasive. She wished the earrings were here in London, instead of at Thurlong Lodge, tucked under his mattress.

Georgette was satisfied with her ravishing appearance. "That will do, I fancy. See that the town carriage is brought to the door without delay."

"Yes, m'lady."

Georgette glowered at the maid as she left the room. What was the matter with the girl? She was as nervous as a mouse.

When Tilly returned after telling the butler the carriage was required, Georgette stood for her to bring her gray velvet cloak with the white fur trimmings. The cloak would be required this morning, not only because of the cold, but because it boasted a hood she could raise over her head when stepping from the carriage into Stephen Mannering's lodgings. It was one thing to call at such an exclusively male address at night, when one's identity was more easily concealed, but quite another to do so in broad daylight.

Stephen was already up when she arrived in Conduit Street, although only just. He had overindulged in Scottish dew the previous night and felt a little the worse for wear. He looked bedraggled and seedy as he sat at the table in the drafty room. The window, as always, was slightly open, and the December chill breathed constantly and soothingly over him. He wore a crumpled blue paisley dressing gown over his shirt and breeches, his hair wasn't combed, and he surveyed the coffeepot and warm bread rolls with some distaste. What he fancied was something good and spicy to drive the ill feeling away—a kedgeree, perhaps. But a kedgeree would mean going to his club, and he didn't feel in the mood. God alone knew what mood he was in. Why, oh, why, had he kept drinking that damned whisky last night? If he'd had company, it would have been understandable, but on his own?

He heard the carriage outside, but paid no attention. The lodging house was large, and there were many other tenants besides him. It wasn't until he heard the knock at the door that he looked up, first at the door and then at the clock on the mantelshelf. Who on earth was calling at this hour?

His valet went to answer, and Stephen's heart sank like a stone as he recognized Georgette's voice. The Belvoir *chienne*? What did she want? Surely she didn't imagine Nicholas was here? He rose reluctantly to his feet as she was shown into the room. "Lady Georgette?" he murmured politely, marveling at her continuing willingness to take risks with her reputation.

She suppressed a shiver of cold as she inclined her head in response to the greeting. "Mr. Mannering." She moved judiciously closer to the fire, and then faced him, waiting to be invited to sit down.

He felt like forgetting his manners, but then grudgingly chose to observe them after all. "Please take a seat, Lady Georgette. May I offer you a cup of coffee?"

"Er, no. Thank you." Her lilac eyes flickered with clever anticipation.

"To what do I owe this honor?" he inquired, resuming his seat and pouring some coffee for something to do. God, the woman unnerved him. So lovely, and yet so deadly, like some poisonous butterfly from the tropics.

"Honor? Well, I do not know that that is how you will regard it once you hear, sir."

His heart sank still further, but he gave no sign. "Oh?"

"I will not beat about the bush, sir. My brother, Geoffrey, no longer holds your notes, I do."

He put the coffeepot down with a clatter. "Why?" he asked uneasily.

"Because I require your assistance."

"Concerning what, precisely?" He was now thoroughly on edge and wishing more than ever that his head were completely clear.

"Concerning the estate of the late Lord Cranham."

Ah, so that was it. She was still intent upon anything that concerned Nicholas. "Lady Georgette, I am not at liberty to—"

"Oh, but you are at liberty, sir. For the moment, anyway," Georgette interrupted smoothly, glancing deliberately toward the open window.

The implication was only too clear to Stephen. The woman was threatening him with debtor's jail unless he cooperated! He swallowed. "Lady Georgette, I—"

"Before you come the noble and refuse my request, perhaps you should hear me out," she observed in a reasonable tone.

He sat back. "As you wish."

"Have you inspected any papers at Cranham House yet? I am interested in any papers that might relate to the recent acquisition of Howard property."

Stephen looked curiously at her. "Of what concern is this to you?"

"Just answer me, sir."

"Yes, there are various papers, IOU's and the deeds

to Mr. Howard's Oxfordshire property, Chalstones. And some jottings in Lord Cranham's diary."

Her eyes sharpened. "Is there any reference to a letter from Lord Cranham to Mr. Howard concerning a possible exchange of Chalstones for some properties in the Indies?"

Stephen was unwillingly curious. "There isn't a letter, only a note in the diary about an intention to accept such an exchange."

"No mention of having formalized such an agreement?"

"No, just an intention so to do."

Georgette exhaled slowly and then rose, moving restlessly to the window for a moment. "Are you quite certain?"

Stephen watched her. "I've only had a brief time in which to inspect things, but yes, I think I can be reasonably sure that there hasn't been a formal finalization of the exchange. I can't be categoric, you understand. It is clear, however, that Lord Cranham certainly meant to proceed, and would have done had he not met with his death so suddenly."

"Oh, I think we can say there wasn't any formal written agreement, sir, and that is what matters. I don't give a fig for what his late lordship *may* have intended to do, for that isn't of any consequence now." Georgette glanced back at him. "Mr. Mannering, I require you to destroy the relevant note in the diary."

Stephen was shocked. "I can't do that!"

"No?" Smiling slightly, she closed the window.

The exclusion of fresh air made the room like a tomb to him. All sound was deadened, and everything felt as if it was pressing him down. He endured for less than a minute, before he got up to swiftly raise the window again, and gulp in huge breaths.

Georgette was at her most deadly. "I am told that the Marshalsea prison is not only horridly confining, but also dreadfully damp. It will play havoc with your health, both mental and physical, will it not?" She leaned closer to him, her voice a malevolent whisper. "I will call in your debts right now unless you do as I wish, sir. And do not make the mistake of taking me lightly, for I mean every word."

The serpentine voice filled him with dread. Perspiration shone on his forehead, his face ashen. For a moment he struggled to recover, and then at last was able to face her again. "All you want me to do is destroy the record in the diary?"

"Oh, no, sir, there is more than that. You see, it doesn't suit me that to a certain extent it has got out in society that Lord Cranham had an exchange in mind. Because there are whispers you are almost certain to receive a visit from Mr. Howard's representative, probably his daughter, since Howard himself is apparently ill. When that happens, I want you to state quite categorically that as the *new* Lord Cranham's agent, you cannot possibly be bound by anything the *late* Lord Cranham may have been contemplating."

"I don't understand. If his father intended such an exchange, I am almost certain Nicholas would—"

"You are missing the point, sir. I want you to say that you happen to know Nicholas wishes to keep Chalstones. You are to say that before he left London for Cheltenham, he already knew of his father's winnings at Mr. Howard's expense, and that he told you he wished to eventually reside at Chalstones himself. It is a very beautiful property, you understand, and far more pleasing than Cranham Castle. Furthermore, I want you to say that Nicholas mentioned both Mr. Howard and his daughter, Sarah, by name, saying that he dispensed with any concern over what happened to them. It must appear to her that he had always known who she was, and that he'd callously amused himself with her. She must be made to think him the cruelest lord in creation."

Stephen stared at her. "Are you telling me that there is something between Nicholas and Miss Howard?"

"Yes."

His eyes cleared with understanding. "And you are out for jealous spite because you cannot have my cousin yourself, is that it?"

Her face became as cold as ice. "I despise them both. I mean to make them suffer, and have already embarked upon a stratagem to that end. I have bribed a footman at Thurlong Lodge to see that Nicholas's letters don't reach her, and I have myself destroyed his first note. Sarah Howard therefore already believes herself to have been deserted by her fine new love, but that isn't enough.

I don't just want her to think he has forgotten her; I want her to think true ill of him. She must be made to think he is knowingly and deliberately depriving her of her beloved Chalstones by canceling his father's intention to agree to the exchange.

Stephen looked away in disgust. "You are entirely without principle," he breathed.

"Your opinion is of no interest to me, sir," she replied.

"What do you imagine will happen when Nicholas returns and finds out?"

"He won't be back in England for months yet, and then it will be up to you to cover your tracks."

"Me?"

"Point the finger in my direction, sirrah, and I will deny everything. It is quite simple. All you have to do if he questions you is deny that you ever mentioned anything about him knowing all along who Sarah Howard was, or about him desiring Chalstones for himself. It then becomes a matter of your word against someone else's. You must merely say you acted in good faith, regarding it as your duty to look after the entire Stanhope family estate until such time as he returned. He will not be able to find fault with that, I promise you. He appointed you to act for him in the protection of his interests, and that is precisely what you will appear to have done." Georgette was the soul of reason. "Come now, sir, be sensible about this. By the time Nicholas returns, the detestable Howard and her father, should he survive his present illness, will be long gone from London, and living as best they can in their reduced circumstances."

A nerve twitched at Stephen's temple, and he felt quite sick. "I won't do it," he said at last.

"Then the Marshalsea awaits," she replied, turning to walk toward the door.

He was drenched in terror. "No, wait!"

"Sir?" She turned by the door.

"I have no choice. I will oblige you."

"Good, and when all is accomplished, I will return your notes."

"When will I be required to do it?"

"At any time. The Howards are in town, staying at Thurlong House. Just remember the story I've invented, and as soon as you go next to Cranham House, make absolutely certain that there is nothing untoward in any of the papers there."

He nodded, despising himself. "Very well."

As she left, he glanced out the window toward the south. Last night he had urged Nicholas to return with all speed; now he prayed he would remain there indefinitely—perhaps forever.

Unaware of what was being perpetrated in his name, Nicholas was at that moment seated comfortably in the conservatory at Cambridge Crescent. The wind gusted against the glass, and the trees in the garden swayed, but it was warm inside because the stoves had been lit. Nicholas had reluctantly given in to Lady Worthington's determination that he should have a good breakfast and then rest properly for several hours before setting off on the open road again.

His grandmother was thoughtful. Elegant in a brown silk gown and ribboned day-bonnet, she surveyed him as he finished a hearty meal of eggs, bacon, sausages, fried bread, tomatoes, and toast, washed down with some of her excellent Turkish coffee. Then she spoke. "I am sure you will be better equipped for a resumption of your journey once you have eaten and rested properly."

He folded his napkin and laid it on the white-painted wrought iron table. "You're right, of course."

"I'm also sure that Miss Howard will not disappear if you delay for a while."

"I know." He glanced at the weather outside.

She watched him. "What is on your mind? Is there something you have neglected to mention to me?"

He smiled. "Is there anything you fail to observe?"

"Precious little. Well?"

"I am concerned that Sarah may not have received either of my letters. In short, I fear she may think I have chosen to end things between us."

"Why? Because your letter from Padstow did not arrive? Surely you sent word to her before then, prior to leaving Cheltenham?"

"That's the rub."

"You mean, you didn't notify her?" Lady Worthington was appalled. "Oh, Nicholas, how could you have been so remiss!"

"I did write to her, but I'm afraid I entrusted delivery of the letter to Lady Georgette Belvoir." He briefly explained the circumstances, and Georgette's apparent penitence.

Lady Worthington was dismayed. "You actually believed that vixen? Nicholas, there are times when I despair of you. She was besotted with you, and nothing on this earth would have moved her to actually deliver such a letter to your new love. I think you may be certain that your note did not reach its destination, and that your unfortunate Miss Howard spent a very unhappy evening waiting for a call you failed to make."

Nicholas got up restlessly. "That's what I fear, too. I regretted giving Georgette the note almost as soon as I'd done it, and so I was careful to write again at the first opportunity, but when the butler at Thurlong Lodge told me the second letter had failed to arrive either . . ."

"I suspect Belvoir fingers at work again. That creature would stoop to anything. However, from what you tell me of your Miss Howard, she is as in love with you as you are with her. She will not lightly spurn you, and I think that the moment you are with her in London, all will soon be well again."

"I sincerely hope so. Grandmother, I wish to marry her."

"I had already guessed as much." She smiled, but then became more serious. "Nicholas, there is something I have to tell you."

"Oh?"

"Your father is dead. Stephen sent a messenger to me yesterday afternoon. It seems there was an accident, a fall down the staircase at Cranham House. It was mercifully brief."

Nicholas stood. "Which was not how it was for my mother. She suffered for years at his callous hands."

Lady Worthington lowered her eyes sadly.

"I would be a liar if I pretended to be sorry in any way grief-stricken that he's gone."

"Will you wear any black?"

"No."

"It is entirely up to you, of course, but I do not blame you. He was a very cruel man."

"Cruel Lord Cranham." Nicholas gave a short laugh. "I must be sure never to earn the same sobriquet."

His grandmother smiled. "That would be impossible, for you are a gentleman to your fingertips, a man of honor and integrity, and I am more proud of you than you will ever know."

He bent to kiss her on the cheek. "And I am more proud of you than you will ever know," he said softly.

She patted his hand. "Go to bed for a while now, and be rested in readiness for going to London."

As he walked from the conservatory, she spoke again. "Will you live in Cranham House?"

"I would as soon reside in Purgatory."

"What of the castle?"

"I intend to sell both and purchase anew. I loathed every moment ever spent in my father's houses, and I will never take Sarah to either of them. The homes I share with her will be *our* homes, with no bitter memories to spoil them."

23

IN her sleep Sarah was lying in Nicholas's arms, their naked bodies warm and close. His breath was soft upon her cheek, and she was encircled by his loving embrace. His eyes were dark with desire, and when he whispered her name she knew he loved her. He caressed her breasts, and intoxicating new feelings tingled through her as she raised her lips to meet his.

Their kiss was slow and luxurious, the prelude to yearned-for consummation. She was his, utterly and completely, and did not merely submit, but met him with a rich desire that ached unendingly through her. This was ecstasy, and she was weightless, carried away on waves of heady fulfillment. They were one, and the pleasure was so intense that she cried out. There were tears on her cheeks, and her skin was warm and damp, still quivering with exquisite contentment. She wanted to lie there forever, to be one with him forever, to be loved by him forever . . .

He whispered tenderly. "I love you, Sarah, I love you heart and soul."

"As I love you," she whispered back, reaching up to touch his hair with her fingertips.

Suddenly the dream was shattered by the firing of a cannon salute at nearby Horse Guards. With a startled gasp she awoke, sitting up in bed with her dark blond curls tumbling in confusion about the shoulders of her lace-trimmed nightgown. The dream fled, and she was alone.

The wind moaned dismally around the eaves, and through a chink in the green brocade curtains she could see that it was about midmorning. She hadn't meant to sleep this late! Her thoughts turned anxiously to her father. How was he? Flinging the bedclothes aside, she got up and pulled on her frilled pink muslin wrap before hurrying from the room. The dream that a moment before had engulfed her completely, was now but a sensuous echo on the edge of memory, fading further into infinity with each heartbeat as she hurried to her father.

The wind outside was so strong that a draft seemed to creep through the whole house, and as she entered her father's bedroom, the fire glowed fiercely for a moment until she'd closed the door again. Lady Thurlong was already seated by the bedside. She wore a dainty maroon-and-white striped gown with long sleeves gathered at the wrists, and her powdered hair was pinned up beneath a neat morning-cap. Sarah was struck anew by how little her appearance went with her reputation in political circles. It was almost impossible to believe that she was such a fierce High Tory that even Mr. Pitt himself listened to what she had to say.

Sarah's father was propped up on his mound of pillows. His face was still sallow and drawn, but by the light from the window she could see that he had a little more color this morning. His recovery was evidently still continuing. She smiled and went to him. "Good morning, Father."

"Good morning, my dear."

She turned to Lady Thurlong. "Good morning, my lady."

"Good morning." The older woman got up. "Did you sleep well?"

"Too well. I didn't mean to be as late as this."

"The rest will have done you good, my dear, and I am here to sit with your father." Lady Thurlong smiled fondly at him.

He returned the smile. "You are far too good to me, Euphemia."

"Don't call me that, for goodness' sake. I much prefer Phemie, as you well know," she chided.

Sarah sat on the edge of the bed, and took her father's hand. "You are looking a little better," she said.

"I feel better, my dear. There is no doubt that I turned a vital corner when I received Cranham's letter. Now that I know I haven't lost Chalstones, I feel able to apply myself to the business of recovery. Until then, I was so disheartened and wretched that there was no hope of my ever improving."

Lady Thurlong pursed her lips. "Well, at least the late Lord Cranham performed one charitable act in his otherwise detestable existence," she murmured. "Still, enough of him, for I do not wish to give your poor daughter indigestion before she has a chance to enjoy her breakfast."

Sarah smiled hesitantly. "I thought perhaps I was too late for breakfast."

"Not at all; Julia and Thomas have only just gone down. Which reminds me. When they looked in here a few minutes ago, I mentioned that Thomas and I have been invited to a grand dinner at the Mansion House tomorrow evening. It is a simple matter for me to acquire two further invitations for you and Julia, and I would very much like you to come as well. Would you care to join us, my dear?"

"A grand dinner?" Sarah was slightly daunted.

"Well, that is the title under which it rejoices, but I can promise you an excellent feast, and an agreeable amount of pomp and ceremony. I think you will enjoy it."

"Then of course I will come. Thank you for asking me, Lady Thurlong."

"Not at all, my dear. Now, you go on down for breakfast, and I shall sit here. You can take my place when you've eaten, if you wish."

"I will do that." Sarah bent to kiss her father again, and then went to the door, where she paused for a moment. "Would it be possible for me to see the letter from Lord Cranham?"

Her father nodded, and Lady Thurlong smiled. "Yes, of course, my dear. I put it on the writing desk in the library, which is the room immediately to your left at the foot of the staircase. There are many papers there, I fear, but you will recognize it, for the late Lord Cranham was given to using yellow sealing wax. A regrettable habit, in my opinion, but at least his correspondence is easy to find."

Sarah retraced her steps to her bedroom, where Annie was now waiting to attend her, and shortly afterward she emerged again to go down to breakfast. She wore a sky blue merino morning gown embroidered with white daisies, and her hair was tied back informally with a wide white satin ribbon. With a warm, dark blue shawl drawn closely around her shoulders, she went down the staircase, for the house was very drafty indeed in such inclement weather.

The library door was closed, and as she opened it there came a rush of cold air that made her breath catch. One of the housemaids had been assigned to the malodorous task of cleaning the windows with raw onions, and to keep the smell to a minimum she had closed the door and opened the window slightly. Sarah's entry into the room caused a tremendous draft as the wind outside swept eagerly through the room. All the papers on the writing desk fluttered in confusion until Sarah quickly closed the door behind her.

The maid gave a gasp. "Oh, I'm sorry, madam," she said tearfully, for the onions had long since begun to make her cry.

"It was my fault entirely," Sarah said quickly, bending to pick up some of the papers from the carpet.

"The smell is so dreadful, but onions do make the glass shine," the maid explained, hastily closing the window.

Sarah was about to reply when a sudden brightening of the flames in the fireplace made her look quickly toward it. She stared in dismay as she saw the remnants of a document with a yellow seal curling up into ashes. "Oh, no!" she cried, and knelt to take the poker to save what she could. But it was too late; all that was left was a fragment of rapidly melting yellow sealing wax.

The poker fell from her horrified fingers. Lord Cranham's letter! She was so numb with shock at the swiftness with which it had happened, that she could only kneel there, staring at the flames as they died down once more.

The maid looked curiously at her. "Are you all right, madam?" she asked.

Slowly Sarah got to her feet again, still gazing wretchedly at the fire. The letter had gone, destroyed in the blinking of an eye. She looked accusingly toward the heedless wind outside, and then gathered her skirts to hurry out once more. She had to tell Julia and Thomas without delay!

They were still at the breakfast table as she burst into the room, and Thomas lowered his knife and fork with concern as he saw how distraught she was. "Sarah? What is it? Is your father—?"

"It's the letter from Lord Cranham. It's been burned." Fighting back the tears, she told them what had happened in those few fateful seconds.

Julia hurried to put her arms around her. "Are you quite certain it was the letter from Lord Cranham?" she asked gently.

"Lady Thurlong said he always used yellow sealing wax. I saw sealing wax like that melting in the flames."

"We'll go and make certain," Julia said, ushering her from the room.

Followed by Thomas, they returned to the library, where the window was still closed and the maid was endeavoring to gather all the papers that had blown from the desk. She hurried out as they came in, and they began to swiftly go through everything on the desk, but there was no sign of a letter sealed with yellow wax.

Sarah cast around desperately, praying that it was still lying somewhere on the floor, but there was nothing. Of all the documents on Lady Thurlong's desk, the only one that had blown into the fire had been the precious letter from Lord Cranham.

A sob caught in her throat. "What am I going to do? My father is relying upon that letter, and now that Lord Cranham is dead—"

Julia put a reassuring hand on her sleeve. "We'll think of something," she said, looking pleadingly at Thomas.

He drew a long breath. "All I can think of is approaching Stephen Mannering, who usually acts for Nicholas Stanhope. There is bound to be some record in Lord Cranham's effects."

Sarah wiped her tears, trying to regain her composure. "Can I come with you when you see him?"

"Yes, of course. I cannot go this morning because Mr. Pitt expects me shortly, but we can go this afternoon. I'm reasonably well acquainted with Mannering, and I know where he lodges. Please don't worry, Sarah, for I'm sure we can sort this out."

"I . . . I can't tell my father."

"There isn't any need to. As soon as we have confirmation from Mannering, all will be well again."

*   *   *

It was almost two o'clock that afternoon before Thomas returned from Whitehall, and he and Sarah were able to set off in his town carriage for Stephen's address in Conduit Street. They drove up St. James's Street to Piccadilly, where Sarah couldn't help glancing toward Cranham House. The black hatchments and drawn curtains seemed much more oppressive now. What if there wasn't any record there of the late lord's decision about Chalstones? What if it would all be up to Nicholas on his return? She couldn't bear the thought, not when he had made it so silently clear that he didn't wish to have anything more to do with her. If it hadn't all been so sad, she would have laughed at the irony of the situation. Of all the men in England, she had had to fall hopelessly in love with the new Lord Cranham. Fate had a grim sense of humor.

The carriage made its way up Old Bond Street, and then into Conduit Street, soon coming to a halt before the lodging house. Thomas assisted her down to the windswept pavement, and then looked up at the windows above. All but one were tightly closed against the weather.

He smiled at her. "Well, unless someone else is cleaning with raw onions, I think our man is at home."

"You know which are his rooms?"

"No, I merely know that he has a completely irrational fear of being shut up anywhere. He always has a window open, even when it's icy outside. How he hasn't succumbed to a mortal ague before now, I really don't know. Come on."

Taking her hand, he drew it over his sleeve and they went inside.

Stephen was feeling dreadful after his unpleasant dealings with Georgette. He was tense with guilt about having given in to her demands, but such was his dread of prison that he knew he'd make the same shabby decision again.

He was dismayed when his valet informed him that Thomas and Sarah had called. He had tried to convince himself that he wouldn't actually be called upon to carry out the loathsome task that had been forced upon him, but he was already face-to-face with the situation he dreaded. From this moment on, he was well and truly Lady Georgette Belvoir's creature.

As they were shown in, he hardly knew he was uttering the usual civilities, and when they first mentioned the letter, he was immeasurably relieved, for if Nicholas's father had sent a formal letter after all, the onus of lying was lifted from him. But then, as they went on to relate the letter's fate, his elation evaporated again, and the weight descended once more.

It was some time before he could bring himself to look Sarah properly in the eyes, but when he did, he knew why Nicholas loved her. How delightfully fresh she was, and how affectingly anxious over the fate of her home. He despised himself more and more as he responded to what they said.

"There was a letter from Lord Cranham about exchanging Chalstones for some property in the Indies? I fear I know nothing about it, and I also fear that there doesn't appear to be any record . . ." He spread his hands helplessly to indicate his inability to be of any assistance.

Sarah's blue eyes beseeched him. "It was delivered at Thurlong House only hours before Lord Cranham died," she said.

"I am not questioning the veracity of what you say, Miss Howard, but if there is no record of such a communication, or indeed of his late lordship's intention to change his mind, I am afraid there is nothing I can do."

Thomas cleared his throat. "Look, I'm sure that if we put our minds to it we can settle this satisfactorily—" he began.

But Stephen interrupted him. "Normally I would have agreed, but on this occasion there is a slight obstacle."

"Obstacle?" Thomas repeated.

Sarah looked uneasily at Stephen. "What do you mean, sir?" she inquired.

"I have been appointed to act for the new Lord Cranham, and in the absence of any legal proof of what you say, I fear I must carry out what I know his wishes to be." Stephen shifted uncomfortably. "You see, my cousin knew of his father's gambling acquisitions before he left for Naples; indeed he knew before he left London for Cheltenham. When he asked me to handle his affairs while he was away, he mentioned being delighted about Chalstones. He said he looked forward to one day residing there." Stephen paused, and then exhaled slowly. "Forgive me for what I am about to say Miss Howard, but I fear it places my cousin's wishes beyond dispute. He not only specifically said he intended one day to live at Chalstones, but he also mentioned you and your father. As I recall, his exact words were: 'I feel sorry for Mr. Howard and his daughter, Sarah, but life can be cruel, and if Howard was fool enough to sit at a gaming table with my father, he does not deserve consideration.' "

Dismayed beyond belief, Sarah could only stare at him. Nicholas had not only shown such cruel indifference to the fate of the former owners of Chalstones, but he'd actually known a Sarah Howard was involved? When he'd met her, surely it must have crossed his mind to wonder if she was the same Sarah Howard?

She looked away sharply as another even more disagreeable thought struck her. Had the absence of such a natural inquiry indicated that he had no need to ask because he knew already? Had he gleaned some despicable amusement for deceiving her into such foolish indiscretions with him? Maybe he found it immensely diverting to attempt to seduce the daughter into surrendering herself, when the father had already surrendered virtually everything else to the Stanhope family! She closed her eyes weakly. Please don't let it prove so. Please . . .

Seeing her pain, in that moment Stephen knew her every thought. Swallowing, he continued. "I'm afraid the matter must rest there, Miss Howard. My cousin expressed a wish to reside at Chalstones, and I must abide by that wish. It is my duty to protect his estate until he returns. If he should then decide to honor what appears to be his late father's wish, that is a matter for him, but I very much doubt that he will choose to do that."

Thomas put a comforting arm around her shoulder. "Come, Sarah, there is nothing more to be gained from this."

She nodded, trying to stem the tears brimming in her eyes.

Stephen felt as if he had crawled from beneath a stone. "I'm truly sorry, Miss Howard," he said truthfully.

Thomas looked at him. "I quite understand the position you are in, sir. We will have to hope that the new Lord Cranham isn't resolute upon this matter. Do you have any notion when he might return?"

"None at all."

Thomas nodded, and ushered Sarah from the room.

As they left, Stephen sat down at the table, and leaned with his face in his hands. May God forgive him for what he'd just done.

Sarah was in a daze as Thomas assisted her back into the carriage. That Nicholas Stanhope was callous she had already known, but she hadn't believed him capable of such calculated cruelty as now seemed the case.

But even that paled into insignificance beside her more immediate concern. What was she going to tell her father? He had only begun his recovery because he believed Chalstones had been saved. Now Chalstones was gone after all.

24

ON their arrival back at Queen Square, Sarah was still too upset to go into the house. She paused at the door with Thomas.

"I can't go in yet. I think I'll take an airing in the park."

"I'll come with you."

"No, I'll go alone." She looked at him. "I've decided not to tell my father anything yet. He'll have to know soon of course, but I want him to be stronger first."

He nodded. "I quite understand."

She drew a shaking breath. "I still cannot believe that I was so mistaken about Nicholas. I find it impossible to credit that he knew who I was, that he paid court to me and charmed me, when all the time he had such intentions regarding Chalstones. It is so utterly heartless."

"I find it hard to believe as well. I know the man, only slightly, of course, but nevertheless I know him, and I would never have dreamed him capable of such conduct. Maybe there is some mistake; maybe Mannering has it wrong."

"His words were clear enough," she said quietly, pushing a stray curl of hair back beneath her hood as the wind gusted around the square.

Thomas fell silent.

"Besides," she went on, "if Nicholas knew of me by name before he left London, surely he would wonder a little when he met someone of the same name while he was actually on his way to Cheltenham? I do not say that Sarah Howard is so unusual as to be noteworthy, but under the circumstances I would have thought . . ." Her voice trailed away into nothingness. She had to face facts. She'd misjudged Nicholas Stanhope completely. Her first impression of him had been more accurate than anything she'd experienced subsequently. Until now, that is. Now she knew him for the toad he was, and she knew that Chalstones would never again belong to her family. The past weeks had taught her something about herself; she was an appalling judge of men. First there had been her dismal assessment of Oliver, and now this.

Thomas kissed her cheek. "Please don't be too sorrowful, Sarah. You and your father have a home here with my aunt, you know that, don't you?"

"We cannot impose forever, Thomas. Sooner or later we will have to find somewhere else. My father's holdings in the Indies will have to be sold, and we will have to exist upon the proceeds."

"All in good time. Meanwhile, we must see that your father regains all the strength he can. You may rest assured that no one will mention anything to him, and whenever you decide he must be told, we will support you."

"You're very kind, Thomas."

"You are Julia's dearest friend, and therefore mine as well. As for my aunt, well, her feelings toward your father are fairly clear, I think." He smiled.

The wind caught her hood, almost wrenching it from her head as she glanced toward the broad flight of steps leading down from the square to the park. "I'll go for my walk now," she said.

"Stay within view of the house, for I don't like to think of you walking alone. St. James's Park may be all that is fashionable, but it isn't really a place for a lady to be on her own." he said.

She nodded, and then turned toward the steps. Her cloak fluttered around her ankles as she made her way down to the trees lining Birdcage Walk. Crossing over the carriageway, she went through the gate in the railed fence beyond, and then she was in the park.

Georgette was also in the park, strolling with some fashionable friends along the Mall, where it was always the thing to be seen. After her earlier good mood, she was now irritable again. Not only had Mason sent word postponing their assignation until the following night, but it was now becoming increasingly clear that her favorite earrings were missing. She had also received a message from Fitzcharles Place, informing her that Oliver would call upon her the next afternoon so that they could drive together in Hyde Park. That had been the last straw, and her temper had become very waspish indeed.

Her lips were downturned as she walked, and there was a stormy look in her eyes that matched the skies above. She wore a vibrant pink pelisse and matching hat, and coal black plumes streamed from the hat. She carried a black reticule and frilled black parasol, which she did not dare to open in such a wind, and her hands were thrust into a large pink muff that was trimmed with black feathers. No one looked more stylish or up to the mark, and no one more vile-tempered. Her friends no longer included her in their idle conversation, and many of them wished she'd go home, for she was difficult company at the best of times. They knew only too well that she was looking for an argument, and they were each determined not to be her victim. They were therefore almost relieved when she halted suddenly, her attention drawn to a woman in a hooded gray velvet cloak who was walking across the park on her own.

The wind had briefly snatched the cloak's hood back, and a predatory glint appeared in Georgette's eye as she recognized Sarah. She waited with gloating anticipation as her prey drew unsuspectingly nearer.

"Well, if it isn't Miss Howard again," Georgette said.

Sarah gasped and halted.

Georgette's friends lingered nearby, wondering what was about to happen. They knew the taunting tone she used, and would have felt some sympathy for her quarry had they not been so glad to have escaped themselves.

Georgette gave a cool smile. "I trust you are well, Miss Howard?"

"Well enough. Thank you." Sarah's response wasn't very forthcoming.

"Really? I confess I'm surprised, for I would be feeling positively crushed if I'd suffered as you have at a certain gentleman's hands."

Georgette's companions glanced at one another.

Sarah raised her chin. "I don't know what you mean, my lady."

"Oh, come now, you were used most cruelly by the new Lord Cranham. He whispered sweet words in your innocent little ears, and you believed him. Was ever a woman more deceived than you? How amused he was. To be sure, he enjoyed a grand diversion at your expense."

Fiery color suffused Sarah's cheeks. "I am not interested in Lord Cranham's notion of amusement, Lady Georgette."

"That cannot be true, not when it is clear he knew who you were, and even as he laid siege to you was aware that his father's good fortune at the gaming tables had made you homeless. What a very salutary lesson you have been forced to learn. Life can be so very unkind, can it not?"

Without another word, Sarah turned and hurried back across the park toward Thurlong House. Georgette's mocking laughter trilled after her.

That evening Thomas persuaded Lady Thurlong and Julia to accompany him to the theater. He wanted Sarah to come as well, but after the strain of spending the rest of the afternoon trying to pretend to her father that all was well, she felt too tired and unhappy for anything as lighthearted as a performance of *She Stoops to Conquer*. Thus she was alone when Nicholas at last arrived in London in his grandmother's traveling carriage, which had been instructed to drive directly to Thurlong House.

She wore a simple olive green velvet gown with a square neckline and long sleeves, and there were pearls at her throat. Her long hair was brushed loose because she had a slight headache, and she was in the drawing room, reading, when the chaise halted in the square outside. She looked up as a gentleman's cane rapped at the front door.

Lady Thurlong's butler hastened to answer the knock, and Sarah froze as she recognized Nicholas's voice.

"Would you inform Miss Howard that Stanhope, I mean, Lord Cranham, has called?"

Sarah stared at the door. It was impossible! How could he be here when he was supposed to be in Naples? A thousand thoughts milled confusingly in her head, and her hands trembled as she closed her book and placed it carefully on the table beside her chair.

The butler came to the drawing room. "Miss Howard, Lord Cranham wishes to see you."

"Please inform his lordship that I am not at home," she replied quietly.

"Madam." The butler withdrew to conveyed her response.

There was a moment of stunned silence, and then suddenly she heard someone striding along the passageway, and Nicholas flung the door open to look at her. "Sarah?" His perplexed gray eyes searched her pale face, seeking a reason for her refusal to see him.

The butler hurried after him. "Please, my lord, Miss Howard does not wish to receive you—!"

"I'm sure she will speak to me now," Nicholas interrupted quietly, still holding her unwilling gaze.

"Madam?" The butler hesitated.

Slowly she nodded at him. "That will be all."

"Very well, madam." The butler withdrew, not certain if he was doing the wise thing. He was careful to leave the door slightly ajar, and to linger within earshot, should she require him.

Nicholas looked concernedly at her. "What's happened, Sarah? Is it your father? My grandmother told me he was gravely ill, and—"

"It isn't my father, sir," she replied coldly, getting to her feet.

"Then what is it? Why did you refuse to receive me? If something is wrong, I do not know about it because I've literally just arrived in town and come straight to see you."

"I refused to receive you because we have nothing to say to each other, Lord Cranham," she said, her voice choked with an overwhelming conflict of emotions. Part of her was overjoyed to see him again, and wished only to drink in every loved feature. The other part despised him. She pressed her hands against the folds of her velvet gown to hide how they trembled.

He paused for a long moment, and then slowly put his hat and gloves on a table and then advanced toward her. "There is a great deal we have to say to each other, Sarah, beginning with why you are so inexplicably cold toward me. When we last parted you called me by my first name and said you loved me. What has changed?"

The puzzlement in his eyes was so very credible, but he was a masterly actor, as she now knew to her cost. "I have changed because I now know you for the reptile you are, sirrah," she said, her chin raised in defiance.

Her coldness dismayed him, for it far exceeded the reception he had feared if she had failed to receive either of his letters. Something else lay behind this. But what? "Sarah, I trust you mean to explain, for as God is my witness, I do not understand. If it is because I appeared to leave Cheltenham without informing you, let me assure you that I *did* write a note to you, but I very foolishly entrusted it to a Lady Georgette to deliver. There was very little time, barely an hour, and I wasn't even able to say good-bye to my grandmother. I also wrote to you from Padstow, where my ship put in briefly, but that letter failed to reach you either. Other than my apparent remissness of this count, I have no idea why you should treat me like this."

"You amaze me, sirrah. In Cheltenham you pretended to cast convention to the winds in the name of true love, and then you left without telling me. But there was much more to your vile deceit, wasn't there? You knew all along who I was, and it amused you to toy with my affections. And now you come here intending to continue your shabby conduct, but it's all up now, for I have had my foolish eyes opened. I find you hateful Lord Cranham, and I don't wish to ever see you again."

He was thunderstruck. What was she talking about? What did she mean that he'd known all along who she was? What shabby conduct was he guilty of? "Sarah, you have my word that I have no idea at all what you are saying."

"Your word? Sirrah, I would not give a fig for your word." How could he continue to lie like this? Her heart was breaking. With each beat it gave, it crumbled more toward dust. . . .

He drew a long breath, still determined to get to the bottom of whatever it was that had so changed her. "Sarah, what is it that I am supposed to have done?"

"Don't insult me, sirrah, for you know perfectly well what you've done.

He crossed toward her then, seizing her by the arms and forcing her to look at him. "Damn you, Sarah! Just explain what all this is about, for I will not leave until you do!"

His touch almost weakened her resolve. She loved him even now, and the dream she'd had before awakening that morning suddenly pervaded her thoughts again. She wanted him, dear God how she wanted him. But he must never know that! Her blue eyes were filled with scorn. "Pretend you are innocent if you wish, sir, and if it amuses you to continue with his playacting, let me humor you by suggesting you call upon your agent, Mr. Mannering, for he can illuminate your so-called darkness."

He was completely bewildered. "Stephen? What has he to do with this?"

"Oh, spare me this!" she cried, trying to pull free of him.

"What has Stephen Mannering to do with this?" he asked again, still holding her.

"I'm sure the word 'Chalstones' conveys everything you need to know, sir," she replied, meeting his eyes with as much cold loathing as she contrive.

"Chalstones?" The name conveyed nothing.

"Oh, *please* stop pretending, for I cannot bear it any more!" she cried, struggling to make him release her.

"You haven't told me what I need to know." He shook her, desperate to put matters right between them if he could. He hadn't done anything. As God was his witness, he hadn't done anything!

He was too strong for her, and she gave up struggling against him, for there was no point.

He misinterpreted her resignation. To him it was as if she'd suddenly softened in his hands, and the change touched something deep inside him. The ugliness of the present was extinguished, leaving only the honeyed sweetness of the past. He drew her toward him, his arm slipping tightly around her waist as he pressed his lips down upon hers. His body ached with a desperate need for her, and he was vaguely conscious of hoping that if his words had not convinced her of his innocence, then his kisses would.

Her treacherous senses betrayed her, but only for a moment. As her lips softened with desire, and her body urged her to succumb, she was reminded who he was and what he'd said and done. With a huge effort she forced him away, at the same time dealing him a furious blow that left stinging red marks upon his cheek.

"Get out of here!" she cried, raising her voice for the first time.

The butler heard, and hurried into the room. "Madam?"

"Please show Lord Cranham out," she said, her voice shaking with distress.

The butler came hesitantly toward Nicholas. "My lord?"

Nicholas's gray eyes were bright and angry as he looked at her. "I do not deserve this, Sarah. I've repeatedly asked you to tell me what all this is about, but you've refused to explain properly."

"Please go, sir," she said quietly, turning her back toward him.

Without another word, he turned to snatch up his hat and gloves and then strode out of the house.

Behind him, Sarah flung herself on to a sofa and gave in to her misery. Her whole body shook as she wept, and the startled butler hurried to find Annie.

Outside, Nicholas was angry and hurt. What on earth had been going on during his absence? What could be so dire that Sarah now regarded him with such loathing? One thing was certain, he intended to find out, and if Stephen knew anything at all, it would be wrung out of him if necessary.

He opened the door of the waiting carriage. "Conduit Street, if you please," he said to the coachman, before climbing into the vehicle. A moment later he had driven out of Queen Square to go to confront his cousin.

But as he arrived at the lodging house and alighted, he saw not only that his cousin's rooms were in darkness, but that the windows were all closed. Stephen couldn't be at home. Lowering his glance to the apartment on the ground floor, he saw there were lights in plenty, and the sound of male laughter. Someone might know when Stephen was expected to return.

Hunching himself against the bitterly cold wind, he hurried across the pavement into the building. He emerged a few minutes later with the information that Stephen had gone to Windsor to visit friends and wasn't expected back until the following evening. It seemed an

age away, but there was nothing to be done except wait
until then.

In the meantime he had to attend to his duty regarding
Whitehall. The appropriate ministers had to be informed
of the success of his mission. As the vehicle bowled along
the cobbled streets, he leaned his head wearily back
against the drab upholstery. Somehow or other he had
to clear his name with Sarah. Whatever she believed he'd
done, he was innocent. He loved her, and wanted things
to be as they had been before. The moment he'd held
her again and kissed her lips, no matter how unwilling
those lips had been, he'd known she would always be
the only one for him.

When it was time for Julia, Thomas, and Lady
Thurlong to return from the theater, Sarah pretended to
have gone to bed. The marks of her tears were too great
to hide, and she could not face the thought of explaining
what had happened. Fortunately her father had remained
asleep, and there had been no need for her to go to him,
so that she was able to avoid saying anything to anyone

She lay awake in the darkness, listening to the moaning
of the wind outside, and thinking about the man she still
could not help loving. He was detestable, but she remained under his spell. His kiss had almost destroyed
the vestiges of her resistance, and only she knew how
huge an effort she had had to make to thrust him away.
But she would continue to make that effort; she had to
if she was to save her pride and protect her integrity.
Nicholas, Lord Cranham, was treacherous and unprincipled, and she would never again allow him to come too
near.

As she drifted into a restless, tormented sleep, she
decided never to mention his visit to anyone. She would
remain silent and spare herself the pain of explanation.

25

LONDON awoke the following morning to a beautiful December day. The wind had died away, the sky was clear and ice blue, and the pale winter sun bathed everything with a cool light.

The perfect morning gave way to a perfect afternoon. Georgette, who still had no idea that Nicholas had returned, stood at her bedroom window looking out over Park Lane toward Hyde Park, where a constant procession of elegant carriages conveyed the *beau monde* upon its daily pageant. It was ideal weather for driving, especially in landaus and barouches, because their hoods could be lowered for the ladies better to display their finery, and under any other circumstances Georgette would have reveled in such an opportunity to show off her beauty and exquisite taste in fashion, but there was no pleasure to be gleaned at all from such a drive in the company of Oliver Fitzcharles.

She was waiting for him now, and she was in a sulk. Her foot tapped impatiently, her lilac eyes were stormy, and her lips were pressed angrily together. She had tried to cry off this wretched drive; indeed she'd endeavored to move heaven and earth to avoid it, but her father had held firm, telling her that she would drive with her husband-to-be, and that was the end of it.

She wore a close-fitting gray velvet spencer over a flimsy white muslin gown that clung to her long legs as she moved, and the spencer was unbuttoned to reveal the gown's low-cut bodice and wide pink sash. The flouncy pink plumes in her gray silk hat trembled as she gazed darkly at the fashionable concourse opposite. It wouldn't have been quite so bad if the nasty weather had continued, for then she would have been able to hide inside the carriage, but Oliver was certain to come in the Fitzcharles's barouche with the hoods lowered, and everyone would see her seated beside him. The mere thought of being in such close proximity to him set her teeth on edge. God, how she hated him. He was so spineless, dull, and uninteresting in every possible way. Her only consolation was that tonight she would go to Mason.

Oliver arrived at that moment, and to her relief she saw that he hadn't come in the barouche, but in his father's small town carriage, which had no hoods to lower. Taking a deep breath to fortify herself for the coming hour or so, she turned from the window to go down. As she did so, she caught a glimpse of Tilly, who had been trying to keep out of her way ever since the subject of the missing earrings had been brought up again in connection with tonight's secret assignation at Cavendish Square.

The maid's furtiveness reminded Georgette, and she halted at the door. Something told her that the maid knew more than she was admitting. "On my return I intend to speak to you again about the earrings."

Tilly's lips parted with dismay. "Yes, m'lady."

"I suggest you search diligently between now and then, for it would be better for you if they were found. Is that amply understood?"

"Yes, m'lady."

Tilly swallowed as the door closed behind her mistress. She couldn't produce earrings that were in Cheltenham! Oh, why had Andrew had to take them? She was going to be in trouble now, and it wasn't her fault.

Oliver waited for Georgette in the green-and-white entrance hall. He wore a particularly modish doublebreasted coat made of kingfisher blue wool, and there were shining golden tassels on the front of his Hessian boots, so that he appeared very much the eager and dashing man-about-town, but the expression on his face was eloquent of the unwillingness with which he had come.

Hearing Georgette's light steps, he turned to see her descending the curving marble staircase, and he concealed his distaste. Whispers had been reaching him about his future wife, scandalous whispers about how openly and persistently she'd pursued Nicholas Stanhope, and he was beginning to wonder if she could still lay claim to any virtue. He had striven to cry off this afternoon, but his father had insisted that he must be seen with her. Very well, he was doing as he was told, but it wasn't mere chance that had led to him arriving in the closed town carriage instead of the expected barouche, for he had no more desire to be seen with Georgette than she had with him.

He bowed as she approached. "Madam."

"Sir."

He offered her his arm, but she ignored it as she swept out past him. He gritted his teeth and almost snatched his hat and gloves from the waiting footman. Then he followed her.

The drive was accomplished in stony silence. They sat in diagonally opposite corners and kept their faces averted throughout, only managing a fixed smile if they caught the eye of a passing acquaintance. Two circuits of the park had been achieved when suddenly Oliver couldn't endure any more. Lowering the window glass, he abruptly ordered the coach to return to Hayden House, and when the carriage drew up at the door, he alighted with insulting alacrity, thus conveying to Georgette that he was as eager as she to bring a disagreeable occasion to a close.

Georgette hadn't thought that he might feel the same about their match as she did, and the sudden realization infuriated her. How dared he! He should be flattered that she had deigned to accept him! Shaking with rage, she again ignored his proferred arm, and swept into the house as regally as she'd swept out over an hour before.

Oliver made no move to follow her, but climbed swiftly back into the carriage to return to Fitzcharles Place. His fingers drummed upon the window ledge. This match was too awful to contemplate. What a fool he'd been to relinquish an angel like Sarah Howard. He closed his eyes. She was so often in his thoughts that he was always conscious of how much he still loved her. If only he'd shown a little backbone for once! If only he hadn't let her down, and forfeited her love. He could remember the very moment in the grotto when her affection for him had died. She'd asked him to defy his father for her, and he had offered excuses—the excuses of a fool.

He wondered if she ever thought about him, or maybe

even still had some feeling for him. There was only one way to find out, and that was to call upon her. He knew she was in London, for he'd happened upon Thomas Thurlong in Whitehall the previous morning. Yes, that was what he'd do, he'd call at Thurlong House tonight when his father was otherwise occupied with the grand dinner at the Mansion House.

A smile at last returned to Oliver's lips, and he hummed lightly to himself as the carriage drove across Mayfair.

The drive, coupled with the realization that Oliver had the temerity to dislike her, had brought Georgette's temper to a supreme pitch. She had been savage enough before, but now she was positively vicious, and she wreaked her spite upon the hapless Tilly the moment she went up to her room.

"Well? Have you found the earrings?" she demanded, teasing off her gloves as if they offended her.

Tilly stood wretchedly before her. "No, m'lady."

"Have you looked?"

"I've looked everywhere, m'lady."

"I see. Well, Tilly, it's quite clear that you know something about the disappearance of those earrings, and since you have resolutely pretended to the contrary, I am left with the distasteful conclusion that you are not to be trusted."

"Oh, that isn't so, m'lady! You *can* trust me, I swear it!" the maid cried, beginning to see what was coming.

"Then tell me what you know about the earrings."

"I . . . I don't know anything," Tilly answered, only too conscious of the giveaway hesitation.

"I know when I'm being lied to. Very well, you leave me no choice but to dismiss you."

Tilly's breath caught. "Please, m'lady—!"

"You are to leave this house immediately, and you will not receive a reference."

The maid swayed a little. No reference? But how could she find another position if she didn't have a recommendation to show her new employer? "Please, m'lady, don't dismiss me like this," she begged.

"My mind is made up. I cannot have someone like you in a position of trust. You may be thankful that I do not have you charged with stealing, for that is within my power, believe me."

Tilly was as white as a sheet. "Please don't dismiss me, m'lady," she whispered again.

"Get out of my sight. I want you out of this house within the hour, is that clear?" Georgette snapped.

The maid flinched, trembling so much she couldn't think properly.

"Get out!" Georgette screamed, picking up a hair-brush and flinging it at the girl.

With a choked cry Tilly ran from the room and along the passage to the back stairs that led up to the servants' quarters in the attic. As she reached her own little bed, she flung herself facedown, her whole body racked with sobs. But gradually the sobs subsided, and slowly she sat up, mopping her tear-reddened eyes. Her anxiety had given way to bitterness and a desire for revenge upon such a mistress. Lady Georgette wasn't going to get away with this! She was going to regret having treated Tilly Brown like dirt! There were things Her High-and-Mighty Ladyship would prefer to keep secret, things like her assignation that night with Sir Mason Thackeray!

A retaliatory smile appeared on the maid's lips, and she got up to go to the chest of drawers she shared with several of the maids. She took out a crumpled piece of paper she'd stolen from the earl's writing desk to write to Andrew, and the pencil she'd taken from the count-ess's card table. Her writing was awkward and childish, but the message was short and to the point.

Ld. Fitscharls. If you want to no about Ldy. G. and Sir M. Thakry, hide in the mewse lane behind his house tonight at 8.

She read it through with a feeling of immense satisfac-tion. If Lord Fitzcharles caught his future daughter-in-law with Sir Mason, whom he hated above all others, there would be a very sharp ending to Lady Georgette's match, and it would be a scandalous ending, with Lady Georgette's reputation in tatters. And serve her right!

Mindful that she'd only been given an hour to pack and leave, Tilly hurriedly packed her few belongings into her battered valise, and then put on her cape and bonnet.

She'd wait until dark before pushing the note under the
door at Fitzcharles Place, and then she'd go to the
Gloucester Coffee House in Piccadilly to buy an outside
ticket on the next stagecoach to Cheltenham. She'd go
to Andrew now, since it was on his account that she'd
lost her position. Besides, he'd said the earrings were for
their future, and now he would have to prove it.

Shortly afterward, with the anonymous note tucked
safely into her reticule, Tilly left Hayden House. The sun
was beginning to sink toward the horizon. Soon it would
be dark, and the note would find its way beneath the
front door at Fitzcharles Place.

Lord Fitzcharles was dressing for the dinner at the
Mansion House. His corpulent person had been squeezed
into the formal evening clothes required for such an occasion, and his discomfort made him snappy as his valet
struggled to achieve the desired knot with his neckcloth.
He was therefore somewhat impatient when the butler
brought Tilly's note.

"Yes? What is it? Well, don't just stand there, man!"

The butler was uncomfortable. They'd deliberated for
some time below stairs as to whether or not to give such
a disreputable communication to his lordship, but in the
end had decided he should see it. "This, er, item, was
pushed beneath a door a short while ago, m'lord," he
said.

"Eh? Pushed under the door, y'say?" Lord Fitzcharles
took the piece of paper and read it. Then he read it
again, and his face went red with rage.

Sensing that all was suddenly not at all well, the valet
stepped back from the neckcloth, prudently deciding that
the knot, such as it was, would now suffice.

For a long moment Lord Fitzcharles was ominously
silent as he mulled over the contents of the note. It
wasn't the hand of an educated person, that much was
obvious, but whoever it was was very precise. Well, if
Lady Georgette Belvoir was seeing his arch-enemy, she'd
pay a very high price!

He turned to the butler. "I won't take the landau tonight after all. I'll use the small town carriage instead.
See that it's brought to the door at half-past seven."

The butler nodded. "M'lord."

The valet was concerned about the grand dinner. "But, m'lord, if you don't leave until then, you'll be late for the Mansion House."

"I'm not going to the Mansion House anymore." Lord Fitzcharles looked at the butler. "Do not inform my son of this."

"No, m'lord."

As Lord Fitzcharles changed his plans in order to see what might or might not transpire at Cavendish Square, Nicholas's carriage arrived at Conduit Street. Stephen's rooms were still in darkness, with every window closed, and so Nicholas settled back to wait. His cousin would return soon, and when he did, there would be questions to answer.

26

STEPHEN was tired as he drove his curricle into Conduit Street at the end of a long day in Windsor, and he stared in disbelief as he recognized Nicholas's carriage outside the lodging house. Nicholas? But he couldn't possibly be back from Naples yet!

Then the disbelief turned to deep dismay, and for a moment Stephen was tempted to turn around and drive away, to turn tail and run, in fact, but then he knew that sooner or later he'd have to face up to it. Nicholas might already have found something out, and if that was the case, he wouldn't let matters lie. Reluctantly Stephen continued along the street, driving past the waiting carriage and then into the alley and stableyard behind the lodging house, where a sleepy groom emerged from the stables to take care of the curricle.

Stephen paused for a moment to steel himself for what promised to be one of the most difficult meetings of his life, and then he strolled out of the alley to the pavement, where Nicholas had now alighted and was waiting for him.

"Nicholas? Good God, what are you doing back so soon?" Stephen was relieved at how convincingly astonished his voice sounded.

"Stephen."

"I thought you'd be away for some time yet."

"I didn't get as far as Naples. The ambassador happened to be at Gibraltar."

"What a stroke of good fortune," Stephen murmured, wishing the ambassador in Hades itself.

"Indeed. Stephen, it's important that I have a word with you."

There was no mistaking his cousin's manner. Stephen's heart began to beat more swiftly. "Er, yes, of course.

Do come inside." He gestured toward the lodging-house door, and then followed Nicholas up the stairs.

The rooms were warm and firelit, but Stephen immediately opened the window before going to light some candles and then take off his outdoor things. "My damned valet has the evening off, but at least he attended to the fire before he left. A glass of *aqua vitae*?" He picked up the decanter of whisky.

"Yes. Thank you." Nicholas removed his hat and gloves and tossed them onto a table.

Stephen pressed an amply filled glass into his hand and then sat down by the fire. "Before we go any further, I'd like to offer my condolences regarding your father."

"And I suppose I should go through the motions and express my thanks," Nicholas replied dryly, sitting down in the seat opposite. "But I'm not a hypocrite, Stephen, and I feel no grief at all that the old bastard is dead. I certainly don't mean to wear mourning for him."

"You were ever honest," Stephen murmured. "Now then, what is it you wish to speak to me about?"

"What does the name 'Chalstones' convey to you?"

Stephen's frantic heart almost stopped within him, but he managed to remain level. There was nothing for it but to reply truthfully, well, as truthfully as possible. "Chalstones? Why, it's part of your father's winnings."

"Winnings?"

"He was on a golden streak just before he died. I did try to tell you about it before you left for Cheltenham, but you didn't want to know. Chalstones is a very fine estate somewhere in Oxfordshire. Or is it Berkshire?"

"I don't give a damn where it is, I just want to know what it has to do with Miss Sarah Howard."

Stephen swallowed. He had to keep control of the situation, he mustn't give in to the alarm that was beginning to seep through every pore! "Actually it was from her father that your father won so heavily. Chalstones was her home."

Nicholas stared at him. "Tell me everything you know, Stephen."

"There isn't much to tell. As I said, your father won a great deal from Mr. Howard, and when I commenced acting on your behalf, I received a visit from Miss Howard and Mr. Thurlong, who is—"

"I know who Thurlong is," Nicholas interrupted impatiently. "Just get to the point. What did Miss Howard say to you?"

"She claimed that your father had agreed to exchange Chalstones for some Caribbean property still in her father's possession, but since she had no proof of this agreement, and there was no mention at all in your father's effects, I had no option but to tell her that such an exchange would have to wait until you returned." Stephen felt sick. He couldn't carry this off, and was certain to make a mistake before long.

Nicholas was silent for a moment. "Stephen, you must have known that neither Miss Howard nor Thomas Thurlong is the sort of person to invent such a story. If they said there was an agreement, then there was."

"Possibly, but they had no proof. What was I supposed to do? Just proceed on their word alone? Nicholas, it was my duty to look after the Stanhope family's interest, and in my book that meant protecting it at all costs. What you decide to do about the Howards is your business, but my conscience is clear. As the guardian of your affairs, I did what I felt was right." Stephen's hand trembled as he raised his glass to his lips. A cool draft from the open window breathed over him, reminding him of the horror that would await if he should be despatched to jail.

Nicholas remained silent as he thought about what he had learned.

His silence alarmed Stephen. "Look, Nicholas, if you are displeased with my conduct in this—" he began.

Nicholas smiled then. "No, of course not. You behaved honorably, and now it's up to me to put matters right with Miss Howard and her father. It's clear to me that my father did indeed agree to an exchange of property, and I intend to settle matters as they should be settled."

Stephen looked away, his guilt suddenly overflowing. He hadn't behaved honorably, indeed his conduct had been the very opposite. He got up agitatedly, putting his empty glass on the mantelshelf and then leaning a hand upon the chimney breast to stare down into the fire.

Nicholas studied him. "What is it, Stephen? Is something wrong?"

"Everything is wrong."

"What do you mean? Is it your debts? Has someone called you in?"

"In a manner of speaking," Stephen replied wryly. Then he faced his cousin. "Nicholas, I haven't acted honorably; in fact I have been entirely *dis*honorable, and I certainly don't deserve your praise."

Nicholas set his glass aside and looked more closely at him. "I'm sure you mean to explain."

"I've been lying to you. Your father *did* agree to the exchange. There was a note in his diary that confirmed it, and I am sure that if I search at Cranham House, I will find a copy of the letter Miss Howard claims her father received on the matter, but which was unfortunately destroyed." Stephen closed his eyes for a moment. He was finished. The Marshalsea awaited, as sure as night followed day.

Nicholas got up slowly. "Why, Stephen?" he asked coolly.

"Because Lady Georgette Belvoir now holds my notes from her brother, and threatens to call them in immediately unless I do her bidding. It seems she hates both you and Miss Howard and wishes to cause as much misery and mischief as she can."

Nicholas was nonplussed. "I can understand why she hates me, for I spurned her more than once and in no uncertain terms, but what has Sarah done to warrant her spite?"

"Won you, probably. Unless it has something to do with Oliver Fitzcharles."

"Fitzcharles?"

Stephen nodded. "Before being betrothed to Lady Georgette, he was briefly betrothed to Miss Howard. At least, that is what I have heard on the grapevine. I gather the first engagement was never made public, and was ended when Lord Fitzcharles found out that due to your father's phenomenal luck, Miss Howard was no longer the heiress she had been. It's only a whisper, of course, but it has the ring of truth."

Nicholas stared at him. "Sarah Howard was to have married Oliver Fitzcharles?" he repeated.

"Yes. Look, Nicholas, that probably hasn't got anything to do with it. The real point of this is that Lady Georgette has been plotting, even to the extent of paying a footman at Thurlong Lodge to intercept any letters you might have sent to Miss Howard."

"I did write to her," Nicholas replied. So that was what had happened to the letter from Padstow! He looked angrily at his cousin. "Damn you for helping her in this, Stephen!"

"I was a very unwilling accomplice, I promise you, and only did it because I was terrified of being locked up, but I haven't the stomach to go through with it." He gave a dry laugh. "Maybe I have a little honor left after all."

"Maybe. Is there any more you have to tell me?"

Stephen looked reluctantly at him. "Yes. Nicholas, I didn't simply tell Miss Howard there was no record of your father's agreement to an exchange. On Lady Georgette's explicit instructions, I said much more than that."

Nicholas's gray eyes were cool. "Go on."

"I said that you'd known about her and about her father's losses *before* you left London for Cheltenham. In other words that you'd cultivated her trust and friendship under vilely false pretenses. More than that, I also told her that you'd specifically mentioned Chalstones, saying that you were glad your father had won it because one day you intended to live there yourself, and to hell with Mr. Howard and his daughter, Sarah. Please forgive me, Nicholas."

Nicholas was livid. "Forgive you? I could gladly extinguish your treacherous life. Thanks to you and that Belvoir she-cat, Sarah Howard now believes me to be the greatest monster that ever lived!"

Stephen couldn't meet his eyes. "I'm so very sorry, Nicholas. If . . . if you want me to repeat all this to Miss Howard herself, then I will, but don't expect Lady Georgette to admit to anything. She has already warned me that she will deny it all."

"May you rot in hell for this, Stephen."

Stephen's wretched gaze moved to the open window. "I soon will, for the *chienne* will call my notes in now, of that you may be sure," he whispered.

Without another word Nicholas snatched up his hat and gloves and strode out just as the clock on the mantelshelf struck eight.

There were tears on Stephen's ashen cheeks, and he

bowed his head. He had salved his conscience, but he had forfeited the friendship and respect of the man he thought most of in all the world.

Lord Fitzcharles's small town carriage was drawn up in the shadows of the mews lane behind Cavendish Square. He had just glanced at his pocket watch. It was eight o'clock, the time mentioned in the anonymous note. He shivered a little, and looked toward Sir Mason's house through a door that had been opened a short while before in the high wall bounding the rear grounds. The lights of the house were clearly visible at the other end of the garden. Curtains had been drawn at the windows of the ground-floor rooms, but from time to time he caught a glimpse of someone through a crack between the heavy draperies. He was certain that it was Thackeray.

Suddenly the sound of a carriage came from farther along the lane, and Lord Fitzcharles carefully lowered the window glass to look out. An anonymous hackney coach was approaching, and it halted almost alongside, causing him to draw swiftly back out of sight. Someone alighted, and the hackneyman leaned down to accept the fare. Then the whip flicked, and the coach drove away again.

Lord Fitzcharles leaned forward once more, and was in time to see a cloaked woman hastening up the garden toward the house. Opening the carriage door, he climbed quietly down, and then followed.

He made his way toward the lighted ground-floor windows and took up a position by the convenient gap between the curtains. He saw his hated foe inside, looking very much the dandy in elegant evening clothes, and appearing more vulpine than ever, with a predatory smile on his lips. Reynard was anticipating a delicious feast to come!

The door of the room opened, and the woman was shown in. In the candlelight, Lord Fitzcharles could see the cloak was made of rich blue figured velvet, with white fur around the hood and hem. At first her face was in shadow, but then she lowered her hood, and he saw that it was indeed Georgette. So the note had not lied.

Lord Fitzcharles watched with silent fury as she hastened toward her lover. Mason took her in his arms, his parted lips pressing down upon hers. Then he undid the ties of the cloak so that it fell away from her, revealing the glittering, clinging, gold tissue gown she wore beneath. Or only just wore, Lord Fitzcharles thought contemptuously, noting how low the flimsy garment plunged over her breasts, and how it outlined every small curve of her beautiful body. It was a shameless garment, the garment of a *belle de nuit,* and the conduct of its wearer was also that of a *belle de nuit.*

Lord Fitzcharles watched for a moment more, and then left the window to make his way toward the kitchen door of the house, where a minute or so earlier Georgette had gained admittance. He didn't knock, but simply opened it and walked in. The servants stared at him for a moment, and then the butler made to hurry to the stairs door to warn his master, but Lord Fitzcharles spoke sharply.

"I wouldn't do that, if I were you!"

The man hesitated.

Lord Fitzcharles gave an unpleasant smile. "You would all do better to pretend you haven't seen me."

The butler stepped back from the doorway and resumed his place by the table. No one else had moved.

Lord Fitzcharles walked past them all, and went up the staircase to the sumptuous entrance hall above. There was no one else around as he made his way toward the room at the rear of the house where he knew he would find the illicit lovers.

He could hear Georgette's playful laugh as he paused at the door, before suddenly thrusting it open and striding into the room.

They leapt apart. Georgette's gown had now joined the cloak upon the floor, and she was naked except for her gartered white silk stockings, her long white gloves, and a diamond necklace. Her face drained of all color as she saw who it was, and with a cry of dismay and humiliation she snatched up the cloak to hide herself.

Mason was startled as well, but then swiftly recovered. The clever smile returned to his lips, and he leaned back against a heavy chair, his arms folded as if he relished the coming minutes.

Lord Fitzcharles's face was red with rage and loathing as he looked at his old foe, for he knew only too well the purpose behind this. "So, Thackeray, this is your revenge for Icarus, is it?"

"So it seems, Fitzcharles."

Georgette didn't hear. She was so panic-stricken that she could barely tie the cloak or bend to retrieve her gown. Her eyes were filled with tears, and she couldn't think properly, but she was coldly aware of one thing. When she instinctively reached out to her lover for support, he ignored her.

Lord Fitzcharles's mouth twisted furiously as he turned his attention to her. "Breaking your vows *before* the wedding, eh? How fortunate that I was warned in time."

"Warned?" Her lilac eyes were huge with disbelief.

"By a well-wisher, I believe the phrase goes. An ill-educated well-wisher, but an accurate one, it seems."

"Ill-educated?"

Lord Fitzcharles took the note from his pocket and placed it upon the table."

A glance told her that it was Tilly's writing. The maid had inflicted a very telling reprisal! Georgette could almost have laughed aloud, for if anyone had ever brought this upon herself, she had. Her temper and spite had overreached at last, and this was the result. But there was still Mason. She turned to her lover, her lovely eyes beseeching him. "Mason?" she whispered.

"Don't look at me, my darling, for I have no intention of taking you on," he replied coolly.

Her lips trembled. "Don't I mean anything to you?"

"Oh, yes, my dear, for you are an admirable weapon."

"Weapon?" Her voice was faint.

"You don't imagine I was ever prepared to let Icarus go without retaliating, do you?"

She stared at him. "Icarus. You mean, all this was because of a horse?"

"What else? I feel nothing for you, sweetheart, you are far too available and eager to interest me for long."

A sob escaped her, and fresh tears sprang to her eyes. "You don't mean it," she whispered.

"I mean every calculated word, my dear. My sole purpose in seducing you now has been to embarrass Fitzcharles, and that, I believe, I have achieved rather nicely."

Lord Fitzcharles gave a dismissive grunt of laughter.

"Embarrass me? You delude yourself, Thackeray. All I mean to do is put a stop to the betrothal, and say precisely why. I shall broadcast it far and wide, and the lady will not have a character left. Nor will you, for I will embellish it greatly, you may be sure of that."

Georgette gave a cry of anguish. "No! Please, no! I will do anything you ask, I will be a model daughter-in-law in every way!"

"Nothing would now induce me to allow you in my family, madam. You are little better than a whore, and I must thank Thackeray here for proving the fact so completely. Prepare yourself to be at the center of a monumental scandal, for I will make sure the whole of society knows about this. Dear God above, and to think that I actually regarded Sarah Howard as unsuitable!" Lord Fitzcharles gave an ironic smile, and then held out his hand. "The ring, if you please."

Her hands were shaking so much that she could hardly obey, and when the ring was off her finger, she fumbled so much that she dropped it.

It fell with a tinkle that echoed in the silent room, and then it rolled over the floor and came to rest by Lord Fitzcharles's feet. He bent to pick it up, and then walked out to return to Fitzcharles Place and once again inform his son that his betrothal was at an end.

Georgette turned to Mason. "Please tell me that you didn't mean what you said," she begged.

"You are beginning to be tiresome, madam. I meant every word."

"Damn you!" she cried, raising her hand to hit him, but he caught her wrist.

"I wouldn't advise it, my dear, for I may forget I'm a gentleman and return the favor. I've used you, just as you've so frequently used others, indeed as you used me when you wished to make Stanhope jealous. My advice to you now is to take Fitzcharles's warning seriously. Your name is going to be on all lips tomorrow, and if you want to avoid the scandal, I suggest you leave London. Your father's Scottish estates would seem to offer an ideal destination, and a lengthy stay there would seem to be the sensible thing. You can sit at your embroidery frame with your brother's unfortunate wife, who has yet to find out about his constant indiscretions with actresses.

Who knows, you may find it stimulating and amusing to gradually inform her what's going on. Yes, you probably will, for that is your way."

"I despise you," she whispered.

"Good, for I would hate to be the object of your true affection." He released her wrist and thrust her away at the same time. "Go home, madam, and pack to leave as quickly as possible, for Lord Fitzcharles won't be the only one spreading tittle-tattle tomorrow. I intend to have a little amusement as well."

Turning, he strode from the room.

Georgette stared after him, and then lowered her eyes miserably. Her glance fell upon Tilly's note, which still lay upon the table. With a savage cry she snatched it up and flung it into the fire.

The clock on the mantelpiece whirred and began to strike the half hour. Georgette's breath caught, and she swiftly gathered all her things and then hurried out. Mason's advice about Scotland was sensible. She couldn't possibly stay in London and face the laughter and humiliation, and she meant to be on her way north before morning.

27

OLIVER wasn't at home when his father returned, but was at that moment steeling himself to approach the door of Thurlong House and request to speak to Sarah.

She was in the library at the rear of the house, selecting a book to read to her father. The library curtains were undrawn, and the room brightly lit as she examined the shelves for a suitable volume. She wore a jonquil yellow dimity gown, and her hair was pinned up, with yellow ribbons fluttering behind.

Lady Thurlong, Julia, and Thomas had gone to to the Mansion House dinner, but she had kept to her decision to cry off. She'd also kept to her decision not to tell anyone about Nicholas's visit, and she was striving with all her might to keep him out of her thoughts, so that her dismay was very great as she heard someone knocking at the front door of the house. Please don't let it be him again. Please.

She turned reluctantly as the butler entered the room. "Yes?" If it was Nicholas, she was determined this time to deny him any chance to speak to her.

"Mr. Fitzcharles has called and wishes to speak to you, madam."

She stared at him. Oliver? But why on earth did he wish to see her? "I, er . . ."

"Do you wish me to tell him you are not at home, madam?"

"No. I will receive him."

"Madam." The butler withdrew again, and a moment later two sets of footsteps returned. The door opened once more. "Mr. Fitzcharles, madam."

She faced her unexpected caller with complete composure. "Sir?"

Oliver waited until the butler had gone, and then smiled a little awkwardly. "I hope you are not offended by my call, Sarah." How refreshing it was to be with her again, for she was everything that Georgette was not.

"Offended? No, but I am a little surprised."

"I, er, heard that you father was taken ill. I trust he is not in danger?"

"We hope that he will recover fully," she replied, pushing thoughts of losing Chalstones to the back of her mind.

"How is Julia?"

"Very well. Look, Oliver, why have you really called? I'm sure it isn't simply to exchange all the usual civilities."

"I wish to make amends for having failed you so singularly in the past."

She was conscious of the warmth in his eyes. "Oliver, that is all over now."

"Not for me. I am ashamed of my conduct in the grotto, and of my subsequent behavior in Cheltenham. All I want is to beg your forgiveness, and ask if we may at least be friends again."

"I have no objection to being friends, Oliver."

He came a little nearer. "I wish with all my heart that I'd shown more backbone, for we should never have parted."

She drew back. "You are betrothed to Lady Georgette now," she reminded him.

"I cannot deny it, since you were present when the match was announced." He searched her face. "Do you have someone else now, Sarah?"

"No." No, no, no.

"Do you regret our parting?"

She looked at him again. "I see nothing to be gained by raking over the cold ashes."

"Are you so certain they are cold?"

Her lips parted. "Of course."

"Maybe they are for you, but they will never be for me."

She stared at him. "Oliver, I think it would be better if you left."

"I'm not in my cups, Sarah, I'm telling you the truth. I still love you, and if I had the chance again, I would never have abided by my father's wishes over our betrothal."

"It's too late now, Oliver."

He gazed at her, longing to reach out and touch her. Suddenly he couldn't resist the temptation, and put his hand to her cheek.

She moved away. "Please don't, Oliver, for I no longer feel anything for you."

"I can't believe that that is the truth."

"You don't want to believe it," she corrected. "Oliver, you asked if we could be friends, and that is all I can ever offer you from now on. You must believe me."

He looked into her eyes, and knew with dismay that she meant it. "Oh, Sarah, if only—"

She interrupted quickly. "We wouldn't have been happy together, I know that now."

"How can you say that?"

"Because I met someone else for a short while, and what I felt for him was far far more than I'd ever felt for you."

"Who was it?"

"It doesn't matter, because it's over now. Let us be content with friendship, Oliver."

"If that is your final word, then I have to bow to it, but I tell you this, I have no intention of marrying Lady Georgette Belvoir, nor do I intend to ever again submit to my father's wishes. I've learned my lesson a little late, but at least I've learned it."

She stared at him. "I can't believe I'm hearing you correctly. You actually mean to defy your father?"

"Yes. I'll face up to him the next time I see him."

"He won't let you have your way."

"He'll have no option. I have a little income of my own, enough to support me wherever I chose to go. I've always had a fancy for America, for Boston, to be precise."

She smiled a little. "They may throw you into the harbor. I seem to recall that they have a penchant for such things there."

"Ah, but I am a mere Englishman, not a cargo of East India Company tea." He returned the smile, loving her so much that his heart ached, but he knew he'd forfeited her forever. "When I eventually return, I will call upon you as a friend."

"I would like that. I'm glad you called tonight, Oliver, for we were once too close for it to be right that we stay at odds now. We had a close call, but I think in the end you will admit, too, that we wouldn't have gone on well as husband and wife."

"I have yet to be convinced of that." He took her hand and raised it to his lips. "Good-bye, Sarah."

"Au revoir, I think, for we will meet again."

He paused, and then pulled her close to kiss her. They held each other for a long moment, and then he left, hardly pausing in the hall for the butler to assist him with his things.

The entire scene in the brightly lit, uncurtained library had been witnessed from the park—witnessed, and completely misinterpreted. After returning to Duke Street from Stephen's lodgings, Nicholas had decided to walk to Thurlong Lodge to explain everything and prove his innocence to Sarah. As he crossed Birdcage Walk and approached the steps up to Queen Square, he was able to see everything that had taken place in the brightly illuminated library. He saw how tenderly Oliver had put his hand to Sarah's cheek, and how lovingly they'd kissed and then stood in an embrace.

As he stared at every apparently incriminating moment, Nicholas's desire to explain had died within him. So that was how it was. Far from being the innocent he'd believed, Miss Sarah Howard was accomplished in the art of flirtation. She had accused him of shabbiness, but that was something of which she herself could justly be accused. She had told him that her former betrothed no longer meant anything to her; that was patently not the case. Not a word about Fitzcharles had passed her lips in Cheltenham, not even when she'd watched his ring being placed on Lady Georgette Belvoir's finger! Had she been seeing Fitzcharles all along? Yes, that had to be it. They had secretly defied Lord Fitzcharles, continuing their liaison even though their betrothal had been ended.

Nicholas remained rooted to the spot with shock and disbelief. What a fool he'd been to be taken in by her.

She had accused him of having known all along who she was, but maybe the shoe was on the other foot, and she had known who he was! Had it been her intention to recoup her father's losses by winning the heart of the next Lord Cranham, and at the same time keep her true love, Fitzcharles?

Suddenly he turned to walk back to Duke Street. He couldn't bring himself to face her yet, but in the end he'd confront her, if only to return everything his father had won. He wanted nothing that was tainted by the Howards, nothing at all. Chalstones and everything else would be returned, and the slate wiped completely clean. And then he'd wipe sweet Sarah Howard from his memory as well.

The moment he returned to Duke Street, he sent a running footman to Stephen, instructing him to go to Cranham House first thing in the morning and then bring him every document, note, page, and scrap of paper that might pertain to the late Lord Cranham's dealings with Mr. Howard.

Oliver returned to Fitzcharles Place, and found his father waiting impatiently. "Father? I thought the Mansion House do would keep you occupied until well after midnight."

"Where in hell's name have you been?" Lord Fitzcharles demanded.

"Out."

His father's face became cold. "Don't come the wit with me, my laddo, for you haven't got the brain."

"I have brain enough to see the light before it's too late," Oliver replied, surprising himself with the ease with which he at last stood up to the despot who'd held sway over him since the day of his birth.

It suited Lord Fitzcharles to ignore his responses for the moment. There were must more important things on the agenda than his son's mood. Taking the betrothal ring from his pocket, he placed it on the table in front of Oliver.

"Your engagement to Lady Georgette Belvoir is at an end," he said flatly.

Oliver glanced at the ring. "Indeed? Can't the lady bear the thought of being between the sheets with me?"

"I caught her *in flagrante delicto* with Thackeray."

Oliver could not have cared less.

Lord Fitzcharles frowned. "Are you listening to me, boy? I said that I caught her in the very act of surrendering her all, such as it still is, to that scoundrel Thackeray!"

"I'm not interested, Father, for I had already decided not to marry her."

"You'd what?" Lord Fitzcharles's face darkened with anger at his son's attitude.

"I'm my own man at last, and I'm telling you, cordially, to go to hell from now on."

"I'll trim your allowance if you continue in this vein," Lord Fitzcharles began, still hardly able to believe his ears. His spineless son was answering back?

"I don't give a damn what you do with my allowance, for I have sufficient for my purposes."

"What purposes?"

"I'm not sure yet, except to inform you that I have a fancy to try America for a while. They declared their independence from us, and now I'm declaring mine from you, which suggests to me that our former colony is an appropriate place for me to commence my new life."

Lord Fitzcharles was now so shocked that he couldn't speak.

Oliver was enjoying himself immensely. For the first time in his life he'd taken matters entirely into his own hands, and the feeling was good. "I won't thank you, Father, for there isn't much to be grateful for. If it hadn't been for your bullying over the years, I wouldn't have been such a milksop as to allow you to part me from the woman I love. My slavish obedience to you cost me Sarah's love, and I will never forgive you or myself for that."

"I'll disinherit you!" Lord Fitzcharles breathed.

"Do so; it makes no difference to me." Oliver smiled then. "Find yourself some poor female to marry to give you another heir. Make someone else's life an unspeakable misery, but do so in the knowledge that in the end your sins will catch up with you. And now, I think I'll pack. I've already ordered a post-chaise, so please do not waste your breath forbidding me the use of your carriages." With a civil nod of his head, he turned and left the room.

Lord Fitzcharles stared apoplectically after him.

Half an hour later, with the barest minimum of belongings, and only his faithful valet for company, the Honorable Oliver Fitzcharles left his father's house and was soon en route for Falmouth, and the first vessel upon which he could obtain passage for America.

He set off on the king's highway at the same time as Georgette, but whereas he was making for the West Country, she was on the Great North Road on her way to distant Scotland. She hadn't stopped crying since she had left Cavendish Square, and she had her parents' indescribable fury ringing in her ears. A dreadful scandal loomed on her every horizon, and she knew that it would be some time before society's interest was diverted by something more titillating than her indiscretions with Sir Mason Thackeray. Too late she realized she'd made some monumental errors of judgment, and too late she accepted that her foul temper had at last plunged her into the trouble she had courted so carelessly for so long.

As her carriage drove swiftly away from London, she had no thought for Sarah and Nicholas and all the mischief she'd done to them. They were a million miles away now, and she was entirely preoccupied with herself—as she always had been, and probably always would.

28

AFTER traveling throughout the night on an outside seat on the Cheltenham Flying Machine stagecoach, Tilly was bitterly cold and stiff as she at last alighted at the Plough Inn in the High Street. Morning light was beginning to lighten the skies, and the spa was stirring. Carrying her battered valise, the maid walked along the pavement toward Thurlong Lodge to tell Andrew what had befallen her. She shivered, for the cold seemed to have seeped right through to her bones, and when she looked up at the sky she saw that the clouds were a dull yellowy-gray, snow clouds.

The only person to be up at Thurlong Lodge was a kitchen boy, who let her in in the mistaken belief that she was the new parlormaid Julia had engaged before leaving for London. The moment the boy's back was turned, she left the kitchens and tiptoed up to Andrew's attic room. A floorboard squeaked beneath her foot as she went softly past the other doors, and the latch felt chill to the touch as she carefully raised it, intending to awaken him by slipping in between the sheets. The hinge groaned as she pushed the door open, and at the sound two figures in the bed sat up with startled gasps.

Tilly stared, for in the cold gray light that came in through the dormer window, she saw that Andrew was with a very buxom blonde with pink cheeks and rosy lips. Both of them were naked, and it was only too clear what had been going on.

Tilly's heart turned over with dismay. "Andrew?" she whispered accusingly.

"Tilly?" He was so shocked that he could only sit there, pulling the bedclothes up to his chin.

The girl gave him a suspicious look. " 'Ere, who's she?" she demanded.

Tilly didn't wait to hear his reply, but fled tearfully back to the stairs. The sound of her running steps awoke everyone, and when she reached the kitchen and flung herself onto a chair and hid her face in her hands, it wasn't long before Hemmings and some of the other servants came down as well to see what was going on. Of Andrew and his new ladylove there was no sign at all.

Hemmings looked at Tilly in puzzlement. "You're Lady Georgette Belvoir's maid, aren't you?" he asked, trying to look dignified as he buttoned his coat over his nightshirt.

Tilly wiped her eyes and sniffed. "I was," she replied. Just as with Georgette, she had already decided how to exact her revenge upon Andrew for his faithlessness. She looked at the butler. "Are you Mr. Hemmings?"

"Yes, butler to Mr. and Mrs. Thurlong," he answered importantly, frowning a little at her. "What are you doing in this house, my girl? You've no business being here. How did you get in?"

The unfortunate kitchen boy shrank back into the shadows by the pantry door, but Tilly had no intention of telling tales on him. She was far too intent upon paying Andrew back. He'd be sorry for what he'd done, just as Lady Georgette was probably sorry now for what she'd done. No one treated Tilly Brown shabbily and got away with it!

She met the butler's gaze. "There's something you should know, Mr. Hemmings. Andrew stole Lady Georgette's diamond earrings. They're hidden under his mattress right now."

There were gasps, and in the confusion as the shocked butler despatched one of the footman up to the attic to look, Tilly slipped craftily away. She didn't intend to get caught as well, but she was certain now that Andrew would pay a very high price for his infidelity.

She lingered on the corner by the lane that led to the mill and saw another footman hurrying from Thurlong Lodge to find the officers of the watch. Half an hour after that she had the supreme satisfaction of seeing Andrew and his loudly protesting new love being hauled away to the town jail.

As she watched, Tilly's elation died away. She'd had her revenge on those who'd been bad to her, but now she was alone and without a position. All she could do was go to her aunt in Worcester and hope for a roof over her head. It was a long way, and she'd have to walk because she'd spent all her money on the stagecoach fare.

With a heavy sigh she picked up her old valise and began the journey. As she did so, the first snowflake fluttered idly down from the leaden skies overhead.

It had begun to snow very lightly in London as well, as Sarah saw the moment Annie drew back the curtains. Scattered flakes drifted slowly past the window, too few as yet to settle at all, but there was a heavy look to the skies that promised a great deal more to come.

"Good morning, Miss Sarah," Annie said, plumping up her pillows so that she could sit comfortably and drink her cup of morning tea.

"Good morning, Annie. How is my father?" It was her first question every day.

"He's still getting better, Miss Sarah."

Sarah sipped the tea. Was it right to continue keeping the truth about Chalstones away from him? She didn't know. Sometimes she thought she should tell him everything, but then she changed her mind, and felt it was best to protect him.

"What shall you wear today, miss?" Annie asked.

"Oh, the lime dimity, I think." It was a warm gown, with gathered sleeves that were long and trimmed with lace at the cuffs, and was ideal for a chilly December morning like this.

At that moment a tap came at her door. "May I speak to you, my dear?" It was Lady Thurlong.

"Yes, of course," Sarah replied, her heart leaping as she feared something had befallen her father after all.

Lady Thurlong came in, her charcoal taffeta gown rustling, and on seeing her guest's anxious face, she immediately smiled reassuringly. "It's quite all right, my dear, your father is well."

"I . . . I thought—"

"I know, and for that you must forgive me. I don't usually come in to see you like this, but there is something I wish to say to you before you go to your father. It has been clear to me that you are torn between telling him about Lord Cranham's wishes, or keeping it to yourself for a little longer. I merely wish to reassure you that whatever your decision, both you and he are more than welcome to remain in this house."

"You are truly kind and thoughtful, Lady Thurlong."

"Kind and thoughtful? What rubbish. I'm entirely selfish in this. You see, I have become very fond of you, and I have always been far more than fond of your dear father. Believe me, if it were considered acceptable, I would not hesitate to ask him to make an honest woman of me after all this time. However, it isn't the thing, and so I must content myself with endeavoring to keep him in my clutches by other means." Lady Thurlong smiled at her. "I love him far too much, d'you see?"

"I am sure that he is more fond of you than he has admitted," Sarah replied.

"Oh, if only that were true, I would be the happiest creature on earth. Anyway, that is all I wished to say to you, my dear. Be assured that my home is your home for as long as you require it."

Sarah reached out and took the older woman's hand, squeezing it gratefully. "Thank you so much."

"Not at all, my dear."

Sarah glanced down at her cup of tea. She still did not know what to do. If she kept the news from her father, would it possibly be a greater shock in the end? Or if she told him now, would his health be up to such a devastating setback?

After receiving Nicholas's message the evening before, Stephen went early to Cranham House to search for any papers connected with Mr. Howard, and he then went to Duke Street with what he'd found. The deeds to Chalstones were foremost in the bundle of items, and so were most of the IOU's, although some had already been redeemed. There was no sign of any copy of the letter concerning the proposed exchange of properties. He brought the diary, for although he had already torn out and destroyed the page concerning the exchange, the rest of the book contained references to those IOU's that Mr. Howard had succeeded in settling. As he drove his curricle from Cranham House to Duke Street, the snowstorm that had been in the offing since before dawn had yet to commence, and there were still only isolated flakes floating on the brittle air.

Nicholas was already up and taking a light breakfast of coffee and fresh bread rolls when his cousin arrived. His anger over Sarah burned relentlessly, and he'd slept very badly. As a consequence he was feeling tired and far from his best when Stephen placed what he'd gathered on the white-clothed table before him.

"That's everything?"

"Yes,"

Nicholas sifted through the items. "Are you aware if Mr. Howard was in any other way in debt to my father?"

"I'm sure he wasn't, and according to the diary he'd already redeemed some of the IOU's by selling his house in Brook Street."

"So if I return all this to Mr. Howard, the whole sorry business will be at an end?"

Stephen looked at him and then nodded. "Yes."

"Then that is what I intend to do, and as quickly as possible."

Stephen drew a long breath. "You'll never know how sorry I am about all this, Nicholas. If I could turn the clock back, I would."

"I know you would," Nicholas replied, not unkindly. "I'm fully aware of how the threat of jail would terrify you."

"Let's face it, I'm simply a coward."

"We all have our nightmares."

"I don't deserve your understanding."

Nicholas gave an ironic smile. "Perhaps you do, Coz, for if it hadn't been for you, I would still be a fool."

Stephen stared at him. "I . . . I don't understand."

"If you hadn't confessed to me when you did, I wouldn't have crossed that damned park last night, and I'd still have been ignorant about Miss Sarah Howard's true character." Nicholas got up from the table and went to the window, looking out toward Thurlong House. "I went over there last night to try to explain the truth to her, but I saw her with Oliver Fitzcharles, and to say they were cozy would be to put it excessively mildly."

Stephen's jaw dropped incredulously. "Miss Howard and Oliver Fitzcharles?"

"Yes. The creature is worthless, as the evidence of

my own eyes proved conclusively. The moment I have returned these papers to her father, I will wash my hands of her entirely, and I would be grateful if you'd never mention her name to me again."

Stephen was silent for a long moment, for he found it hard to believe that Sarah Howard was capable of such duplicity. He left the subject for the moment, but decided to return to it in a short while. "What do you wish to do about me, Nicholas?" he asked then.

"You?"

"Yes. Do you wish to know me after this?"

"Blood is thicker than water, Coz, and I know that dear Georgette would have worded her threats with supreme care. Here, these are yours." Nicholas went to a desk and took out a small sheaf of papers, which he thrust into his hands.

Stephen stared at them, for they were his own IOU's. Then he looked up at Nicholas. "But, how——?"

"I paid Geoffrey Belvoir a visit late last night and told him that unless he retrieved them from his odious sibling, I would personally tear him limb from limb. He obliged. It seems the lady herself left London in a tremendous hurry last night. Geoffrey declined to say why, but in her haste she left your notes behind."

Stephen was overcome. "I . . . I don't know what to say."

"I suggest you burn the wretched things without delay." Nicholas indicated the fire.

Stephen gladly tossed them onto the flames.

Nicholas watched them turn to ashes. "I trust this has all been a lesson to you?"

"It has. I don't want to *see* a green baize table again, let alone *sit* at one." Stephen turned to him. "Nicholas, are you quite sure about Miss Howard?"

"Sure? In what way?"

"That you're right about her."

"I'm certain beyond all shadow of doubt. I was an idiot to have ever fallen for her."

Stephen shrugged a little. "If you insist, but it seems to me that you are a little too adamant."

"There speaks the expert on the fair sex?"

Stephen smiled ruefully. "I know I'm not well versed in such things, but nevertheless——"

"Nevertheless you are wrong, Coz. The lady is scheming and lacking in all virtue, and I wish Fitzcharles well of her." Nicholas drew a long breath. "Stephen, I not only know her to be faithless, but I also suspect her of having deliberately set about courting my acquaintance."

Stephen gaped. "What do you mean?"

"Yesterday she accused me of having known all along who she was, but I believe that it is the other way around, and *she* knew who *I* was. It isn't beyond the bounds of possibility that she saw me as an ideal way of recouping all that her father lost."

Stephen stared at him, and then gave a slight laugh. "That's ridiculous!"

"Is it?"

"Yes, and if you weren't in such a hurt dudgeon, you'd see it for yourself. If she was doing that, I hardly think she'd give you your congé the moment you arrived in London; on the contrary, she'd welcome you with open arms. Be sensible."

Such plain common sense couldn't be denied, and after a moment Nicholas nodded, feeling a little foolish. "Yes, I suppose you're right."

"There's no 'suppose' about it, I am right."

"Very well, I concede that particular point, but that doesn't make her innocent on the other count as well. I saw her, Stephen, and my eyes did not deceive me. She and Fitzcharles are lovers, and I believe they have been all along."

"You may be wrong," Stephen insisted, a doubt nagging away at the back of his mind. He had met Sarah Howard and didn't believe her to be the sort of young lady who would deceive in such a way. If anything, she was the complete opposite.

Nicholas sighed. "Stephen, if I'm wrong, why would Georgette Belvoir quit London so suddenly?"

"I, er, don't follow the connection."

"If Fitzcharles has clung to his old love, Georgette must needs save face as best she can. She's been rejected in a humiliating and very public way, there will be chitter-chatter all over town, and both fathers will be furious. Ergo, Georgette rushes off to Scotland to sit it out until the fuss dies away again, and society has someone else's bones to chew over."

It sounded too likely to be denied, and Stephen nodded resignedly. "On this occasion I cannot find anything to say to the contrary," he murmured.

Nicholas looked across at Thurlong House again. "I think I'll go there now. When I get back, I, too, will leave London for a while."

"Where are you going? Cranham Castle?"

"Good God, no, I loathe the place. I intend to go back to Cheltenham and Grandmother's soothing company. On the way I think I'll have a look at this famous Chalstones, just to see what it was that I might so very justfiably kept for myself." Nicholas's lips pressed together bitterly. "After all this, I fear I'll probably require the Cheltenham cure to settle my bile."

"That I doubt very much." Stephen paused and then smiled a little. "I take it you don't want me to handle your affairs here in London?"

"I think you've done enough recently, don't you?" Nicholas responded dryly. Then he turned to call his valet.

Shortly afterward he hurried through the garden gate into St. James's Park and began to walk through the lightly falling snow toward Thurlong House.

29

AFTER arising and having breakfast, Sarah had adjourned to the library to think about whether or not to say anything to her father regarding the loss of Chalstones. She spent an hour of heart searching and deliberation, and then decided that he had to be told the truth. It wasn't an easy decision, and she felt sick with apprehension as she got up from the fireside chair. She wore the lime dimity gown, with its long gathered sleeves and froth of lace spilling over her wrists. Her hair was twisted up into a simple knot from which it then tumbled in a single heavy ringlet, and the knot was adorned with a wide bow of bright lime satin ribbon. She looked bright and cheerful, but those were the last things she felt as she emerged to go to her father's bedroom.

When she crossed the entrance hall toward the staircase, there was a sharp rap on the front door, and she turned as the butler hastened to answer it. Her heart tightened within her, seeing Nicholas standing there.

He did not see her as he addressed the butler. "I wish to speak to Mr. Howard, if that is possible."

The butler was uneasy about admitting him after what had happened during his last call. "I, er, am afraid that Mr. Howard is too unwell to receive visitors, my lord."

Sarah spoke then. "Perhaps you should speak to me if your purpose concerns my father, Lord Cranham."

Nicholas's gray eyes were veiled as they turned toward her. "It is entirely up to you, Miss Howard, although I must point out that it was neither my intention nor my desire to speak to you."

"Do not imagine that I am eager to find myself in your company either, sir, for I am not, but if this has anything to do with my father, then I regard it as my duty to hear whatever it is you wish to say." Her tone was cool, as

were her eyes, but her gullible heart was pounding foolishly in her breast. "If you will come this way," she went
on, returning to the library.

Nicholas handed his hat and gloves to the butler, and
then followed her.

In the library she turned to face him. "Well, sir?"

For a moment he didn't respond, for he could only
think that this was the room where the previous evening
she had been alone with Oliver Fitzcharles, where she
had smiled tenderly into that gentleman's eyes, and
where she had kissed him.

"Sir?"

He took the diary and small sheaf of papers from his
pocket and placed them on a table. "This is all that exists
concerning your father's debts to mine, including the
deeds to Chalstones. My father's diary contains references to redeemed notes, and I would be grateful if it
could be sent back to me as soon as you have checked
everything of relevance, but the rest I return in its en-
tirety because I am canceling your father's obligation. I
trust that this will be the end of any connection I may
have with your family."

She stared incredulously at the papers. "You . . . you
are canceling my father's debts?"

"Yes."

She could hardly believe it. A moment or so ago she
had been on the point of telling her father that all was
lost, but now . . . She looked quickly at him. "May I
know why you are doing this?"

"Because, contrary to your unpleasantly expressed
charge, I had no knowledge of my father's gambling affairs, and I did not know anything about this matter until
I returned to London the day before yesterday. The
name 'Chalstones' conveyed nothing to me, and I hadn't
heard anything about your father's irresponsible conduct
at the gaming tables."

She stiffened. "Please do not refer to my father in that
way, sir."

"Madam, it seems to me that you think it proper to
refer to me in any way you choose, but I am not to point
out certain uncomfortable truths to you. Your father *was*
irresponsible, Miss Howard, and no amount of posturing
on your part will alter that fact. I am sure that he is

usually a model parent, and that you love him dearly, but that does not excuse his foolishness in persistently sitting at the gaming table with my father, who was a far from model parent, and whose relentless capacity for pressing home an advantage was positively legendary."

Sarah lowered her eyes. She didn't like what he said, but could not gainsay his right to say it. Her father hadn't shown wisdom, and said so himself.

Nicholas drew a long breath. "As I have said, I did not know anything about this until I returned to London, but although you think you have been given good reason to believe ill of me, I equally think I have good reason to be savagely disappointed in your lack of faith or trust. I do not intend to dignify your mistrust with an explanation as to what really happened, or who was responsible, for it no longer interests me what you think. All I am concerned with is returning everything to its original owner."

His words stung. "If you wish me to express my gratitude, then I will oblige. Thank you, Lord Cranham."

"How easily the platitudes slip from your lips, Miss Howard, almost as easily as expressions of love."

Her blue eyes flashed angrily at him. "Are you calling my integrity into question, sir?"

"Integrity? Madam, in my opinion you do not have any."

"If I have been wrong about you, then I sincerely apologize, sir, but that is *all* of which I am guilty."

"Indeed?" He gave an mocking laugh. "You amaze me, madam, indeed your gall positively staggers me."

"Gall? What gall?"

"Miss Howard, you stand there looking the very picture of purity and innocence, and yet last night you were far from innocent with Oliver Fitzcharles in this very room."

Color flooded into her cheeks. "How do you know that?"

"Those who wish to conceal their activities should take the elementary precaution of drawing the curtains."

Her glance flew toward the windows, and then back to him. "I had not realized you were a Peeping Tom, Lord Cranham."

"I was on my way here to try to put matters right

between us, but fortunately I was diverted by your rather public exhibitions of affection."

Her cheeks felt as if they were on fire. "You misunderstood everything you saw, sir."

"I am not that much of a fool, madam. I know what I saw, and I now know you for the abandoned creature that you really are, and I bitterly regret ever having been persuaded to love you."

She gasped. "Abandoned?"

"Yes, madam, for how else can your conduct be described? Indeed, I now begin to suspect that the unfortunate dandy at the Frogmill was less at fault than I realized. No doubt you encouraged him." He was so bitter that he allowed his anger full rein.

"How dare you!" she breathed, shaking so much that she had to steady herself by putting a hand on the back of a chair.

"I dare because I despise you, Sarah Howard. Your sweet lies have caused me more pain that you will ever know. I only hope that one day someone will deal you similar pain, for as God is my witness you deserve it."

"Please leave." Her voice was a whisper.

"I intend to, and I trust that this will be the last time we ever meet. Good-bye, madam." Turning on his heel, he strode from the room.

Sarah was so stricken that she could not move. She loved him, but he despised her. His parting look of hatred and contempt would live with her forever.

Walking swiftly back across the park through the lightly falling snow, Nicholas returned to Duke Street and immediately ordered his phaeton to be made ready for the journey to Cheltenham. He wanted to kick the dust of London from his heels and escape from all proximity with Sarah Howard. How enchanting she had looked in her lime dimity gown, and how beguilingly unspoiled. If he hadn't observed her with Fitzcharles, he'd never have guessed the truth. She was a viper, and in her way as poisonous as Lady Georgette Belvoir. He prayed he would soon be able to forget Miss Howard, and he would commence laying the ghost by pausing on his journey to inspect Chalstones, the property which had been the cause of so much heartache.

Within half an hour he was on his way, urging the team of black horses out of the capital along the Oxford road. The skies overhead were still a thick yellow-gray, and the snow was beginning to fall more heavily, lying in the thinnest of white carpets over the countryside.

Nicholas drove like the wind, flinging the team along the highway as if the hounds of hell itself were giving chase. But it was the memory of Sarah Howard that pursued him. She was all around him, her perfume filling his nostrils, her gentle voice echoing in his ears, and her eyes taunting him with their loveliness.

Having made his peace with Nicholas, Stephen had driven his curricle to his club in St. James's, not to renege on his promise not to indulge in gambling anymore, but to enjoy an hour or so playing billiards with his cronies.

Smoke hung in the air, and there was a low murmur of male voices from the various tables. The tap of cue upon ivory balls was heard from time to time, and Stephen was soon immersed in a game with his old friend, Jerry Pankhurst. All the anxiety of the past few days had lifted, and he felt almost light-hearted, although he couldn't quite put Sarah Howard from his mind. There was something about her that inspired trust, and he couldn't help thinking that Nicholas was wrong to doubt her in any way. Whatever had taken place between Fitzcharles and her, Stephen was sure it wasn't what it appeared to be. And whatever Lady Georgette Belvoir's reason was for leaving London so hurriedly, Stephen suspected that it had nothing to do with Fitzcharles and Sarah Howard.

After a while there was a sudden burst of laughter from the table nearest the door, and Stephen looked up to see that Sir Mason Thackeray had come in, and was busy relating an amusing anecdote. Another roar of laughter ensued as the story was conveyed to the next table, and Stephen leaned curiously on his cue, wondering what was going on.

Mason left after a while, but the mirth he had encouraged continued, until at last Stephen's companion went to the next table to try to find out what it was about. He returned to relate the story of Georgette's humiliation the night before.

Stephen's jaw dropped. "Lord Fitzcharles actually found her in the buff?"

"So it would seem. The match is certainly off, and the lady has taken to her heels. From all accounts, she was traveling at such a pace that she must already be in Scotland, possibly to the extent of having been unable to halt in time to prevent driving over the cliff at John o' Groats!" Jerry replied with a chuckle. He felt no sympathy for the lady, having on several times felt the edge of her vitriolic tongue. She was long overdue for a downfall.

Stephen put his cue on the table. "Let me get this straight. Someone tipped Fitzcharles off that Thackeray was entertaining Georgette Belvoir, and he discovered them practically in the very act?"

"Yes."

"And that is why the lady has left London?"

"Yes. Look, why are you so interested in the precise details?" Jerry looked curiously at him.

"Because I was given to understand that her reason for leaving was that she'd lost Oliver Fitzcharles to someone else."

Jerry shook his head. "She left because she knew her name was going to be all over town today, and she couldn't stand the scandal. Besides, Fitzcharles has left as well, and certainly isn't enjoying good fortune in the arms of another love."

"How can you be certain of that?"

"Because I spoke to him late last night on my way to town. He was at the Red Cow in Hammersmith, sinking his umpteenth tankard, and getting himself blissfully drunk. He was on his way to Falmouth, and thence to America."

"He's leaving the country?"

"Definitely. He mentioned the ending of his match and seemed highly delighted about it, although, to give him credit, in spite of his inebriation, he wasn't ungentlemanly enough to relate the tale of La Belvoir's indiscretions with Thackeray. He must have known, though, because he said his father had confronted him with certain details that made the continuance of the match impossible. It seemed to me that the ending of the betrothal was of no consequence at all to him, for he was far more interested in telling me how he'd at last found the courage to tell his father what he could do."

"And there was no mention of another woman?"

"Well . . ."

"Come on, Jerry, this is important."

"He did say something about having always loved someone called Sarah, whom he had tried to win back, but couldn't because she wouldn't have him. That's why he's hightailing it to America. I don't know who this Sarah is, but—"

"I know who she is," Stephen interrupted. "Jerry, are you absolutely sure about all this?"

"Yes."

"Georgette Belvoir has left town because she fears all the talk about her dealings with Thackeray, and Oliver Fitzcharles is on his way to America after having failed to win someone called Sarah?"

"Yes." Jerry was becoming irritated. "Look, Stephen, I hope you're going to offer an explanation for all this?"

"Perhaps I will one day, but first I have something I must do. In a way I've been responsible for a great deal of harm being done, and I think I see a way of redeeming myself. Forgive me, Jerry, but there is someone I must see without delay."

Snatching up his coat, hat, and gloves, he ran from the crowded room, and was soon driving swiftly back along Pall Mall. His destination was Thurlong House, and the person he wished to see was Sarah.

30

SARAH had at last managed to collect herself sufficiently to take Nicholas's documents to her father. She pushed her private heartache into the background as she watched his relief and delight at knowing his troubles were so providently at an end.

"Oh, my dear, I can only say that the new Lord Cranham is a man of great honor and consideration," he murmured, running his loving fingertips over the deeds to Chalstones as he lay propped up on his pillows.

Sarah did not reply, but glanced unhappily out at the snowflakes drifting past the window.

Her father looked at her. "I trust you expressed my gratitude, my dear?"

"Yes. Of course."

"Is something wrong, Sarah?"

She made herself smile. "I'm quite all right, truly. Just a little tired, perhaps."

He nodded. "This has all been a great strain upon you, my dear. I know that you have forgiven my foolishness in continuing to play when I knew I was losing, but I will never forgive myself. I still do not know what madness came over me for those dreadful nights, but I do know that it will never happen again. After coming so close to losing Chalstones and most of my fortune, I have learned a very sharp and salutary lesson. I will write a note to Lord Cranham now, and I will make a point of calling upon him personally the moment I am well enough."

She remained silent.

He studied her again. "Am I to take it you do not particularly like the new Lord Cranham?"

"I have no opinion of him," she replied. Liar! You love him and you always will!

"Well, at least we will not now have to impose upon Phemie, I mean Lady Thurlong, anymore."

"She does not regard it as an imposition," Sarah pointed out with a faint smile.

He cleared his throat. "I'm sure she was merely being polite, my dear."

"Do you really expect me to believe that?" she inquired, looking forthrightly into his eyes. "You have been less than honest with me in the past, sir; indeed you have been less than a gentleman."

"Eh? Sarah, my'dear, how can you say such things!" he protested.

"Because it's true. The first time you mentioned your affection for Lady Thurlong was that time at Chalstones when you asked me to go to Cheltenham with Julia. I had no idea before then, and now that I've been here and have heard how Lady Thurlong speaks of you, it's quite clear that you and she were once very close indeed."

"I wouldn't say we were all that—"

"Very close indeed," she repeated. "I would go so far as to say that you should have married each other when you had the chance, instead of going your separate ways and settling for less."

"Sarah! Your dear mother meant everything to me."

"You were exceedingly fond of her, Father, but I know now that you never loved her in the truest sense of the word. Lady Thurlong is your real love, and you are hers. You would both be very foolish to go your separate ways again."

He stared at her. "You appear to have given this a great deal of thought, my dear," he said at last.

"No, I haven't thought about it at all until now," she replied truthfully. "But now that it has occurred to me, I see it all very clearly indeed."

"You speak almost as if from bitter experience," he murmured, his eyes very shrewd and thoughtful.

"Perhaps I do."

"Who is he?" he asked.

"Who?"

"The man who has broken your poor heart?"

She turned away from the bed. "There isn't anyone."

"Now who's bring less than honest? Come now, I know it isn't young Fitzcharles, so who is he?"

"There isn't anyone," she insisted, "but for you there *is* someone. Don't let her slip through your fingers again. She loves you and you love her. In her own words she wishes you would make an honest woman of her after all this time. I think you should."

With that she gathered her dimity skirts and hurried from the room. Her father gazed after her, and then looked at the documents on the bed before him. For a moment he did nothing, but then he reached out for the little handbell on the table by the bed.

A footman came hurrying in response. "Sir?"

"Would you kindly request Lady Thurlong to come to me without delay?"

"Yes, sir."

A few moments later Lady Thurlong hurried anxiously in, the lace tippets on her day-bonnet fluttering as she crossed the room to the bed. She knew all about the returned documents and settlement of the debts, and could only think that something was wrong. "Whatever is it, Henry? Is something wrong?"

He smiled fondly at her, thinking how very beautiful she still was, and how much cream silk became her porcelain delicateness. "Wrong? Yes, Phemie, something has been very wrong, but I trust it will soon be put right."

"Please tell me what it is," she said, still anxious.

"I think the time is long overdue when you should spare my reputation by marrying me."

She stared at him.

He smiled again. "Be my wife, Phemie."

Tears of happiness filled her eyes, and she reached out to put her hand gladly over his. "Nothing would give me more joy, my dearest," she murmured.

Sarah joined Julia in the drawing room. Thomas had once again gone to assist Mr. Pitt, and Julia was endeavoring to work at her embroidery frame. She wore a mauve merino gown that usually looked very good on her, but today it made her look pale and unwell. Indeed, Sarah thought, she had looked pale and unwell for a day or so now, and certainly wasn't eating as heartily as she might.

Sitting down opposite her, Sarah watched the busy needle flashing in and out of the canvas. "How are you feeling?" she asked after a moment.

"To be honest I feel absolutely awful, most peculiar in fact. I think I must have eaten something at the Mansion House last night."

"Julia, you were unwell this time yesterday," Sarah pointed out.

"Yes."

Sarah smiled a little. "Has it occurred to you to wonder when you had your last . . . ?" She allowed her voice to die away.

The needle halted as Julia thought for a long moment. Her lips moved as she silently counted back, and then she suddenly looked at Sarah. "It must be six weeks," she said incredulously, for in all the upheaval of recent days she hadn't given the matter any thought at all. Her eyes cleared and an astonished smile broke over her face. "Sarah, I'm overdue! I'm always exactly on time, but I'm two weeks' late! Oh, I hardly dare to hope, for Thomas and I so want to have a family. Do you think I might be?"

Sarah couldn't help laughing. "Julia, I'm not an expert on such things; indeed if I were, there would be disapproving tutting, but it seems to me that there is every possibility. I recall how it affected my cousin Maria when she and her husband stayed with us two years ago. She was just as pale and wan as you, she was ill every morning, and felt most peculiar all day. Seven months later she had a beautiful baby boy. That is the full extent of my knowledge, but it seems to me that you are exactly the same, and as I recall it is about six or seven weeks since Thomas left Cheltenham to come here. No doubt you made full use of your last few days together."

Julia reddened. "Yes, we did rather." She was about to say something more when Stephen's curricle drew up outside. She was surprised. "It's Mr. Mannering," she said.

Sarah got up and watched as he alighted from the vehicle. "I wonder what he wants? Perhaps Lord Cranham has changed his mind and wants all the documents back again!

"I hardly think so."

They listened as Stephen's knock was answered, and they heard his anxious tone as he asked if Miss Howard was at home.

Julia glanced at her. "I will stay with you if you wish to hear what he has to say."

Sarah hesitated. "I'd be grateful if you would."

The butler came in and bowed to Sarah. "Mr. Mannering has called, madam, and craves your indulgence on a matter of great urgency."

"Urgency? Very well, please show him in."

"Madam."

He withdrew and then returned with Stephen.

"How may I be of assistance, Mr. Mannering?" Sarah asked.

"You can answer what may at first appear to be a very impertinent question, Miss Howard."

"I am not in the habit of responding to impertinent questions, sir."

"This is very important, Miss Howard. Believe me, I wouldn't ask it at all if I did not know how much may hang upon your answer." Stephen looked earnestly at her. "I have been responsible for much mischief, albeit unwillingly, and now I wish to make amends if I can. Will you answer my question?"

"That depends upon the question, sir," she replied noncommittally, wondering what on earth could be on his mind.

He drew a long breath. "Will you tell me if you are in love with my cousin, Lord Cranham?"

Sarah stared at him, and Julia gave an indignant gasp. "How dare you, sir!" she cried.

He held up his hand to her, his attention remaining on Sarah. "Please tell me, Miss Howard. Do you love Nicholas?"

Julia was angry now. "Mr. Mannering, it is none of your business what Miss Howard's feelings may or may not be toward Lord Cranham!"

"It's Mrs. Thurlong, isn't it?"

"Yes."

"Mrs. Thurlong, please believe that I am not here to upset Miss Howard, or indeed to cause any more mischief. I truly wish to right certain wrongs." Stephen looked at Sarah again. "Will you answer me, Miss Howard?"

"Yes, I will answer you. I do love Lord Cranham, Mr. Mannering, but I know beyond all doubt that he does not love me."

He smiled. "I think you are wrong, he does love you. You are both wrong about each other. He hasn't lied to you, or deceived you in any way, and he certainly isn't guilty of any cruelty toward you. He thinks you have found solace with your former love, Mr. Fitzcharles, but I know that that isn't the case. I'm sure you have been faithful to Nicholas in every respect, and that if I could show you both the error of your ways, it would not be long before all misunderstandings and recriminations were things of the past."

Sarah met his gaze. "I wish I could believe you, sir, but I cannot. When Lord Cranham and I last parted, he made his feelings more than just plain, he made them crystal clear."

"As I'm sure you did as well."

She looked away.

"Let me take you to him now, Miss Howard."

"No . . ."

"If you love him, you will come."

Julia searched his face, and then looked at Sarah. "Do as he asks," she said quietly.

"Julia, I—"

"Go with him. You will never forgive yourself if you don't."

Sarah stared at her for a moment, and then suddenly nodded. "Very well. I'll go and put on my cloak."

Stephen exhaled with relief. "Be quick, Miss Howard, for we may already be too late. Nicholas is leaving London for Cheltenham today."

The curricle wheels were almost silent upon the snow as Stephen reined in outside Nicholas's house in Duke Street. Sarah remained in the vehicle as he alighted and hurried to the door.

She was ice-cold with trepidation as she huddled in her fur-lined cloak, her hands thrust deep into a muff. Her blue eyes were large and nervous as she watched Stephen speaking to Nicholas's butler, and then her heart sank as she saw the servant shake his head.

Stephen returned to the curricle, and put an urgent hand on her arm. "I'm afraid Nicholas has already left for Cheltenham, Miss Howard, but he hasn't been gone all that long and is using his carriage, which doesn't travel as fast as we can."

"You . . . you are suggesting we follow him?"

"Yes. He said he was going to stop at Chalstones on the way, and I think we will catch him there. What do you say? Shall we try?"

She hesitated. "Mr. Mannering, what if you are wrong, and Lord Cranham feels nothing for me? I don't think I could bear the mortification of—"

"Miss Howard, if I were not a reformed character, I would lay odds that my cousin still loves you. Trust me."

She nodded. "Very well, Mr. Mannering."

31

STANDING at the window in the gallery, Nicholas's musings on recent events were brought sharply into the present as he saw the curricle approaching. He recognized it immediately as his cousin's, and in the fading light his gaze went to the vehicle's passenger. Even without seeing her face, he knew that the woman in the crimson cloak was Sarah.

Damn Stephen for bringing her! He turned sharply from the window, his glance moving instinctively back to the portrait. The colors were indistinct now that the candlestick stood upon the table, but the painting's lovely blue eyes seemed to be looking more intently at him now, as if challenging him to stand his ground.

His ground? An ironic smile played briefly upon his lips as he looked around him. This was *her* ground, and he was the intruder.

He heard the front door of the house open, and the sound of voices. Then light steps came hesitantly toward the entrance of the gallery. He saw her the moment she appeared. She no longer wore the cloak, and the lime color of her dimity gown was bright and clear in the uncertain light. He thought how well the gown became her. But then, everything became her . . .

His silent thoughts betrayed him into weakness, and he stiffened his resolve. He must not give in to the spell she cast over him, for that way lay unhappiness and betrayal. Inwardly he cursed his cousin again for forcing this unwelcome meeting upon him.

She came slowly toward him, her steps soft upon the gallery's gray-and-white tiled floor. It was as if she had stepped down from the portrait, canvas and paint becoming living flesh and blood.

"Nicholas?" Echoes took up her voice, and his name

was repeated all around, whispering to him from every corner.

He steeled himself against her. "I trust you will forgive my presumptuousness in coming to this hallowed place, Miss Howard, but I fear my vulgar curiosity got the better of me." He spoke evenly and without expression, offering neither invitation nor rebuff—offering nothing at all, except the barest bones of civility.

"You are very welcome to come to this house, Nicholas."

"I find that hard to believe, madam."

"I have so much I must say to you."

"Nothing I wish to hear."

"Please, Nicholas, for we may never have another chance. I am so very sorry that I believed ill of you. I should have known that you had no idea at all that I was the daughter of the man from whom your father had won so much."

"Madam, I did not know anything about the entire business. My involvement was Lady Georgette Belvoir's invention."

"I know that now. I wish only I could prove to you that I am equally innocent. Nicholas, there is nothing between Oliver Fitzcharles and me, I swear that I—"

He interrupted sharply. "We've said all that is necessary, madam. and will merely be laboring the point if we continue." She was affecting him too much. He wanted to believe her, and was in danger of giving in to the overwhelming desire he felt whenever he was near her. It was madness to remain in her company like this. He glanced at the window. Darkness was almost complete, but the roads must still be passable, or Stephen's curricle could not have reached here. "If you will excuse me, I must continue my journey," he murmured.

With a start she followed his glance. "You surely do not intend to travel again in this weather?"

"Yes, Miss Howard, I do."

"There is no need."

He raised an eyebrow. "I would prefer not to be immured here overnight; indeed I think this is the very last place in the land I would choose to stay."

"Please don't hate me, Nicholas, for I haven't deceived you."

"Oh? So I imagined it when you kissed Fitzcharles?"

"No, you did not imagine it, but what you saw was a farewell kiss between friends."

"And you really expect me to believe that?"

"Yes, because it is the truth."

"So he's just a friend, is he? Forgive me for choosing to doubt, but I don't recall your ever mentioning him to me before, and yet he was, until recently, your fiancé. Did it slip your memory?"

"No, of course it didn't. I didn't wish to talk about him, that's all. My love for him was in the past, and I preferred not to bring him back into the present."

"He was very much in the present in the library at Thurlong House," he reminded her coolly.

"I will not pretend that he didn't wish to resume our former closeness, but I told him it could never be. He accepted that fact, and now he is on his way to America. There is nothing between Oliver and me, Nicholas, and I certainly haven't felt anything for him since knowing you." She held his gaze. "Your cousin has explained absolutely everything to me, and I now know exactly how far Lady Georgette was prepared to go to drive a wedge between us. I fell into her trap, and the absence of any communication from you served only to confirm it all. I am no longer in that trap, Nicholas, and everything is clear to me. I wish only that it was as clear to you. If I thought it would further my cause, I would go down on my knees to beg you to believe and trust in me again."

"What a truly touching scene you conjure, madam," he replied, his dry tone belying the doubt which was beginning to steal over him. Was she really a serpent with the face of an angel? Or was she telling the truth?

"Mock me if you wish, Nicholas, but I am trying to convince you of my innocence, and of my continuing love for you. I desperately want to win you back, and if those moments by the Chelt meant anything at all, then you will listen to me now."

Her voice died away, and he said nothing in the hollow silence that followed. After a moment she couldn't bear it anymore. Choking back the sob that rose in her throat, she gathered her skirts to hurry out of the gallery.

His tormented gaze swung to the portrait. The painted eyes accused him, and suddenly he knew that he could never escape from his love for her. She wasn't the serpent, she was the angel, and he needed her more than he had ever needed anyone in his life. She *was* his life!

He ran to the entrance of the gallery and called after her as she fled across the vast hall beyond. "Sarah?" Her name was very soft upon his lips, but the echoes heard, and took up the sound. "Sarah, Sarah, Sarah . . ."

She halted without looking back.

"Please come back to me, Sarah."

Her eyes shimmered with tears, and slowly she turned, afraid to believe that there was hope after all.

"Forgive me for hurting you, my darling, forgive me for my blind male anger, and above all for my damned pride." He held his hand out to her. "I love you, Sarah, and I know that you've told me the truth."

With a cry of joy she ran back to him, flinging herself into his arms and raising her lips to meet the passion of his kiss.

Their bodies melted together as he crushed her close, and his fingers curled into the warmth of her hair. He wanted to cry with happiness as he cherished her. She was the most precious gift he had ever been given, and he would never again relinquish his hold.

She shivered with ecstasy as his lips moved to her throat, and she abandoned herself to the rich, luxurious desires he alone could stir in her. Only a heartbeat before she thought she had lost him forever, but now they were one again.

At last he cupped her face in his hands, his gray eyes dark with feeling as he looked at her. "I want you with me forever, and I've known that since the moment by the Chelt when I first kissed you. When I wrote to you from Padstow, I asked you to be my wife. I ask you again now. Will you marry me, Sarah?"

Her breath caught. "Marry you?" she whispered.

"Yes, for you are the only woman who can be my Lady Cranham."

Tears of happiness wet her cheeks, and she nodded. "If that is your wish," she breathed.

"It is my most earnest wish," he murmured, kissing her again.

As they stood locked in each other's arms in the entrance of the gallery, the candlelight swayed on the paintings behind them. Sarah's portrait seemed to smile.